ALTERNATE SOURCES

LAMAR BRANTLEY

RAMAL CIRE CREATIVE LLC

Ramal Cire Creative LLC

ramalcirecreative.com

ISBN: 979-8-9941341-0-8 (paperback)

ISBN: 979-8-9941341-1-5 (ebook)

Cover art and design by Jay Montgomery

jaymontgomery.com

1

The rain had been Biblical; a storm reminiscent of Old Testament vengeance. The downpour had been relentless, and the dark clouds patrolled the sky threatening to unleash even more, as if the transgressions of those beneath their gaze required additional punishment. The sirens had finally faded to silent without any immediate reports of a touchdown, but tornado watches were still in effect for DeKalb, Henry, and Fayette counties. Carl braved the storm's violent assault in his rig; failure to pick up the load was not an option.

Carl's slender, brown face was familiar, but nameless. The night-shift security guard had one duty, and it did not entail small talk or acquainting himself with every driver seeking to gain access to the receiving docks of the pharmaceutical distributor which employed him as a contractor. If it was an unfamiliar face or if he had suspicions, he would ask questions, but he had seen Carl's cautious face enough times to remain stoic and go through the motions. Carl always looked nervous, like he was constantly in the crosshairs of a rifle scope, but he had proven to be harmless. The guard handed Carl the clipboard so he could scribble his signature next to the time the security guard had just written down on the log. It was 1:27AM; well within the 1:15 to 1:45 window Carl usually arrived to pick up his load. Carl nodded as he handed the clipboard back to the guard, but the gesture, as usual was not returned. The guard stepped back into his shed and pressed a button releasing the large magnetic lock allowing the gate to slowly roll open.

Security protocol called for the drivers to open the doors on their trailers prior to backing into the dock, but this was rarely enforced and thus seldom done; that early morning was no exception. The trailer was aligned perfectly with the dock door, and Carl slid down from his cab and chocked the wheels per safety protocols. The threat of more rain hung overhead, and the sky could be heard rumbling somewhere in the distance like a bloated stomach with a sour bowel. He thought he witnessed a raindrop splatter on the ground, but it was just a bead of sweat which had fallen from his forehead when he bent over to secure the wheel. He wiped his forehead with the back of his hand and wondered if he had been sweating at the guard shack. He didn't know why he was nervous; it was not his first time executing the arrangement, and all previous jobs were without incident. He shook it off and returned to the cab of his truck and waited.

The dock door was raised first, immediately followed by the trailer door. The masked men were heard before they were seen.

"Everyone get down on the ground!"

"Flat on your stomachs with your hands extended in front of you!"

Nine men exited the trailer holding semi-automatic assault rifles. Three men quickly secured the loading dock making sure everyone complied with their orders, and the other six dispersed to predetermined areas of the warehouse. One went to the shipping supervisor's office which was near the dock. He was like a deer frozen in headlights of a vehicle still accelerating toward him.

"Press that button and you'll die right here, right now."

The supervisor stood and walked out of the office with his hands above his head. He did not press the panic button under his desk. He had been on the job less than a month and was not willing to die trying to protect it. He joined the others on the concrete floor with his hands extended. He had to lay on his side due to the size of his stomach but was still very uncomfortable and struggled to breathe.

Three other masked men went to the break room and gave the employees on break the same orders which had been given on the shipping dock. The other supervisor was in the break room as well. Everyone complied without incident. Fear in the room was airborne and spread like a contagion.

The nightshift operations manager, for whatever reason, tried to be a hero. When the armed masked man arrived at his office, he charged the man and tried to disarm him; thinking that his size and strength would give him the advantage. The adrenaline rush allowed him to land a few admirable blows, but it ultimately ended with a blade lodged in his abdomen. It was not intended to be a fatal wound, but the blood loss was already significant. The sight of the blood and the knife protruding from his body when he was dragged into the break room served as ample deterrent for anyone else contemplating hero status. No one rushed to his aid to offer assistance; in fact, several employees unknowingly smiled at the sight of him bleeding on the floor.

The remaining masked men roamed the warehouse in search of stragglers, quickly rounding up anyone they found. The night shift was a pick, pack, and ship operation, while day shift focused on receiving, stocking, inventory, and returns. The front office was closed at night so there were far fewer employees in the building than dayshift.

Once the armed intruders had a degree of certainty that everyone was accounted for, they moved from seize to the scavenge phase of the operation. Everyone from the shipping dock was moved to the break room.

"Who has access to the cage and vault?" The question came from the masked man who was charged with leading the incursion. It was obvious who was in charge, he had been the one barking the orders. No one answered his question.

"The controlled substance cage, who has access? I won't ask again."

A distraught female voice answered from the back of the break room. "I work in the cage and vault."

"Get up and come with me."

Another man jumped to his feet with his arms raised and at least four assault rifles were immediately pointed at him. "I work in the cage and vault too; I'll go with you, take me instead."

"Look here boys we got ourselves a real man's man, protecting the women and children. I can respect that... alright, you can come with her; just don't try to be a hero. We're just here for product, not souls; no one has to die tonight. But make no mistake, you fuck with us, and you *will* be put down."

Four armed men, including the leader, followed the two employees to the massive, controlled substance cage. The female employee placed her badge on the badge reader which released the magnet allowing the massive door to roll open. There were shrink-wrapped pallets of stacked totes filled with schedule III – V controlled substances lined along the metal fencing of the cage and totes filled with schedule II narcotics in a staging area of the vault. The controlled substances were not removed from the cage until they were ready to be loaded directly onto the truck. A fact which was obviously known to the masked men.

"Go grab a couple forklifts." The order came from the leader, and two masked men hustled to the shipping dock and came back driving forklifts. One by one they drove the pallets to the dock. There was a total of eleven pallets.

'FINALLY,' Carl thought as he felt the weight of the forklifts loading pallets of drugs onto his trailer. It had taken much longer than usual but he maintained his composure. Another truck had just arrived at the gate and Carl envisioned the stone-faced guard tediously performing his routine without uttering one word. Other trucks seeking to pick up their loads would soon follow. Carl anxiously glanced at his watch; the window was closing, but there was still time to make the drop.

The product from the cage and vault was loaded first, followed by several wrapped pallets of sealed cooler boxes which were sitting on the dock. These styrofoam lined boxes were filled with vaccines and other vials of life-saving medicines with frozen icepacks barely keeping the temperature within the acceptable range, some relying on acceptable excursions to be compliant. The pallets of OTC product and prescription drugs left behind on the dock would be picked up by other regular drivers and taken to cross-docks where they would be sorted and loaded onto vans for delivery to pharmacies and hospitals.

Once all the targeted product was loaded, the armed leader followed the two employees back to the break-room. The stench of fear laced perspiration dampening human bodies permeated the room, and everyone was on edge.

"Give me your badges," the leader ordered. He grabbed a garbage bag and walked up to each employee and watched as they dropped their badge into the bag. Without the badges, they would be locked in the break-room, unable to enter the warehouse nor the front office area.

"Once first shift arrives, you'll be able to leave this room."

"What about him?" The voice came from a young man standing next to the wounded operations manager. The armed men looked around at each other and then gazed at the leader, who had not contemplated what to do with the man who would surely bleed to death. After considering the limited options he realized there was only one.

"He attacked one of my men; it was self-defense. If he dies, it's his own fault."

A TRACTOR TRAILER backed into the dock two bays from where Carl was parked. The driver climbed out of the cab and chocked the wheels. Carl watched intently as he walked in front of his truck and climbed the stairs leading to the truckers' entrance. He rang the buzzer and waited for the lock to be released. After pressing the button for the third time, the driver looked around perplexed. He pulled on the door handle, but it was locked. Carl peeked at the man in his side mirror; deliberating what his next move would be. He was not surprised when he saw the man walking toward him.

"Anybody in there?" He asked after Carl lowered his window.

"Yeah, they've been loading my truck. Takin' 'em a long time though."

"They usually open the door on the first ring."

"They probably all took a break. They haven't been on the trailer in a while."

The man looked at his watch perturbed. "Break? I'm on a schedule, they need to open that damn door." Carl shrugged and smiled awkwardly. The man returned to the door and leaned on the buzzer.

. . .

CARL HEARD and felt his trailer door close just as another truck pulled up to the security gate, and Carl did not hesitate to pull away from the dock with his cargo. The security guard was preoccupied with the other driver, but Carl managed to wait patiently until the guard finished and walked his way. His nerves were on fire and his heart pounded against his chest, but his facial expression remained calm. He was running behind, and the consequences would be dire. He was allowed to exit without incident. It was not until the second driver failed to gain entry to the building that the two disgruntled drivers walked over to the guard shack and alerted the guard. He made a call to the night operations manager, but it went unanswered as did the calls to the two supervisors. He called the emergency contact number and awakened the site general manager from a deep sleep.

An ambulance rushed the critically wounded manager to the hospital, and the Henry County police officers took statements from everyone locked in the break room. A DEA form 106 for theft and loss of controlled substances would be filed with the DEA along with a call later that morning to the local DEA field office in Atlanta. No one wanted DEA Diversion investigators combing through their security SOPs and tracing every misstep and violation, but failure to report would be career ending; and the fines and potential loss of DEA registration would be devastating to a company with just two distribution centers on opposite sides of the country.

THE DROP LOCATION was a remote field roughly thirty miles south of the distribution center in McDonough Georgia. There were no buildings or other structures visible from the field, and there was even an absence of light thanks to the looming clouds blocking the usual illumination from the moon and stars. Carl did not mind, the darker the better. He smiled in misguided relief at the notion that even God had His view obstructed of what was taking place on the small patch of earth.

Three cargo vans and two box trucks were waiting when Carl arrived. The three cargo vans were familiar, but the two box trucks were anonymous, and they made Carl uneasy. He was not aware of any changes to the arrangement, but then again no one told him anything anyway; pickup at X location and drop off at Y location. He had never asked questions and was not about to start. He climbed down from the cab and his boots sank down into the mud. He glanced at the two box trucks, but it was too dark to see faces. As he plowed his way to the rear of the trailer, he knew the ground condition would make the transfers hazardous, but it wasn't his job, so he didn't care; he was just the driver.

The three cargo vans slowly maneuvered to the rear of the trailer and two men exited each van. They were the usual suspects, and this gave Carl a portion of comfort but the two box trucks still lurking behind bothered him. There was no seal on the trailer door, not even the temporary one he had become accustomed to removing. Something was off; his first thought was to run back to the cab of his truck and haul ass back to Interstate 75. He gazed again at the two box trucks, and although he could not see them, he felt the mysterious men gazing back at him. If he ran, he would have to keep running, ducking and dodging someone he had never seen, but had proven they could reach Carl whenever and wherever. Carl took a deep breath and released the locking mechanism on the door. He jumped back when the door rolled up without his assistance. Nine masked men jumped from the back of the trailer. Carl stopped breathing or at least lost the ability to exhale.

"What took you so damn long?" The leader shouted as he found his footing in the mud. "

"Who the hell are you?" Carl asked startled. The faint words sounded as if they were Carl's last breath.

"Who we are is not important," the leader exclaimed, "what's important is that I know who you are. Do you understand what I'm saying?"

Carl's eyes focused on the assault rifles the men had secured to their shoulders. Their identities were hidden behind masks, and Carl hoped they remained that way. He did not want to see their faces, that would make him a witness, and there was no way he would survive the night as a witness.

"How did you get on my truck?"

"Shut the fuck up!" The leader barked.

He knew better than to ask questions, but nerves had taken over. He knew there were only two possible answers. They were either on the trailer when he first picked it up or they had boarded the trailer at the distribution center. The question he did not ask out loud was the most important question. What had they done inside the warehouse? That question frightened Carl the most. The less he knew the better.

"Let's get to it!" The leader shouted. He waved at the box trucks, and they slowly made their way over to the trailer. Two masked men slid out of each truck and gathered at the rear of the trailer with the others.

The box trucks were loaded first, while the van drivers loitered near their vans. The masked men formed lines from the trailer to the back of the trucks. The product on the trailer was sorted and distributed appropriately. The controlled substances were distributed evenly on the box trucks. The rest of the product was left on the truck for Carl and the van drivers to do with what they wanted. Usually that meant the van drivers broke down the pallet of 'extra' product and loaded it onto the vans. What they did with it was of no concern to Carl.

Carl delivered the rest of the freight to the cross dock where it was sorted by route and delivered to the pharmacies as regular deliveries.

Carl stood to the side and watched the well-oiled machine operate. His back injury prevented him from doing anything but light lifting. Carl considered light lifting ten pounds or less, and he had a doctor's memorandum to show any shipping supervisor who challenged him. Many challenged, calling him lazy, and he did not dispute their claim. He had spent over twenty years of his life moving freight, and he had earned the right to stay in his truck and let the young backs load and unload his cargo.

Carl had been considering retirement, at least from his legitimate routes and customers he contracted with as an owner operator. The 'envelope' jobs, he had planned on doing a while longer because the money was good, but as he watched the masked men take product off his truck, he could think of nothing else but full retirement. He called them envelope jobs because he received an envelope in his mailbox with instructions and locations. There was no return address and no postage. Payment was in cash, and until that night it had been easy money. He knew getting out of the envelope jobs would be difficult if not impossible. He had tried once and within a week his mother's house was riddled with bullets. She was not home at the time, but the message had been received. She passed away from a heart attack several years later, leaving Carl with no living family. If there was a way out the envelope jobs alive, it had not yet revealed itself to Carl, or had it?

2

The hands of time dripped molasses, and each sticky second struggled to pass as words struggled to breathe life under the smothering weight of the presenter's nervous stutter. He only stuttered when he was nervous, and he had plenty to be nervous about. His name was not relevant, nor were the names of the other operations directors seated at the table, they were all known by the cities in which their facilities were domiciled. It was a practice started by Stanley Forsythe; one he meant as a show of disrespect which had stuck like a bodily fluid stain on an old sofa. He had only been speaking for twelve minutes, but it seemed like an hour to Charlie and the others in the room who were forced to listen to the quarterly report for Davidson Enterprises' Orlando, Florida Distribution Center. It was not only his delivery which was uninspiring, but the numbers also failed to elicit excitement. Sales and profits had been stagnant all year, which the Orlando director of operations attributed to the narrowing, already anemic margins for generic drugs, and the fourth quarter showed little promise to move the needle. 1999 would not be a good year; even with all the pharmacies and hospitals placing larger than usual end of year orders just in case everything crashed when the clock struck 12:01am on January 1st, 2000. They at least wanted to have inventory on hand if the computers stopped working.

Orlando, Florida was not the only distribution center with less than stellar numbers to report, the other two ops directors in the conference room awaiting their turn to present would have similar reports for their facilities in Dallas, and Los Angeles. The one person, managing the one facility which consistently defied all market conditions and produced strong margins for Davidson Enterprises was not present, and Bob Davidson was keenly aware of his absence.

For some it was first contact. There had been a sighting, and the chatter was heavy. Some questioned why he was on site; it could not be good, because Stanley made it clear that he despised the corporate office and hated the Northeast in general. Others hoped it did not affect their bonuses, since most of the company's profits were derived from the Distributing Company, which he presided over. Still others, mostly women, were clamoring to get a peek at the "extremely handsome" loosely married man. Stanley did not disappoint; his tailored suit accentuated his athletic build, and his blueish grey eyes were focused as he strode confidently through the office.

The executive conference room was next to Bob Davidson's office, and one had to pass by Geraldine, Bob's executive assistant, to enter either space. Geraldine guarded Bob's office diligently, no one gained entrance without her permission. She was not as protective of the conference room, but she still paid attention to who entered and exited, making sure it had been properly reserved in advance; of course, the conference room had to be reserved with Geraldine. She glanced down at her watch when she saw Stanley approaching. It was the gold watch Bob had given her for twenty-five years of service, and she was only a few years away from fifty years as Bob's assistant. Her exact tenure was debatable due to several short-lived resignations over the years, but in her mind, it was approaching fifty years. She did not give credence to the number Human Resources calculated; Human Resources did not exist when she started as a young lady in her early twenties as Bob's 'secretary.'

"You're late," Geraldine scoffed.

"How can I be late when the meeting doesn't officially start until I arrive."

"Sounds like they've started to me..." she exclaimed as she glanced in the direction of the conference room. Neither she nor Stanley had a jovial tone or facial expression. "You might be that important in your own world but in this one, time waits for no man."

"Well, I guess I better stop wasting it out here talking to you." Stanley proceeded to the conference room pursued by her scornful gaze.

No one was surprised when Stanley Forsythe marched into the conference room thirty-two minutes late, but eyebrows raised when he immediately started speaking over the Orlando ops director who was still mercilessly stammering through his presentation. Stanley walked over to the podium in his charcoal grey suit and stood next to the bewildered speaker; his six-foot two-inch athletic frame towered over the much shorter and rounder man. Everyone in the room peered at Bob Davidson, the founder, and President of Davidson Enterprises, but he remained silent. His baggy eyes darted around the conference room as if he wanted to say something but was unable to form words; or at least the courage to expel them. Orlando yielded the podium to Stanley who proceeded without apology, for of course he had done nothing wrong.

While the disruption provided a distraction, and was silently appreciated by those in the room, it was still a disruption. A very disrespectful one which Charlie Thomas could not disregard like the others in the room.

"Uhhh excuse me... you can't just barge in here thirty-some minutes late and start talking over people."

Stanley recognized the angry voice of the only female in the conference room, but he did not acknowledge Charlie in any way and continued as if she had not hurled words at him.

"I know you all have your numbers to present," Stanley proclaimed with disdain, "and sadly you're probably proud of them, but you all know that my margins are better than of all yours combined, and because of that, I'm sure Bob here will generously share my wealth with you come bonus time at the end of the year."

"You represent one of four *Davidson* Distribution Centers," Charlie interrupted again, "and all of them are equally important, as are the ops directors sitting in this room representing them."

Stanley paused, which caused an eerie silence like the eye of a storm passing over bringing the anticipation of what was on the other side of it. Charlie did not fear the aftermath.

"What makes you think you're more important than any of them? You're all equals."

The last comment brought a smirk to Stan's face. "Is that true gentlemen? Are we equals?" He eyeballed each director in the room, but none would make eye contact with him; they knew they were not his equal and silently wished Charlie would stop antagonizing him. Everything he said was true. Stanley oversaw the Davidson Distributing Company in Livonia, Michigan, a suburb of Detroit. The Distributing Company was a pharmaceutical distribution center like the other Davidson facilities, but it operated as if it was a separate entity, and Stanley gave himself the title of President. Of course, it was not a separate entity, and Stanley was technically an operations director like the others in the room, but Bob Davidson had given Stanley generous leeway, like he had done in the meeting.

"Charlie, I can't say it's great to see you," Stanley exclaimed as he peered into her brown eyes, "and just because you have a man's name doesn't mean..."

"Doesn't mean what?" Charlie inquired, "that I can speak in a room full of men?"

"Shouldn't you be in the support staff meeting? This is an ops leadership meeting; everyone here runs a facility."

"And I purchase product for each one of those facilities."

"Except mine. I source my own product."

"Source... is that what you call it? That makes it almost sound legitimate, we both know what you do is far more nefarious than that."

"That's enough," Bob finally bellowed, "you two can take it outside after we're finished here." The old man's tone was firm, but his voice was still feeble. He tried to look stern, but his sagging jaws and wrinkled forehead screamed Grandpa. He knew where the conversation was headed, and he sought to derail it while he still could.

"Stan since you hijacked the floor you might as well continue with your presentation."

"Thanks Bob," Stanley said gazing at Charlie. He straightened his tie as if the altercation with Charlie had been physical. He was the only one in the room wearing a suit, but it was his standard uniform. The cape was only present in his mind.

If it had been anyone other than Stanley, or any facility other than The Distributing Company, the numbers Stanley boasted would have been dismissed as inflated. He pompously proclaimed that his net dollars were more in one quarter than the other divisions combined and recited their numbers to them to validate his claim. Charlie glanced around the room and shook her head despairingly; the other directors were too humiliated to be offended.

Despite Stanley's objections, the other ops directors were allowed to present, but the presentations were sheepish compared to and as a result of Stanley's braggadocio. They rushed through the sales and margins and focused more on compliance and safety metrics. Dallas and Philadelphia had stellar DEA inspections and the FDA recall checks at all facilities were flawless. The FDA had been very active due to several class I recalls of popular prescription drugs. Stanley did not include compliance or safety metrics in his presentation; in his mind they were not revenue generating so they were insignificant. The Distributing company had never received a fine or negative finding from a regulatory agency, so Bob did not ask questions. Answers, and accountability, only followed questions, and with Stanley Bob had a do not ask policy.

CHARLIE STOOD before the room full of white men flushed with a feeling of unfortunate familiarity. While it was common for her to be the only female, specifically black female in the room or with a folding chair at the table, the realization still flashed in her mind long enough for her to acknowledge it. She tried not to look at Stanley, but he sat to the right of Bob, positioned as close to the head of the table as possible. Bob instinctively moved over to accommodate him. She hoped she had not actually rolled her eyes.

Charlie opened with a futile suggestion to move the annual meeting to a location with a milder winter climate and received a favorable response from everyone in the room. Even Bob smiled accordingly, but everyone knew it stood a snowball's chance in hell of happening. Bob was too frugal to move the annual meeting offsite to a place like Las Vegas, San Antonio, or South Florida; he even balked at the suggestion to rotate the meeting locations amongst the distribution centers. He insisted on hosting the meeting at the corporate office in Stamford, and always two weeks before Thanksgiving. He believed they needed to come home and break bread together at least once a year, although Stanley never attended the team dinner after the meeting.

Charlie fielded the usual questions from the team and deflected Stanley's snide comments.

"The Distributing Company is able to purchase drugs with more favorable pricing than what you get from the manufacturers, why is that, and how can we leverage the Distributing Company's suppliers to help our bottom lines?"

The question came from the ops director of the Los Angeles Distribution Center. It was domiciled in Rancho Cucamonga, but it was referred to as the Los Angeles location. Charlie always referred to him as the nerd of the group, and his social skills were painfully lacking.

"My suppliers are proprietary," Stanley asserted.

"But we're all one company," Los Angeles blurted out in frustration.

"Are we?" Stanley did not expect a response to his rhetorical question.

"Stanley operates in the shadows of the grey market," Charlie blurted out in haste to the chagrin of her boss. "His product is suspect at best and..."

"That's quite enough Charlie!" Bob scolded. "We will look into the matter. If not sourced directly we can look into transferring more product from the Distributing Company to the rest of the network." The look on Stan's face let everyone in the room know it would never happen.

"I don't think that's a good idea Mr. Davidson," Charlie exclaimed frantically, "not without more checks in place."

"What kind of checks Charlie?" The question came from Stanley, but Charlie continued to address Bob.

"At a minimum all prescription drugs should have a pedigree and every transaction on it should be verified."

"I'm sure the Distributing Company does a thorough job of vetting its suppliers and product Charlie, I see no reason why we can't move more of Stanley's product through our network."

"But..." Bob raised is hand to silence her and she smothered the breath out of the rest of her words, extinguishing them before even more damage could be done. Charlie wanted to protest further, but knew it was not the time nor audience. She had already let Stanley rattle her in front of Bob. Surely Bob was not as naive as he sounded.

There were no additional questions from the group; they were still grappling with what had just transpired. Charlie saw it on their faces, and she was embarrassed. The smirk she saw on Stanley's face as she returned to her seat decimated her. She silently thanked her deceased mother for her temper as she always did when she lost it.

STANLEY'S ENTRANCE had been one of shock and awe, but his exit was phantom-like. After the meeting, everyone instinctively huddled into impromptu conversations. Charlie had seen Stanley shake a few hands, but when she looked for him again, he was gone. It was probably for the better she thought.

CHARLIE WAS FROZEN by Geraldine's gaze before she could follow the others out of the conference room. It was a grimace she had never witnessed in person, but it wielded the weight of disheartened ancestors. Her shoulders sank and she felt apologetic but was unaware of her transgression. Her eyes fell to the ground and before she knew it Geraldine was in front of her. The door shut behind her with the force of a strong wind.

"Pick 'em up!"

Charlie looked up timidly, confused by the command.

"Pick 'em up!"

"Pick up what Ms. Geraldine?"

"What you just laid at the feet of those white men." Her voice had become a strained whisper being forced through clenched teeth. "The power you surrendered that they didn't even have the authority to take. The peace you relinquished, the pride you shed like an old coat. That's what you're looking at on the floor aren't you?"

"I just lost my temper..." Charlie uttered sheepishly.

"You didn't lose it; you got lost in it; there's a difference."

"But he..."

"He jerks you around like a puppet on a string because you're so busy trying to prove you're his equal that you can't see that *he's* the one that can't look *you* in the eye. A man can only look down on you if you kneel." Geraldine turned and walked purposefully toward the door.

"How... how do you know what was said in here?"

"Chile' I thought you knew," Geraldine exclaimed without breaking stride, "I know everything that happens within these walls."

Charlie smiled. Not because the 5 foot nothing elder had set her straight, but because Geraldine was impeccably dressed, and her confident stride would put women half her age to shame.

SEEKING to add value and purpose to the trip to Connecticut, Stanley skipped the team dinner after the meeting, which surprised no one, to have dinner with one of his most valued trading partners. The dinner invitation from Dominic Vanelli, owner of Emperor Drugs, was one Stanley could not turn down. To have dinner at Dominic's palatial home in New Jersey was better than any reservation he could have made at any

Italian restaurant in New York City. Dominic's mother did not cook often, but when she did it was an event. Dominic's wife appreciated her mother-in-law's cooking, but did not appreciate the way Dominic and others carried on even when she prepared something as simple as spaghetti and meatballs. She knew it was the sauce, a recipe the 'old woman' had not yet handed down to her son's wife.

Business was never discussed at the table, but Dominic appreciated the praises Stanley rained down on his mother. It was understood that all was well between the two men, both professionally and personally. There was nothing left but to enjoy a bottle of wine.

3

"Please hold for Mr. Caesar..."

Charlie cursed herself for answering the phone without first checking the caller id. Consequently, she had to sit on hold while Roman's assistant let him know "the bitch" had finally answered the phone and was on hold. Mr. Caesar... what kind of narcissist would change his name to Roman Caesar she thought. Charlie was certain it was not the name printed on his birth certificate.

"Well, you finally answered, I've called several times..." Roman paused to allow her to repent for her transgression. Charlie used the time to calm herself from the attitude stirring her molecules like Bruce Banner's gamma radiation.

"What do you want Roman? Why are you calling me?"

"How is the weather up there in Connecticut?"

"Cold."

"Well, it's sunny and warm down here in South Florida."

Charlie chose silence as her response, and Roman listened to as much of it as he could, but he was first to blink.

"I tried to call the other girl..."

"Christine... her name is Christine; but you already know that because you talk to her on a regular basis."

"Well apparently she's on vacation."

"It's a week before Christmas, that happens."

"I sent her an offer which I forwarded to you when I got her out-of-office."

"I saw it, not interested."

"What do you mean not interested? The other girl jumps on these types of offers."

"Then you need to wait until Christine gets back."

"I could have gone to another company, but I always give Davidson Distributing my best offers first. You can't get this product for a better price."

"I know, that's the problem; this offer is too good to be true. You couldn't have acquired these drugs legally and knowing you they're probably counterfeit. I don't know why the Distributing Company purchases anything from your dirty companies anyway. I don't buy any of your product in our other distribution centers; I don't want to contaminate our supply chain."

The proverbial Line was crossed when she uttered the word "counterfeit," but it was too late to step back over it. The necessary silence that followed felt like an artificial cease-fire to give both sides time to reload or contemplate a truce. It also gave Charlie time to blame her late mother once again for her quick temper and lack of a filter.

"It's the holiday season," Roman stated calmly, "and I am going to end this call so you will have time to find another job before your family gathers around the table for Christmas dinner." They both hung up the phone simultaneously; neither wanted to hear the other's dial tone.

Charlie's responsibilities as director of purchasing for Davidson Enterprises did not include the Davidson Distributing Company. The same was true for all Davidson management in the corporate office. The Distributing Company had its own management team at the facility in Livonia, Michigan led by Stanley Forsythe, and only he had any communication with anyone at the corporate office. All were forbidden to address anyone on his team directly or indirectly, and that included Bob Davidson, the sole proprietor of the company. They were also prohibited from engaging with any vendor, customer, supplier, or any other entity or representative thereof conducting business with the Distributing Company. While none of these guidelines were in writing, they were understood to be gospel. Stanley had this sovereignty because the Distributing Company made more profit than the other four distribution centers combined. Margins were razor thin in the pharmaceutical distribution business but not the Distributing Company. For various reasons, both known and unknown, the Distributing Company printed money; and because of that Stanley had autonomy.

The restrictions on communication were not reciprocal. Stanley could engage with anyone he saw fit and intimidated all but a few people in the company; the woman whose number he had just dialed was one of the few.

"Charlie Thomas..." Charlie greeted in her best customer service voice without looking at the caller id.

"What the fuck is your problem!?" Stanley did not hear the dial tone at first, because his own voice still rang in his ears. It took him a few seconds to realize Charlie was no longer on the phone.

"Who the hell do you think you are!" He yelled into the phone when Charlie answered it a second time. He heard the dial tone immediately, almost expected it. His phone rang and he took a deep breath before answering. Charlie spoke first.

"You called my number a couple times, but I think you were trying to reach someone else; your wife maybe?"

An f-bomb was ready to be launched, but Stanley swallowed it, and it exploded in his throat causing him to cough uncontrollably.

"Are you okay? Do you want to call me back later?"

Charlie waited patiently as Stanley struggled to catch his breath and form the word "no." A full sentence took a while longer.

"I had a conversation with one of my suppliers, and I understand you did too."

"Yes, Roman Caesar called me earlier. Apparently, your buyer was unavailable, so he called me to cut him a purchase order for some Laprin. I refused and the conversation went downhill from there."

"Yes, I heard."

"I let my temper get the best of me, and I apologize, but I will not be associated with criminal activity."

"What criminal activity?" Stanley asked a little too loudly. "Just because the price is better than what you pay from the manufacturers doesn't make it criminal."

"Where did he source the product from in order to sell it to you at that price? I want a paper trail, let me see the pedigree." Stanley's prolonged pause only heightened her suspicion. "You don't have a pedigree, do you? At least not a legitimate one."

"In the future, please refrain from speaking with my suppliers."

"He called me! In the future, please have your suppliers refrain from contacting me... Why didn't he just call you for the order? I'm sure you would've cut him a PO."

The dial tone caused Charlie to smile. She listened for several seconds before silencing it. The sound helped soothe the rage before it fully manifested. She knew there was always someone between Stan and Roman for every transaction. One had to have the ability to always claim ignorance.

. . .

The express train from Stamford, Connecticut made only one stop, as if out of respect, before settling into its slot at Grand Central Station. Harlem, 125th Street; midwife to a cultural renaissance buried under gentrified concrete and brown stones with rents too high to pay from the proceeds of parties serving chicken and waffles while running Bostons in marathon bidding wars for books.

Charlie usually reserved her escapes to Harlem for the weekends, but she was already having a rough week at work, and she needed some fried catfish and jazz to keep her from cutting someone. Ancient bricks, steps from the train station, led to sidewalks guiding tourists through hallowed ground. Storefront merchants competed with concrete vendors with goods displayed on folding tables, as mobile as the currency used to purchase their wares.

Each step was definite, her stride patient, if not reluctant… as if the destination was the familiar journey itself. She inhaled deep and long enough for her lungs to fill with the ancestral breaths that gave creative life to the generations before her. Men gawked and chirped undauntedly as Charlie strolled by, each swollen in their own mating rituals; she smiled in recognition.

The winter air was brisk; snow was forecast for later that evening, but she had plenty of time to have dinner and catch the train back to Stamford before the flakes started falling. As she approached her destination, her stomach growled in anticipation like a full bladder aching to be emptied; the urgency intensified when the relief of release was near.

It was gospel night, and the gospel music had a bebop feel; Charlie found herself nodding her head as she consumed her fried catfish. The quartet was obviously a jazz group, but Charlie appreciated the flavor they gave to the music. She felt no guilt, but she knew her Grandmother would give her the side eye for moving in such a way to the Lord's music. No vocals were needed, the trumpet pronounced every word of the hymn like Gabriel annunciating the Messiah.

Jazz was her vice. Dropping the needle on a Coltrane LP was like rolling a joint and taking a slow drag. Charlie still enjoyed the crackle of an LP over a cassette or cd when listening to jazz.

Charlie knew she had caught the eye of the tall, lean, cherrywood colored man picking apart the stand-up bass, but she was unaware that he had caught her looking as well. Charlie kept a perpetual "approach with caution" look on her face which most intelligent men heeded, but her intercepted gaze emboldened him. He approached her table between sets.

"Excuse me," he said as Charlie looked up at him still chewing her food, "forgive my interruption, but you looked like you were enjoying the music as much as the food, and I just wanted to see if you had a request for our next set."

"No, I mean yes, I am, but I don't have a request; you gentlemen are doing just fine."

"Thank you," he said even more encouraged by her smile, "I might have to try some of that fried catfish."

"If you just want to try food, then you're in the wrong place."

His smile revealed nearly all of his teeth, and Charlie noticed how healthy they looked. A quick once-over revealed a well-groomed and dapper man, and her expression softened even more. If jazz was her high, then the jazz musician was her dealer. It was a weakness, she knew, and one she fought hard to combat. More than one musician had tried to use the product he was pushing to leave her vulnerable.

"I'm Quinton," he proclaimed still flashing his radiant smile, "I won't shake your hand while you're eating, but I would love to put your name on the list for the New Year's Eve show at Bones."

"Bones? That's the hottest jazz club in the city and the hardest ticket to get on New Year's Eve."

"I've heard. I'm playing with a band that's performing that night. If you give me your name and number, all you have to do is show up at the door."

"My name is Charlie Thomas, and you don't need my number; all they need is my name at the door, right?"

"Indeed..." Quinton's smile did not diminish. "Okay Charlie, enjoy your brunch, I hope to see you on New Year's Eve." Quinton turned and walked away, joining the others in the group at their reserved table. Charlie was full of skepticism, fearing she had just been fed a line. Her weakness left just enough cracks in her armor for her to smile unknowingly.

There was nothing left on Charlie's plate for the dishwasher to discard, it only needed to be dipped in soapy water and wiped clean. Charlie left her customary generous tip and vacated the table so another anxious patron could have their name called. It was time to succumb to the city, hoping it would be gentle while hailing its roughness. That's what she loved most about Harlem; it was like a good lover. It could slow grind tenderly all night or grab her by her hair from behind when it wanted to. She did not look back when she reached the door, but she could feel the set of eyes warmly escort her out to the cold sidewalk.

4

The Henry County Police Department was fixated on finding the masked men responsible for the armed robbery. The Georgia State Police had also gotten involved in the case, and both agencies promised to bring the perpetrators to justice. The DEA Diversion Investigators were single-minded in their pursuit of the stolen controlled substances. They had received an inventory of everything taken and the street value was substantial. They were determined to get the pilfered drugs off the street, particularly the narcotics. They were also tallying the security breakdowns and procedure deficiencies that allowed such a bold undertaking. The registrant would have questions to answer and an accountability to reconcile. Certainly, a fine would be warranted, or a letter of admonition at a minimum.

All agencies involved were convinced it was an inside job. Either a current or former employee was most likely involved, based on information obtained from those working at the facility that night. The offenders' knowledge of the cage and vault, and location of the night manager's and supervisor's offices, as well as the timing of the robbery all led to someone with intimate knowledge of the operation. Everyone was a suspect until they were not. There was only one real lead; the driver of the truck. His name was obtained from the log he signed when he entered the gated property.

"What the hell happened!?" The silent response was as brash as the question. Although the voice roared from a speaker-phone and the man on the other end was 250 miles away, his presence filled the room, and the threat of physical harm was still present.

"This was supposed to be a pickup, switch, and drop, just like we've done dozens of times. Who the hell was that on the back of the trailer? How did a routine pickup turn into armed robbery?"

The men looked around at each other, but no one offered an answer. They were just as clueless as the man whose voice bellowed from the speaker.

"The DEA doesn't give a shit about the other drugs, but because someone decided to take controlled substances, they're gonna suit up and get in the game. I don't have anyone at DEA on payroll yet." There was a pregnant pause before the next question crackled from the speaker. "Does anyone know who the men were?"

"No..." One man responded feebly. If there was anyone in the room with any sort of rank, it would have been him.

"So, they knew where the trailer would be parked, what the pickup location was and where the drop location would be, but no one knows who they were..." The voice trailed off, not expecting an answer. "What about the driver?"

"Name's Carl, he's done a lot of jobs for us."

"Think he was in on it?"

"I don't think so. Our guys with the cargo vans said he was surprised and pretty shaken."

"If we don't know who they were then the cops don't know either; but they know who the driver was. We need to find Carl before they do."

Everyone nodded.

"Do we have another driver in that region?"

"No, Carl did as many jobs as two or three drivers in other regions. He has no family that we know of, and he stayed on the road."

"That means he has nothing keeping him tied down, he's probably already on the run. Business doesn't stop, my customers are hungry for product; we need more drivers to replace Carl. Is there someone we can move from another region?"

"We might not have to; I know a guy..."

Carl was like a leaf in the wind, blown in whatever direction the breeze swirled, the scent of fear lingering in the air as he moved. His apartment in Birmingham, Alabama revealed he had left in a hurry. Drawers were still open with garments hanging out and strewn across the floor. The two men surveying the one bedroom dwelling envisioned Carl taking whatever he could stuff into a couple duffle bags and leaving the rest behind. Unlike law enforcement, they did not need a warrant to enter the apartment forcefully, so they knew it had been untouched. The mess was Carl's doing, not the police.

Their findings were received favorably by their employer. If he was running, he was not talking. He did not know any details of the operation, but the blanks left to be filled in by the investigators' imagination would only lead to more questions, and a prolonged investigation. Carl was a loose end that either required assistance or elimination; it had not yet been decided which.

ACCORDING TO THE PROPERTY MANAGER, Carl rented month-to-month and always paid with a convenience store money-order. There was no emergency contact on file, and Carl was an ideal tenant; he paid his rent on the first of the month and was never heard from or about. No, she had never seen a truck or trailer parked on the property and was not aware of any acquaintances. The DEA agents did not find any of the stolen controlled substances inside the apartment, but they also knew they were not the first visitors. The door had been opened without unlocking it first, and they did not know if Carl had been taken or was on the run. The apartment was generic, everything in the apartment was provided by the property management company, from the cheap furniture to the linens, dishes, and the bland art on the walls. Carl left nothing behind of use, and no personal items were laying around, not a photograph, business card, or even a menu from the local Chinese restaurant. It was clear he lived with one foot out the door. The police would come to the same conclusion when they searched the premises the next day.

THE BRIMMING mailbox was only twelve feet from the front door of the rickety double wide trailer near downtown Memphis, but it was only emptied on Sundays, and only out of necessity. It usually contained nothing of interest to those forced to retrieve its contents, and most of the correspondence was past-due when placed in the rusted metal mailbox, so additional idle time would not make a difference.

Clint almost tossed the envelope in the trash with the other mail. Some of the envelopes were pink or blue, indicating they contained final notices threatening legal action or disruption of whatever service was still active. Something about the plain white envelope with no return address captured his attention. It even made him put down the can of cold-enough beer he had retrieved from the decrepit refrigerator. It was a ritual on mail collection day, he had already emptied several cans with prolonged gulps; it helped make the task tolerable if not palatable. Clint wanted solitude in his inadequacy. The total disregard and demolition of one's pride should not be a public spectacle.

Maybe it was seeing his name and address handwritten in blue ink, or the fact that there was no postage on the envelope. It was in the mailbox with the other mail, but it could not have been delivered by the postal service, not without payment. Clint examined it carefully, handling the envelope cautiously, as if the mysterious contents were potentially life threatening.

Clint could feel his wife's presence lurking in the shadows for a soul to torment. His marriage felt more like a haunting and he knew it would take more than a judge to rid him of her, it would take a priest. He glanced around and found his wife, Carol, gazing at him curiously from the entranceway leading into the cramped kitchen where Clint's sloppy, overweight body was entrenched. The kitchen was tiny and untidy, like the rest of the dwelling.

"What's that?" Carol asked inquisitively. She was only interested because of the way Clint handled the envelope.

"Don't know."

"Well, are you gonna open it or not?"

"Hold your horses, your name ain't on this envelope, mine is. Looks suspicious to me; could be poison or somethin'."

"Poison?" Carol mocked, "who would want to do a no-good piece a' shit like you a favor?"

She walked over and snatched the envelope from Clint's hand. He did not resist; better she gets poisoned than him. Carol ripped open the envelope and unfolded the handwritten letter. No powder was present, so Clint moved in close and read the letter over her shoulder. His eyes scanned it quickly and focused on a dollar amount near the bottom of the paper. It was not an amount owed, but a proposed payment amount for his services.

Clint's heart rate accelerated as he read each sentence. There was an address for a pickup location along with a date and two-hour window, and an address for a drop location. Distracted by the amount of the payment for his services, Clint only scanned the paragraph following the payment amount and did not comprehend its meaning. Acceptance of the offer would lead to more assignments, not as opportunities but as obligations.

"Is this some kinda' joke?" Carol asked suspiciously. "Did your brother send this?"

"Roy can't spell this good," Clint proclaimed, "gimmie that."

Clint snatched the letter from his wife's claws and folded it carefully and placed it in his back pocket.

"What are you gonna do?" Carol asked, "There's no number to call and you don't even know who it's from."

"I know enough." With those final words the discussion ended; at least Clint's participation in it. Carol questioned his intellect and hurled a few parting shots, but Clint did not engage and eventually Carol faded into the darkness from which she came.

CLINT HAD ROUGHLY seven miles to decide if he would take exit 79 off the interstate as instructed. He was certain of his plan to follow the directions when he pulled away from the dock with the load, but the road gave him an abundance of time for contemplation. The money was good, but he could not spend it in jail. He contemplated what would happen if he backed out of the deal; but the money was good; it was too late he was already in too deep; he had already picked up the load, and the money was good.

He was not going to take the exit. He decided to keep his foot on the accelerator until he made it to his scheduled drop and report what had transpired to the authorities, end of discussion. He tried not to look at the green sign which informed travelers that exit 79 was in one mile, but he saw it out of the corner of his eye and the conversation inside his head resumed with a desperate fervor. The cab reeked of nervous perspiration and the cheap cologne he had purchased at a truck stop in West Virginia. The exit was upon him; the arrow on the sign reflected in his headlights. He had no intention of stopping or even slowing, but at the last second, he jerked the steering wheel clockwise and slammed his foot on the brake. The tires screeched and the trailer was lifted off the ground on one side, but Clint managed to recover and narrowly avoid the ditch. The rig finally came to a complete stop at the bottom of the hill as the yellow traffic light turned red. Clint took several deep breaths trying to calm himself, and the traffic light ran its course of green, yellow and red twice before Clint made a right turn onto the dark, desolate road.

The building was nondescript and looked abandoned. The only signage announced that the property was private, and that trespassing was not permitted. One had the impression that enforcement would not be by the law but by any means necessary. There was one dock door and a metal man door next to it; neither looked inviting. Clint carefully backed his tractor-trailer into perfect alignment with the dock door. He glanced around nervously and caught a glimpse of a figure putting chocks behind the wheels of the trailer. The figure approached the cab and climbed up on the driver's side. Clint reluctantly lowered the window.

"Got the seal?"

Clint handed the figure the seal which was handed to him when he picked up the load at the pharmaceutical manufacturer's facility. He thought that odd, usually the seal remained on the truck until it was removed at the destination, but he was not going to ask questions. The numbers matched what was written on the bill of laden, and what would be expected at the final destination. The seal currently on the truck would be cut off and discarded; there was no record of it.

"Smells like shit in there."

Clint smiled nervously but never looked him in the face. He could not identify him, and it made him feel safer. It was obvious Clint was very nervous.

"First time huh?"

Clint nodded his head, still afraid to engage.

"Don't worry, you're doing good. Just stick with the plan and you'll be fine." He tossed an envelope into Clint's lap. "This makes it a lot easier to swallow."

Clint was afraid to look down, but he knew what it was. He had no intention of counting the contents until he was back on the interstate and in control of his faculties.

Clint heard the dock door roll up followed several seconds later by the door to his trailer. He could feel the weight of the forklift as it entered and exited the trailer several times. Roughly forty-five minutes passed before Clint heard the trailer door close forcefully followed by a hard knocking on the trailer indicating it was time for him to leave. Whatever they did was complete, and Clint did not ask any questions. He put the transmission in gear and pulled away without looking back; he vowed to the good Lord never to return. He would not stop again until he reached the address he had been given in Louisville, Kentucky.

A poorly painted box truck that had once been part of the fleet of a national rental company, backed up to the dark building several miles from exit 79 off the interstate. What had been unloaded from Clint's trailer was loaded onto the box truck. It would arrive in South Florida the following evening.

5

The closet smelled of lavender. Not a strong perfume, only a soft aroma to keep the cotton and wool fibers from becoming stale. Dresses arranged by occasion occupied half the walk-in space, while curvy-fit jeans, in all washes, claimed most of the other half. All of the evidence at the scene led to a young professional woman with a generational thickness and the confidence of a tease. The first date dresses while conservative, were naughty enough to capture and suspend the imagination in anticipation of what a second date might reveal.

It was not a date by definition, at least not in Charlie's mind, but it did require something "grown and sexy" which usually meant new. She did not have a lot of time, but she would make time for a visit to Angela's Boutique. It had been a few months since she had seen her good friend anyway.

She parked in front of the quaint boutique in downtown Stamford and ventured inside. The bell above the door announced her presence, and Angela, the proprietor of the boutique, greeted her with an affectionate hug.

"Well, if it isn't Miss Black Corporate America." Angela greeted her friend.

"Just trying to be like you when I grow up."

"How is your daddy doing?" Angela asked sincerely.

"He's fine, you know Daddy; still working hard and playin' harder."

"He ain't retired from GM yet?"

"Girl the union got him a cush job. Half the time he clocks in and drives to Canada to the casino. He said he's done his time in the salt mines, and he's earned what he has now. He has thirty-some years in the shop."

They shared a laugh and Angela squeezed her again.

"It's good to see you girl; so, what's the occasion? First date, second date, or trying to get a date?"

"I don't know..." Charlie whined, "none of the above... girl just hook me up with what I need. You know my body almost as intimately as a lover."

"Not for lack of trying," Angela exclaimed flirtatiously.

"You know you don't have what I need."

"I had what you needed that one time in college."

"Girl we were young, and I was drunk."

"Yo' ass is never drunk. As much brown liquor as you drink... you knew what you were doing."

"You took advantage of me, I feel violated..."

"Whateva', so where you goin'?"

"New Year's Eve at Bones."

"Girl, you lyin'!" Angela yelled in disbelief, "those tickets are hard as hell to get; how did *you* get tickets?"

"This brotha was playing at the restaurant I go to in Harlem and he asked if I wanted to go."

"Let me guess... he's a jazz musician...do you know this dude?"

"Never seen him before in my life, but he had great teeth."

"So you goin' out with him?"

"You sound jealous, and we're not going out. He asked me my name so he could leave it at the door. He said he's a musician with the group playing that night."

"And you believed him?" Instinctively, her right hand came to rest on her right hip.

"Girl what do I have to lose? I didn't give him my number or anything. If my name isn't on the list, I turn around and go to one of the house parties I've been invited to."

"You had on a dress, didn't you? That ass and those thick legs, that brotha' couldn't help himself; I know how he feels."

"Girl shut up and find me a dress."

The two friends eventually settled on a little black dress, which was a staple in every refined woman's closet, and agreed on a pair of cranberry stilettos and matching clutch.

Two DEA diversion investigators arrived at the pharmaceutical distribution center in McDonough, GA and showed their credentials to the anxious receptionist sitting behind the thick glass window. The investigators first identified themselves outside when they pressed the button, and a female voice cracked from the speaker asking how she could help them. Before buzzing them in, the receptionist placed a call to the operations manager, and in under ninety seconds everyone in the building knew DEA was onsite. DEA inspections were the subject of much preparation at the facility. Mock inspections were conducted, a binder was assembled with documentation the investigators usually asked for, monthly inventories of controlled substances were performed, and when the DEA investigators arrived the anxiety in the building was still tangible. Few things struck as much fear as an unannounced DEA Inspection.

. . .

"You had to know we were coming," Wanda, the lead investigator and diversion supervisor in the Atlanta office, said as everyone settled around the large faux wood conference table. She could sense the shock and nervousness caused by their presence at the facility. The operations manager, cage and vault supervisor, and the compliance supervisor joined Wanda and her colleague Peggy in the conference room.

"Any time a registrant has a theft of the magnitude you had you can bet money on the fact that we're showing up." Wanda was from Southwest Atlanta, and not even her bachelor's degree or DEA credentials could hide that fact. Her tone was always matter of fact, and she had zero tolerance for 'game playing' as she called it.

"We figured since we had to come out for the theft, we might as well just do a full inspection; you were about due anyway."

"Great," the operations manager stated with as much fake enthusiasm as he could muster, "what do you need from us?"

"You know the routine, let's see the biennial inventory, and let's go count some product and do the reconciliation."

"Do you want to start with the product that had the shrinkage?"

"Oh, is that what we're calling it? According to the 106 you filed, we're talking pallets of 'shrinkage.'" Wanda used air quotes around the word shrinkage. "The level of diversion we're talking about could have only happened with the assistance of someone here."

"Don't you think it's a little premature to form a conclusion without a proper investigation?"

Wanda tilted her head slightly and rested her chin in her hand as she leaned on the arm of the chair. Her dark brown eyes captured his shifting bluish grey eyes and would not let them go, forcing the reddening faced man to look at her as she mused about how he started it, not her. If he wanted to test her, then it was on."

"You know, you're right, let's just get right to the investigation. When was the last time you did a full alarm test?"

The ops manager looked at the cage and vault supervisor who looked at the compliance manager, whose mouth hung open, but no words fell out.

"If I recall correctly," Wanda said in what she called her 'customer service' voice, "your SOP states you conduct them monthly, yes?" A head nod from the compliance manager but nothing more.

"Good, let me see the last six months test results. I can review them when we get back from conducting a full test right now."

"Now?" The operations manager questioned. "We're in the middle of picking and packing orders."

"I'm sorry if this is an inconvenience," she said in an even more professional tone. Peggy looked at her struggling to contain her smirk. "I just want to be sure to conduct a proper investigation in a timely manner." She stood to her feet and Peggy instinctively stood with her. "Ready when you are."

BEFORE WANDA and Peggy left for lunch on their fourth day, Wanda let the operations manager know they would be conducting the closeout meeting later that day. The ops manager was relieved, but only consternation showed on his face. The audit had been brutal, it seemed as if the two investigators had audited every regulation in 21 CFR part 1300 to End. They had undergone several DEA audits, but none like what they experienced that week. He thought back to the first day when he challenged Wanda, and suspected that played a big part in how the week unfolded.

. . .

THE CONFERENCE ROOM table sat ten, and all ten chairs were occupied; there were even two individuals standing in the back of the room. This was no surprise to Wanda and Peggy, it was typical when the registrant knew the audit had not gone well, and this audit had the added "shrinkage" to investigate. Three suits from corporate had flown in on Wednesday after receiving the distress call from the site leader after the first day.

"Well," Wanda exhaled, "I see we have a full house; hello everyone."

The obligatory greetings filled the room, followed by brief introductions. Peggy jotted down the names on her notepad, as did the compliance manager.

"First, thank you for the hospitality, you've been great hosts this week. As far as the inspection, you know... it... well we were quite surprised by some of the observations we found, and I understand you have experienced quite a bit of turnover, but... registrants still have an obligation to maintain adequate security and record keeping during periods of transition." Wanda paused to read the room. A few heads nodded, but she knew they wanted to get to it, enough of the niceties. "Okay, Peggy will be walking us through the observations and potential findings."

Peggy smiled nervously. The closeout was the most contentious part of the inspection, especially with the number and severity of some of the violations they found. She removed her legal pad from her bag and placed it on the table in front of her. She thumbed through to the last page of notes. An audible gasp came from somewhere in the room.

"Are all of those pages filled with observations?" The question came from one of the suits leaning against a wall in the back.

"Mostly, yes." Peggy replied.

"Then I'm gonna need a chair."

"And a drink." Another suit exclaimed.

"Okay," Peggy said regaining control, "let's start with physical security..."

EVERYONE in the conference room was exhausted when Peggy reached the final page of observations. At times the meeting felt like a deposition, and at others like a high-school debate. While interaction was welcome during a closeout meeting, it was not encouraged; especially when it was hostile. More than once the site leader had to be shut down by a suit from legal and reminded that 'there would be opportunity for formal challenges once an official document was presented. This was just an opportunity for the investigators to share their thoughts before deciding what, if anything to allege in writing.' Of course, that disclaimer drew a smirk from Wanda, but she remained silent.

"Is there anything else?" The operations manager asked sarcastically when Peggy had finished.

"Just the matter of the shrinkage..." Wanda exclaimed, "at least that's what your operations manager called it," Wanda added when she saw the furled brows from the suits. "Of course we are still conducting our investigation, but we do have several leads on the location of the product, and we hope to recover as much of it as we can soon as possible. I don't have to stress to you the importance of getting those narcotics off the street."

"Anything the DEA needs from us just let us know. I hope we have proven that we as a company will do whatever it takes to aid your investigation and recover our product." - A suit.

"Of course... Wanda nodded. "One thing that is troubling is the fact that a full inventory was not conducted after the theft. It's my understanding that packing lists were used to do an accounting of the product on the staged pallets that were taken.

Based on the inventory and accountability we did just on the product known to be stolen, we uncovered that more product was lost than originally thought. The true scope of the loss won't be known until a full inventory is conducted in the cage and vault. Obviously more controlled substances were taken than what was reported on the 106." Wanda paused to let it sink in. She could have gone on about the severity of the mistakes and repercussions, but she knew the suits were already doing the math on potential fines. No need to mention what they had learned from interviews they conducted with employees from the night shift; it was still an active investigation.

When the two investigators were off the property the real bloodshed began.

"What the fuck?! The outburst was directed at the site leader. "What have you been doing down here?"

Before he could respond, the operations manager chimed in. "She had it out for us from the beginning. She didn't like it when I challenged her bullshit on day one. She found us guilty before she even looked at a single piece of evidence, I mean record, a single record."

"You look pretty fucking guilty to me;" the suit had shed his jacket and loosened his tie, "and evidence is right, because this is headed before an administrative judge. Forget the fines, we'll settle those down when they throw an outrageous number at us, but we'll be lucky to keep our registration. They'll have an order to show cause drafted before the weekend ends."

"What's this shit about the inventory?" Ron asked his operations manager. "I thought a full count was conducted."

"That's what I thought," he replied looking at the cage and vault supervisor.

"I thought we only needed to count what was on the pallets."

"If he still has a job when I get back to the office tomorrow, his won't be the only head on the ground. Fuck..."

There was a bar at the hotel, and he could already smell the liquor on his breath as he walked out of the building with the other suits close behind.

6

The sound was too voluptuous to be contained and too emboldened to be relegated to simple background behind dinner conversation. There was little air left for patrons to breathe after trained lungs seized every portion and blasted it through brass horns, only to be reclaimed for another note. Swing, as playful as falling in love and as hysterical as a child's laughter. Those fortunate enough to secure tickets were swinging in the new year in style. Bones did not have much of a dance floor to speak of, but those brazen few who did occupy the space soared as if on wings rising to glory after judgement and stepping as if at Heaven's gates trying to break in a new pair of shoes.

Charlie's name was on the list as promised, and she was allowed to enter the club even though the large figure at the door expected a man. It was not her intent to make an entrance, but notes dropped to the ground like groceries in a rain-soaked paper bag when she walked in. The black knit dress was brought to life by her movement. A motif that at first glance appeared predictable, but a more refined gaze revealed its complexity. It was more constraint than flaunt, governed by the fortitude of generations of black women praying not to catch the eye or be disrespected as a distraction. Hopefully no one outside of the musicians noticed the temporary loss of breath of the saxophonist as Charlie found a vacant barstool and settled into her place in the universe as the North star. She found the man responsible for her ticket on stage playing the standup bass.

"A PRETTY DRINK FOR A PRETTY LADY." The bartender exclaimed as he placed an amaretto sour in front of Charlie. Charlie looked down at the drink and then at the bartender with a disapproving look.

"You can save the pretty drinks for some hussy looking to be picked up." She pointed at the brown liquor on the top shelf. "You can pour me a glass of that."

"Oh, it's like that." The bartender smirked as he looked where Charlie pointed.

"I've been drinking Crown with my daddy since I was sixteen. He didn't want some fool thinking he could take advantage after a few drinks. It saved my ass more than once in college... literally."

The pretty drink was replaced with a potent brown liquor with no ice.

"On the house."

"Thanks, but I don't wanna owe the house." She reached into her clutch and retrieved her credit card. "This is on American Express, start a tab."

"What's your name," The bartender asked tentatively, "or should I call you brown liquor?"

"Well, that *was* my nickname in college, but my daddy named me Charlie; and no, he did not want a boy."

"I-I ..."

"You were thinking it."

"Okay, just let me know when your glass is thirsty."

"Stay close."

The bartender retreated to an area where he could watch the carnage. One by one men confidently approached Charlie and retreated with less than they had.

The bass player, she didn't remember his name, held and stroked the standup base like it was a woman. A curvy, sensuous woman like Charlie that purred and moaned with his every stroke of the bow or pluck of the string. He had good hands, and she let herself wonder if he knew how to caress a woman as well as he caressed that instrument. He smiled from the stage and nodded, letting her know that he did. She turned away self-conscious; he had read her mind… or the look in her brown eyes. After a few drinks, the only thing she could not control was the look in her eyes.

THE BAND ANNOUNCED they were talking a break, but they promised to return if it was okay with the audience, and there were no objections. The bass player took the opportunity to join Charlie at the bar.

"I'm almost scared to approach you, you've turned away just about every man in this club tonight."

"They didn't place my name on the list at the door;" Charlie responded graciously, "and it was a short list. Thank you."

"It was my pleasure, I'm glad you came."

"The band is really good," Charlie exclaimed looking for a distraction, "you were stroking that bass like it was your woman."

"Well, it's been a while; I'm out of practice."

"It didn't look like it to me."

"I mean on a woman…"

The bartender returned, and the timing could not have been better as far as Charlie was concerned.

"I just had to come meet the man who has lasted longer than one minute with brown liquor. She's been shootin' 'em down like target practice."

"Brown liquor?"

"Story for another time," Charlie teased.

"Oh, so there's gonna be another time?"

Charlie smiled coyly. "I don't even know your name…"

"You mean you don't remember my name. I introduced myself at the restaurant." He extended his hand to Charlie. "Quinton, everyone calls me Q."

Charlie extended her hand to meet his and he kissed it.

"Oh, a gentleman…"

"Just a gentle man."

"Okay Q, that's my cue," the bartender proclaimed, "just let me know if I can get you anything."

"Actually, I know she has a bar tab, but can you bring her anything she wants for dinner and put it on mine?

"You got it." He handed Charlie a menu. "Take your time." The bartender walked away leaving Charlie and Q to talk alone.

The conversation was mutually satisfying, and the laughter authentic. Q only commented on her beauty once, but the prose was likened to that of a poet. Charlie ordered the only fish selection on the menu, and they toasted the night with a shot of Crown Select.

"I need to get back to the stage," Q said regrettably, "our next set will be starting soon."

"Is your band playing until midnight?"

"Yes Ma'am, we're swinging in the New year. It's finally New Year's Eve, 1999 and we're gonna party like Prince proclaimed."

"Well, I'll have to make an exit before the clock strikes twelve."

"Like you made an entrance? Our sax player lost his breath

and missed a couple notes when you walked in wearing that dress."

Charlie wrote her phone number on a napkin and handed it to Q. "Here's my number. Call me if you want to see a first date dress."

"This wasn't a first date?"

"No, I just wanted to see if you were a man of your word or full of shit."

"Stick around until at least the third song," Q requested, "I have a solo I want to dedicate to you. There's a lot of... I believe stroking was the word you used." Q stood and kissed her on the cheek before walking back to the stage.

EXHAUSTED from the candidates who looked good on paper and had the standard scripted responses to his standard scripted questions, Hank was glad to see the dirty fingernails, cowboy boots, and beer gut sitting across the desk from him. His voice sounded like a Harley, and Hank would bet a paycheck that he rode one when he wasn't driving his pickup truck. Hank was looking at a rounder version of himself, and he could feel his blood pressure headache finally subsiding. Luke Cartwright wasn't from Texas, but hell... he checked every other box; no one was perfect.

"Look out there at those people Luke," Hank instructed as he pointed in the direction of the large window looking out into the warehouse from his office. "I wouldn't give a nickel for most of 'em, and I would want change back for the others. I can count on one hand the ones who give a damn."

Luke nodded like he knew the story all too well. He watched as employees casually pushed carts lined with totes filled with various pharmaceuticals down the aisles and huddled in conversation, presumably out of view. Hank walked over to the window carrying his oversized coffee mug. He found Robert, the supervisor, in the usual place.

"That so-called supervisor over there sittin' on his ass is about as worthless as the rest of 'em. He's too scared to make a decision and he lets his employees walk all over him. I'd fire him but the ol' bastard has been here longer than the cracks in the floors and it would take an act of Congress to get him out of here, damn Democrats. I can't wait to elect George W. You know he's from the great state of Texas, don't you?"

Hank did not wait for him to answer, because he knew it would be in the affirmative.

"Ever been to Texas Luke?"

"Can't say that I have."

"Well, I won't hold that against you, but it's your loss. Texas is the best of these so-called United States. I always say, you better get to Texas before you get to Heaven."

"So how did you end up in Michigan?" Luke asked looking at the large Texas flag hanging on the wall behind Hank's desk. It was the first thing one noticed when entering Hank's office.

"It's a long story," Hank responded with a smirk. "I was going to ask you the same thing; you're a southern boy."

"It's a longer story, and it involves a woman."

"Don't they all... made you leave your last job in Georgia and move up north to the cold. Must be a sweet Georgia peach."

Luke smiled and nodded. Hank walked back to his desk and dropped down into his faux leather chair. He put his coffee mug down on his desk right on top of Luke's resume; the splash would leave a permanent stain. Luke did not flinch as their eyeballs mirrored each other's movements, or lack thereof.

"When can you start Luke?"

"I already have.... I've already seen a few people on the clock who don't need to be."

Hank could not stop the smile from stretching across his

face if he had wanted to. He spent the rest of the interview reciting the company history and briefly discussing the business model at a high level. No need to get into the weeds until absolutely necessary.

Davidson Distributing Company was one of five pharmaceutical distribution centers operated by Davidson Enterprises, headquartered in Stamford, CT. At over two hundred thousand square feet, the Distributing Company in Livonia, MI was the largest facility in the Davidson network. Unlike the other distribution centers in Los Angeles, Dallas, and Orlando, which purchased pharmaceuticals from manufacturers and distributed them to pharmacies, hospitals, and other final dispensers, the Distributing Company purchased the majority of its drugs from distributors and sold them to other distributors, while also supplementing the inventory of Davidson's other four facilities. Luke was confused by the tangled web of distribution, and Hank sought to ease his mind.

"I know you're used to the traditional pharmaceutical distribution model at your previous employer, but there is nothing traditional about this place. All you have to do is make sure the product gets received into inventory when it comes in, that it's picked and packed correctly, and loaded on the truck on time. Don't worry about where it came from or where it's going."

It sounded easy enough and a handshake sealed the deal. He would start immediately; he had no current employer to serve a two-week notice.

ROBERT WALKED into the all-white kitchen and found his wife packing his lunch. The appliances, cabinets, and backsplash were all white, and even the countertops were white laminate. The kitchen was large but dated, no renovations had been made in the forty-three years they had lived in the house.

Breakfast was on the table waiting for him. He walked over and kissed his loving wife before sitting at the table.

"You know you don't have to fix me breakfast every morning. It's too early..."

"If you have to get up this early to go to work, I can certainly get up and fix you some breakfast." She placed a brown paper bag on the counter. "And here's your lunch."

"Now Honey you know I can grab something to eat on my break, I have time, you don't have to pack my lunch every day."

"I know," Barbara whined, "but I just feel better preparing your lunch after your heart attack and all. You know the doctor said you have to be mindful of what you eat."

"And you don't trust me to eat healthy on my own."

Barbara blushed as she smiled sweetly. "I didn't say that."

"Actions speak louder than words."

HANK'S INSTRUCTIONS to Robert had been clear. Two pallets of product wrapped in black shrink wrap with yellow tape would arrive and needed to be quarantined immediately. He was to be notified the moment it arrived. Robert nodded his head like he understood, and assured Hank that he would see to it personally. Hank had no faith in his supervisor, but even he could manage such a simple task.

The product arrived and was signed for at 1:05pm. Robert was in his office with door closed eating the lunch his wife had carefully packed. She stopped letting him take frozen microwave dinners because of the sodium. He had already suffered a minor heart attack and was taking medicine for his blood pressure and cholesterol, but he could not afford to retire. In five years, he would be sixty-five and could possibly start considering retiring then.

It was not uncommon to receive pallets wrapped in black shrink wrap. Davidson Distributing Company routinely shipped its controlled substances with black shrink wrap, which technically was a DEA violation. Controlled substances were not to be marked or identified during shipment and the black shrink wrap identified them. What stood out about the two pallets that were unloaded at 1:05pm was the yellow crime scene tape. At least that's what it looked like to the employees in the receiving area. They were eager to unwrap the mysterious pallets but were disappointed to find boxes that looked like every other box they routinely received. The label identified the contents as a very common medication used to treat hypertension. The only peculiar thing was the lack of a packing slip or any other paperwork, but that also happened on occasion. Initial research was conducted, but no open purchase order was found for the product. Further research would require a call to the purchasing department, and no warehouse employee ever spoke to anyone in the front office; it was unclear if they were even allowed to, but no one felt comfortable attempting communication. They would cross paths in the parking lot or at the vending machine in the break room, but seldom was eye contact made, or words exchanged.

The pallets were moved to the side until Robert returned from lunch. Hank and his two direct reports were the only ones from the warehouse whose badges granted access to the front offices. Robert would have to contact purchasing to determine the supplier. He would create a generic purchase order to receive the product against, if the shipper could not be determined. The purchasing department was unaware of an open purchase order for the product, so Robert created a generic purchase order at 3:25pm.

The first pallet was placed up in the racks intact. It was stored in bulk inventory, so full cases would only be picked from it. The other pallet was broken down and stocked in three locations. Four cases were cut open and stocked in the primary pick location, twelve cases were stocked in a secondary location, and the remainder of the pallet was placed into a backup location.

HANK HAD NOT HEARD anything about his two pallets arriving but that did not surprise him. Robert had probably forgotten to tell him that the pallets were quarantined, so Hank went to the quarantine area to inspect the pallets.

"What do you mean you haven't seen 'em?" Hank responded to the Lead in the Quarantine cage. "Two pallets, black shrink wrap, yellow tape."

The young man shrugged and shook his head. "Don't know what to tell you Sir."

Robert had the same deer in headlights look when Hank walked into his office and asked about the pallets.

"Where is the product wrapped in black shrink wrap with yellow tape that I said would come in today? What did I tell you!?"

Robert stammered but no recognizable words came out.

"I specifically said don't receive it into inventory, don't cut the shrink wrap, don't even look at it too long. Do you remember that?"

Hank looked down at his watch and then back into the leery eyes of his supervisor. It was possible they had not arrived, but it was more likely his supervisor had screwed up. Hank leaned heavily toward the latter.

"TWO PALLETS, black shrink-wrap with yellow tape..." Hank exclaimed when he walked into the receiving area with Robert on his heels. "Anybody seen 'em?"

Robert looked at his receiving team in desperation and knew the answer immediately from the looks on their faces.

"They came in around lunchtime," one of the employees proclaimed, "I unloaded the truck."

"I tried to receive 'em, but there was no paperwork." Another employee exclaimed. Sweat drenched Robert's forehead as he thought about the purchase order he created for two pallets of product. Hank never told him what the product was, and the shrink-wrap and tape had already been discarded when he created a purchase order for the product.

"Where is it now?" Hank asked. It was more of a demand than a question. Two sets of eyes focused on Robert.

"Robert created a PO, and I received them in. All of the product received this afternoon has been stocked already."

Hank also knew there was a good chance that some of it had already been picked and packed for shipment as well.

"Goddammit!" He turned and shot Robert a piercing gaze. "Let's see which you find first, my product or another job."

IT DID NOT TAKE Robert long to discover that product had indeed been picked and packed for shipment. He commandeered every available body in the warehouse to make sure every box was found, cut open, and the product retrieved. When the truck arrived, Robert was too consumed with the search to notice two employees raise the dock door. He did not see Hank until he stood over him.

"Have you found all of it?"

"We're still working on it, but we..."

"The truck is here, and I've never missed a departure time, and I don't plan on starting now."

Robert glanced over and saw the two employees raise the truck door revealing an empty trailer. "We're working as fast as we can," he said exasperated. His voice had raised to the level of a yell, and Hank pulled him to the side away from the others.

"Do we have any more of the drug in stock?"

"Well... yeah," Robert answered curiously, "but it's a different lot number and expiration date."

"I don't give a damn. Take some of it and use it to replace what's still missing from the two pallets that *you* let get received and stocked. Re-stack the pallet and put the different lot number in the middle. Any open partial cases add some of the product to the case and reseal it. I want you to do it; no one else."

Robert was reluctant, and the fear was on his face. "I don't feel comfortable doing that."

"I didn't ask if you were comfortable, just get it done."

"What was wrong with the two pallets?" Robert blurted out unexpectedly. He even surprised himself by asking the question.

"What did you say?"

"What's wrong with the product?" he asked even more emboldened, "why is it quarantined?"

"That's not your concern."

"It is my concern if I do what you're asking."

Hank lunged at Robert as if he was going to strike him, causing Robert to recoil and brace for a blow which never came, at least not physically.

"I'm not asking." Hank turned and walked away, leaving Robert wrestling with his thoughts. It was not the first time Robert was instructed to do something he was not comfortable with, and each time he convinced himself it would be his last.

The FDA was not the only three-letter government agency interested in the two quarantined pallets sitting in the Distributing Company's warehouse. Two FBI agents, both playing the role of bad cop, also wanted to know the story behind the two pallets of counterfeit medication.

The FDA was in and out in a couple hours. They wanted to

take an inventory of the product, get copies of all necessary documentation and arrange a destruction date so they could witness the incineration. Because all product was accounted for, there was no need to issue a recall. Hank gave them everything they wanted and was an accommodating host. That changed when the FBI started their line of questioning.

"Have a seat Mr. Wallace," the senior agent instructed when Hank returned to his office after escorting the two FDA agents to the main entrance.

"Well, this *is* my office," Hank exclaimed as he fell into his chair.

"You from Texas?" The senior agent asked looking at the flag hanging on the wall.

"Born and raised," Hank responded proudly. The other agent wrote something down on his notepad. Hank looked curiously at the two men wearing identical dark grey government suits.

"What happened to the yellow tape?"

"What yellow tape?"

"Come on Hank... Can I call you Hank?"

"No." Hank focused on the senior and taller agent doing the talking and tried not to look at the sidekick taking notes.

"The yellow tape on the black plastic the pallets were wrapped in."

Hank's eyes shifted slightly as he considered his next words carefully. His words were being recorded, at least on paper, and the sidekick may have been recording his thoughts and mannerisms as well.

"We had to take inventory of the pallets to make sure everything was there."

"Those were not the instructions. The pallets were to remain untouched until we arrived."

Again, Hank's eyes shifted, and it was captured in writing.

He briefly considered asking what was just written down but knew he would not get an answer. It was an intimidation tactic he surmised, and it had him distracted.

"Okay look..." Hank said as he leaned forward in his chair. "The receiving crew unwrapped the pallets by mistake when they came in. When I found out about it, I had the pallets rewrapped and placed in quarantine. It was a simple mistake."

"So, you did not unwrap the pallets to take inventory like you stated earlier." It was more of a statement than a question, and Hank made no attempt to answer it. "At any time did the product leave the receiving area?"

"Yes."

"Where did it go?"

"It got stocked, but we quickly retrieved it and took inventory before rewrapping the boxes on the pallets."

"I see," the senior agent said as he nodded at his colleague, "I noticed that several of the boxes had been opened."

"Yes, but we made sure each case was full; nothing was missing."

"How do you know the contents which were removed from the box were replaced with the original contents and not other bottles of like product?"

That was a good question. In his haste to find the product, Hank did not check to verify lot numbers. Shit! He looked at the sidekick to see if he had heard that. He did not hear Hank curse in his mind, but he did make note of the panic in his eyes.

"Do you mind if we have another look?"

Of course he minded, but he did not answer the rhetorical question. He felt like asking for a lawyer.

"So, where did the product come from?" The senior agent asked methodically.

"I don't know. I run a shipping and receiving operation; I don't get into the details."

"So, you routinely receive pharmaceuticals without some kind of packing slip or invoice?"

"These pallets did not have any paperwork when they came in."

"This time..." the senior agent added. "This was not the first time the product hit your dock. This was actually a return because your customer suspected it was counterfeit."

Hank sat expressionless, looking the senior agent squarely in the eye. His jaws were clenched in anger, but the agents were not impressed.

"Surely there's some paperwork somewhere that will tell us where the product originated."

"Surely," Hank answered sarcastically, "but not here. I can direct you to the front office for any documents you might need."

"Would that be Stanley Forsythe?"

Hank's eyes shifted for a third time. "He's our general manager, but there are others who can help you with document requests."

"I'd rather not waste any more time. If you say Stan is the man, then we will tell him you said he was the one to talk to."

Hank could feel his body temperature spike, and his head felt as if it would explode in any second. He reached into his drawer and retrieved a prescription bottle. He twisted the cap and shook out a white tablet into his moist palm. He threw the medicine into his mouth and swallowed hard.

"One more thing before we go have a second look at the two pallets. Have you ever heard of Rome Enterprises?"

"Can't say that it rings a bell," Hank answered quickly before he could shift his eyes or any other part of his body. Maybe he answered too quickly.

. . .

The two pallets were stacked with cases containing four packs of twelve bottles filled with sixty tablets each. All of the cases were sealed with the exception of three cases. After the three cases were inspected, it was discovered that two twelve packs had a different lot number and expiration date than the other packs and cases. Hank's mind immediately started backtracking to the day the product came in and all the mistakes that were made. He cursed his supervisor again and stared wide-eyed at the two agents. No words were exchanged nor needed to convey the gravity of the situation. At least one hundred forty-four bottles of potentially counterfeit product had left the building. Tracking them down was a priority.

"I think it's time to speak with Mr. Forsythe now."

Stanley was not on site, at least that's what the two FBI agents were told, but he was available to speak via phone. The three men returned to Hank's office where Hank dialed Stanley from a speaker phone.

"Hey Stanley, I'm here with..."

"I'm agent Butler and this is..."

"Do you have a warrant?" Stanley asked abruptly.

"Excuse me?"

"A warrant. You've asked for certain documents, so I'm sure you have presented Hank with a warrant."

"We're just talking..."

"Until you have a Judge's autograph, the conversation is over, and we will not be turning over any documents. Hank, please escort these gentlemen out of my building."

"Just one question," the senior agent said as he leaned back in the chair, "What is the nature of your relationship with Roman Caesar, and the apparent partnership between Davidson Distributing and Rome Enterprises and its affiliates?"

The dial tone blared from the speaker for longer than it needed to, as Hank hesitated for effect. Newly empowered, he stood and strutted over to the door and opened it wide.

"We'll be back," the senior agent proclaimed as they stood and walked out of the office.

7

The Davidson Distributing Company was Roman's preeminent trading partner, and Stanley Forsythe was his most loyal accomplice, but a whispered rumor in confidence caused Roman to seek the security of another prime trading partner as a precaution. His source was reliable and discreet and had never been wrong before. Roman had been trying to penetrate the big three distributors for years, and this could either be his golden opportunity, or shut the door permanently. Stanley claimed ignorance when asked, and Roman had no reason to doubt his most trusted cohort. He figured that Bob Davidson would keep it hidden from his team until it was a done deal.

Paul leaked like a faucet and Roman knew he could not keep his mouth shut, but he knew how to move product. He was general manager at one of the largest independent pharmaceutical wholesalers in the country, and their tentacles stretched coast to coast. They were an Authorized Distributor for most manufacturers and their financials were solid. Roman was reluctant to make the call, but he had to ensure he had channels to move product in case Davidson dried up.

"Paul, how the hell are ya?" Roman bellowed when Paul answered the phone on the first ring.

"Roman, what you got for me?" The eagerness in his tone was a bit much, even for Paul. "What fell off the truck and into my lucky hands?"

Roman hesitated, he contemplated his next words carefully. In five seconds, he had confirmed that he could not trust Paul to be the partner he sought and questioned if he should proceed with the conversation.

"Roman?"

"Yeah, I'm here."

"Thought I lost you. What super deal do you have for me today?"

"Sorry, I don't have anything today. Just calling my best customers to say Happy New Year."

"Well same to you Roman. Let me know when you have something good."

"Will do."

Roman hung up the phone and made a mental note to move Paul to the bottom of the list. He dialed Peter LeBlanc at Gulf Coast Pharmapack. Roman's companies did a lot of business with Gulf Coast, and it had always been fruitful for both parties.

"Not interested," Peter exclaimed when he saw Roman's number and picked up the phone. Even those two words carried Peter's thick Louisiana accent.

"Well good afternoon to you too."

"Hello Roman, like I said, not interested."

"You haven't heard my offer yet."

"I hear your offers in my sleep Roman; not that I'm getting any sleep lately thanks to you. The FDA paid us a visit inquiring about some Laprin we repackaged. They claim the lot numbers we sourced and repackaged were of interest."

"Of interest... what the hell does that mean?"

"It means the manufacturer has no record of that lot number."

"Where did you get the product from?" Roman asked audaciously. There was nothing but silence on the other end of the phone. Both men knew the answer.

"The real question is where did *you* get the product from?"

"What did you tell them?" Roman's tone was more threatening than nervous.

"What do you think I told them? I gave them an invoice from one of your companies. I don't even remember which Rome Enterprises company was on the invoice, there are so many. I don't know how you keep them sorted out."

"Do you have a copy of the invoice?"

"Of course, I made a copy of everything I gave them."

"FAX it to me."

"Okay but nothing else for a while. We have too many eyes looking at us right now." Before Roman could respond the call ended.

Roman had newly acquired product to move quickly before it was reported, and without missing a beat he dialed another number. His search for another prime partner would have to wait, he needed the product out of his warehouse.

"Christine, I was hoping you were back from vacation." Roman exclaimed when Christine answered. "I didn't want to have to deal with your counterpart at corporate."

"I heard about your conversation with Charlie, sorry about that."

"How was your vacation?"

"It was..."

"Great, glad to hear it. I have some Testrol that I've been saving just for you. A New Year's gift for my number one customer. I'm sending you the numbers now."

There was a pause as Christine opened the email and attachment.

"Wow, this is well below WAC."

"Like I said, a gift. Since when do we trade at wholesale acquisition cost anyway?"

Another pregnant pause.

"Testrol is hard to get right now, and definitely not at this price, how... where..."

"Jesus Christine, you're starting to sound like the other girl. I assure you, that product came directly from the manufacturer."

"I don't suppose you have an invoice or something..."

"I have a packing slip from the manufacturer if it will put your mind at ease. It has another company's name on it, but you'll know the product is legitimate."

Christine had more questions; the product had obviously been diverted but at least it was not counterfeit; she knew better than to ask. Roman could not get Charlie fired, but one word to Stanley and Christine knew she would be unemployed, or worse.

"We'll take all you have."

"That's my girl. Heather will be expecting your purchase order within the hour." Roman hung up the phone before Christine could utter another word. His next call was to his shipping supervisor.

"Get that shit outta here; it's all going to Davidson Distributing."

BOB DAVIDSON'S corner office was at the end of the hall, but it was closely guarded by Geraldine. Stanley's intent was to walk past her, but she stood and blocked his path to Bob's double doors.

"May I help you?" It was not an offer of assistance, but a warning. The only one she would offer.

"I'm here to see Bob," Stanley exclaimed looking down at

her. Stanley stood a foot taller than the woman standing before him. Her face and posture were stern.

"You don't have an appointment."

"I know he's in there."

"And he probably knows you're out here as loud as you are. Now have a seat and I'll see if he wants to see you."

Stanley took a deep breath and slowly exhaled. He had gone toe to toe with Geraldine before and he knew resistance was futile. He turned and walked over to one of the leather chairs and stood beside it. Geraldine returned to her desk and called Bob.

"Is it him?" Bob asked when he answered the phone.

"Sure is."

"You can send him in."

"No, not yet. I'll let you know when I'm ready. You white men have entitlement issues, and this one has it bad." She hung up the phone and looked in Stanley's direction. "It will be a minute; Mr. Davidson is busy at the moment."

Stanley's eyes protested but his mouth did not. He refused to sit, and kept his eyes locked on Geraldine.

TWENTY MINUTES PASSED as if they were ninety. Geraldine called the owner of the company and was greeted with laughter.

"Has he learned his lesson?"

Geraldine looked over at Stanley who was still fuming. "No, but I'm tired of looking at him."

"Send him in."

"Mr. Davidson will see you now," Geraldine exclaimed in Stanley's direction.

Stanley casually walked into Bob's office and slammed the door behind him. Geraldine smiled satisfactorily; her mission had been accomplished.

"You need to control that old…"

"Stop right there!" Bob roared as he raised his hand in protest. "Whatever you have to say about Geraldine you could have said to her face at your own risk. You will not disrespect her in my presence."

"I've been out there waiting while you were in here sitting on your ass..."

"But you're here now; and I'm an old man whose heart can't take the excitement. Have a seat and let's discuss whatever it is you felt the need to come all this way to get off your chest."

"You know why I'm here."

The two men exchanged gazes like two boxers before a prizefight. Bob was first to show a sign of nerves when perspiration appeared on his brow and his mostly bald head. There were still thin patches of grey hair on the sides, but the top had not seen hair in several years.

"Have a seat," Bob offered.

It was a body blow that took his air briefly, but it did force Stanley to sit in one of the two leather chairs in front of Bob's massive oak desk. Those three words were confirmation; Bob was selling the company.

"I've been in this business for over fifty years," Bob said wearily, "and it's time for me to..."

"Sell the Distributing Company to me," Stanley exclaimed cutting him off. He did not want to hear Bob's life story nor was he interested in why he was selling the company. He was old as dirt, and it was time for him to move on. As far as Stanley was concerned, the old bastard should have called it quits years ago.

"I knew you would propose that, but New Wind Pharma won't do the deal without Distributing Company."

"Of course they won't! They only want Davidson for the Distributing Company. You know they're going to close every other facility."

"They've assured me that they will offer jobs to all field

employees and some of the corporate staff. There will be severance packages for those who decline or who they can't place."

"That's bullshit..."

"We've agreed on the terms of the deal."

Another body blow. It was further along than Stanley anticipated. That infuriated him even more.

"When were you going to tell me? Does anyone else know?"

"I was going to let employees know at the appropriate time. That time is quickly approaching."

"What about..."

"The Distributing Company will remain intact. I know of no plans that impact your team. As far as I know it will be business as usual; as long as you play nicely."

"What does that mean?"

"New Wind Pharma is a Fortune 25 company; you're not going to have the autonomy you have now. You're a spoiled brat who's gotten his way because you made a lot of profit for Davidson. You will be a small fish in New Wind's ocean."

"I can hold my own," Stanley replied with a smirk.

"By the way, you're going to have some visitors over the next few weeks. Show them everything they ask for; nothing is off limits."

"The Distributing Company is still mine. I dictate what anyone can and cannot have access to."

"I expect your full cooperation. You can't kill this deal, but you can kill your chances of being a part of it."

Stanley looked as if he had more to say, but as far as Bob was concerned the conversation was over. He pressed a button on his phone and Geraldine opened the door and stood looking at Stanley. He knew immediately it was his cue to leave, but he did not budge.

"Would you get Charlie please," Bob said to Geraldine.

"Are we done?" Stanley asked with a defiant tone.

"Aren't we?"

Stanley looked at Geraldine who was still standing stoically at the door. One last glare into Bob's ancient eyes and Stanley exited as ceremoniously as he had entered. Geraldine followed to make sure he left the area.

"SHE'S HERE," Geraldine said when Bob answered the phone.

"Okay, bring her in."

The door opened and Charlie walked in wearing a nervous smile.

"Please stay," Bob said to Geraldine as she was turning to walk out. "Please, have a seat ladies."

"Oh-oh, this can't be good. First Stanley shows up and now me, and you've asked Ms. Geraldine to be a witness."

"She's not here as a witness," Bob exclaimed with a chuckle, "I just want to talk to you two young ladies."

Both ladies sat in the two chairs in front of Bob's desk and crossed their legs. Charlie looked around the office and noted that the décor had not changed since the first time she sat in the same chair for her interview. She thought the furniture was old seven years ago, and nothing had changed. When her eyes finally settled on Bob, she could see that he was uneasy. His wrinkled brow was evidence of the thoughts he struggled to bring to words. He finally decided on the direct approach.

"I'm selling the company to New Wind," Bob abruptly blurted out. Charlie immediately looked at Geraldine who obviously was not hearing the news for the first time. Bob could see the panic in Charlie's eyes.

"I want you to go to the Distributing Company," he said to Charlie as calmly as he could, "I know that New Wind is keeping the Distributing Company intact. I want you to go prior to New Wind taking over."

Suddenly, crevices formed in Charlie's brow, as a hurricane of thoughts and emotions swirled violently in a confined space.

"Does this mean I don't have a job if I don't go?"

"I can't promise anything other than a severance package if you say no. Employees at the warehouses will be offered jobs, but I can't say for staff here at the corporate office."

"How much time do I have?" Charlie asked calmer than anyone expected, including herself.

"Sixty to ninety days before the ink dries, but I need your answer within two weeks. I need you there sooner than later."

"That's not a lot of time for a decision like this."

"I know, and I'm sorry. I first thought about asking you a couple years ago, and it has been on my mind ever since." Bob shifted in his chair and chose his next words very carefully. "I need a presence in Michigan."

"A presence?"

"Yes, a corporate employee, someone I can trust."

"To do what?"

Again, Bob paused for a selective word search.

"Oh, you mean be a spy... I'm not a snitch Mr. Davidson. Stan does whatever he wants unchecked, and that's your fault... sir."

Geraldine smiled with pride, and it did not go unnoticed.

"That's not what I mean at all," Bob said defensively, "it's just from a corporate governance perspective we've been lacking with the Distributing Company. I need someone to help manage inventory and have compliance oversight. I know you're more than qualified, and you're the only other person besides Geraldine and I who is not intimidated by Stanley. Not to mention it would save your job. You don't have to give me an answer right now, but I want you to think about it."

Charlie nodded her head, in large part due to the added weight. Geraldine leaned over and put her hand on Charlie's knee. Bob knew that Geraldine had a special relationship with Charlie, and he suspected it was because they were the only two.

Bob did not consider himself racist by any stretch of the imagination. The fact that forty out of Davidson's forty-two corporate employees were white was something he never considered until he watched the two women in front of him interact with each other. The support they showed one another, and the maternal nurturing Geraldine flaunted for Charlie was more than just a friendship amongst coworkers. To his knowledge, Geraldine did not share the same affection for any other employee in the corporate office. Maybe Geraldine was the racist. He shook his head in an effort to reboot his thoughts; why was he thinking about racism anyway.

"Race is never a factor in hiring decisions," Bob blurted out as if they were reading his thoughts."

Geraldine and Charlie looked at each other in bewilderment.

"Where did that come from?" Geraldine asked. She was still looking at Charlie, but the question was directed at Bob.

"I don't know... You've never thought about it? I never thought about it; what does that say about me?" There was a defensive tone in Bob's voice.

Again, the two women looked at each other to see if the other knew what was happening. Both sets of eyes were searching, and Bob's eyes were filled with doubt. Sure, it had crossed Charlie's mind more than once that she was the only one in meetings, and that there were only two at the corporate office, but it was no different from the pharmaceutical conferences she attended or the suppliers she visited. She was either the only black person or one of a handful, and they always acknowledged each other; relieved that they were not the only one.

Charlie did not know whether to respond to Bob's question or just sit uncomfortably until he asked another. The tension in the room was like it was sprayed from a can, and there was no way to get from under its mist. Bob was obviously overcome with sentiment, and Charlie wanted no part of it.

"Okay..." Charlie exclaimed as she stood and looked for the exit. "Thanks for letting me know about the company and I will get back to you with my decision soon." She smiled at Geraldine and walked out of the office without looking back. The other side of the door was fresh air. She inhaled as much as she could and retreated to her office.

"WHAT DO YOU THINK GERL?"

"I think she'll do it," Geraldine said with a knowing smile, "Charlie is loyal, and she has family in Michigan."

Bob nodded in assurance. "What about you? You gonna finally retire for good?"

"Yeah... after years of running this company I'm tired. Or I might start my own with my share of the package."

"How does it feel being a millionaire?"

"I'm not yet. You have to sell the company first."

"The due diligence period is almost over, and you and I have an iron clad agreement. You get twenty percent of my payout, and you've earned every penny. The check will come to you from New Wind."

8

The CCTV screen flickered, and a line stretched across the center of the screen, but one thing was clear. While one of the masked men was hauling pallets of product out of the controlled substance cage on a forklift, two other masked men along with a male employee stacked cases on pallets in the vault. Two pallets in total were stacked seven layers high with sealed boxes of Schedule 2 controlled substances. The labels could not be read on the screen, but from where they were picked, the cage and vault supervisor stated they were mostly Oxycodone.

The employee was identified as Travis Johnson, and Wanda already had agents in route to his last known address. Wanda and Peggy were back on site, but the meeting had been arranged in advance.

"Dumb-as didn't even know he was on camera." The operations manager exclaimed. The usual suspects, minus the suits from corporate, were gathered around the monitor in the security office watching the events from the night of the theft.

"According to information we obtained from other employees present that night, Travis volunteered to go to the cage and vault after a young lady identified herself as having a key. Everyone thought he was being a hero, but now we know he was working with the perpetrators. It was his plan all along to get inside that vault."

"What about her?" The question came from the site leader. He was experiencing a sinking feeling, and he was searching for footing.

"She appears to be an innocent victim," Wanda responded, "but not everything is always as it appears; we will find out the truth. Also, there were three individuals on your access list who are no longer employed here; one of them was a supervisor who had been here for less than a year. Not only was the list not updated, but the vault combination was not changed nor locks changed on the cage door. We're gonna need information on these individuals. In fact, we will need information on anyone who left the company within the last 12 months."

"Sure, whatever you need," the site leader assured her as he walked out of the office to make a call, "excuse me." Everyone in the room knew who he was calling. Wanda and Peggy exited the building ten minutes later.

A LETTER of admonition was issued along with a considerable fine for security and record keeping violations. The investigation into the theft was ongoing, but they had a good lead, and the previous nightshift supervisor was a person of interest. The driver was nowhere to be found, but they had not given up. They had considerable resources at their disposal and the agency was confident all parties involved would be brought to justice. A portion of the controlled substances had been recovered, but there were still narcotics from the heist on the street or worse. Consumption was always a growing risk as time passed.

. . .

TRAVIS COULDN'T TALK FAST ENOUGH. He had been quiet from the time he was cuffed until he arrived in the concrete room with no windows, but once he saw the video he started providing a soundtrack to the events as they unfolded. He did not know names, but he knew they were ex-military. Travis had served himself and he knew the mannerisms of a fellow soldier. Travis had not given the men much information, they had already gotten what they needed from a former employee; someone with knowledge of the night operation and the cage and vault. Travis just confirmed what they already knew, and he was to be ready and available if things went sideways and they needed to improvise. His primary duty was to open the dock door when the truck backed in before the driver had an opportunity to enter the building.

Travis had been approached at the Waffle House near the distribution center. He ate there at the end of every shift on his way home. A man came and sat at the table across from him. He was asked if he wanted to make an easy five thousand dollars and of course the answer was yes. He was given just enough detail to be able to do his part and was not given the date until the night before, again at the Waffle House by a different man. He could not describe the men other than they were white.

As for the four cases of extended-release Oxycodone, the popular brand name that was extremely valuable on the street, he had already sold a case and a half and would be prosecuted for theft, possession, and distribution of a schedule 2 controlled substance. He did not have enough helpful information to broker a deal, even after a court appointed attorney got involved. The woman on the video was indeed an innocent victim and she was still shaken by the experience. She had been on paid leave since the incident.

~

Word was out. The first call came from the Distributing Company's most trusted customer, Emperor Drugs, a pharmaceutical distributor based in New Jersey. The two trading partners conducted fixed business, usually at the end of the month, with the majority of the product purchased returned for credit the beginning of the following month. Few noticed the monthly pattern of pallets of product being returned, and those who did were reluctant to question the transactions.

The relationship was too important for Stanley to reassure his nervous partner over the phone; he had to fly to Newark to hold his hand. The sky was not falling. Yes, Davidson Enterprises was being acquired by New Wind, but nothing would change. New Jersey was the first stop on Stanley's damage control tour.

Dominic Vanelli was sitting behind his desk when Stanley walked into his office without knocking. The receptionist had already announced Stanley's presence when he walked by her without speaking in route to Dominic's office.

"Dom, how the hell are you my old friend?"

Dominic stood slowly and walked around his large desk to greet Stanley. "I've been better Stan; I've heard some troubling news." The two men embrace. Stanley noticed Michael out of the corner of his eye but did not acknowledge him.

"So, is it true?" Dominic asked solemnly.

"Is what true?"

"This is not the time for games Stan, my business is on the line."

"Look Dom, we will continue to conduct business as usual," Stanley exclaimed with confidence, "this changes nothing."

"How can you be so sure Stan?" The question came from Michael, Emperor's chief counsel, who insisted on being in the room. Stan did not look in his direction, he locked eyeballs with Dom, the president of the company.

"Dominic, we've walked through hell without breaking a sweat. I've worked for three different companies, and we have always done business together."

"This is different Stan. New Wind thinks their shit doesn't stink. They are so concerned about their image, once they find out what we're doing they won't hesitate to turn us in."

"Which is why we need to sever ties now," Michael added.

Stanley struggled to remain calm, but the cracks were weakening his resolve. He and Dominic had known each other for over twenty years and had done business for equally as long. Michael was a fly buzzing in his ear that he wanted to swat, step on, pick up with a piece of tissue and flush down the toilet.

"Dom listen to me. New Wind is as concerned with profits as any other multi-billion-dollar corporation. They have a hard-on for the Distributing Company because we make huge profits; hell, we are the only reason they want to buy Davidson Enterprises. Like you said, they're concerned about their image; they don't like getting their hands dirty. As long as I'm bringing in the money, they won't even look my way. They will just cash the checks just like Davidson did."

"What if they do look?" Dom broke eye contact with Stanley. "Maybe we should sever ties..."

"Goddammit quit being such a pussy Dom!" Stanley exploded. "And stop looking at Michael, this is your company! I expect Michael to whine like a child, but you and I have always handled things as men. Now send Mikey to his room so the adults can talk."

"Fuck you Stan," Michael exclaimed in anger. "I'm here because my job is to protect the company's interests. Why are you here? Whose interests are you trying to protect?"

"Everybody's," Stan exclaimed as he looked at Michael for the first time. The scowl on his face gave Michael pause. "We've done deals with the devil that would have you running home to your mother if you knew half of it. You can't sever ties, if one goes down, we all go down. Even if we don't ever do another deal, we've done enough to be joined at the spine. If I pass gas you choke on my shit."

Michael looked to Dom for an explanation, but the look in Dom's eyes said it all. Whatever they had done or were doing had Dom trapped, which meant Emperor drugs was an accomplice.

"Good day gentlemen," Stan said as he stood and grabbed his coat from the back of his chair. "I have a plane to catch, and it looks like Mikey might need medical attention. I'll leave you two to talk." He walked out of Dom's office leaving the door wide open. They watched him until he turned the corner and was out of sight. Michael even walked to the front door and watched him drive away in his rental car. Satisfied, he returned to Dom's office and closed the door; they needed to talk.

FROM NEW JERSEY STANLEY flew to San Juan for meetings with his trading partners on the island. He could have eased their anxiety with a phone call, but he felt a more personal touch was appropriate; with one partner in particular. There was a company owned by an exotic woman who began each of their meetings with a glass of wine and ended them with an orgasm. The wine was refined, but she was intoxicating, and her appetite insatiable. Stanley usually felt inadequate after their meetings.

After his more personal touch on the island, Stanley flew home for a few nights before heading to the west coast to meet with several crucial customers. A gubernatorial candidate in California was making a lot of noise about counterfeit drugs and the "grey market," and she was gaining traction with voters. Some of the Distributing Company's partners in the state were looking for an exit strategy, and New Wind's acquisition of Davidson Enterprises added fuel to a smoldering fire. Some feared exposure, while others feared their low-cost drug supply would diminish; of course, Stanley assured them neither would happen. They still wondered if they should abandon ship while the lifeboats were still available and seaworthy, but the money they were making weighed heavily when mitigating the risk.

THE MINIVAN PARKED in the visitor's space was the first thing Stanley noticed as he parked his 7-series BMW in his reserved parking space. His nostrils flared and his heart rate accelerated instinctively, as if sensing danger, in preparation for what was waiting inside his building. It was an ambush, and he was certain he knew the characters. Retreat never crossed his mind; instead, he was on the offensive. It was still his building and his company. He stormed out of the car and closed the door with excessive force from the adrenaline rush. He looked back to make sure there was no damage to his BMW before marching inside the building.

"They're in the conference room," his assistant exclaimed as he approached her desk in route to his office.

"Who's in the conference room Debbie? I don't have a meeting on my calendar."

Debbie looked frightfully perplexed. Her usual pale skin lost what little color it had. Stanley's tone and facial expression were very hostile. She looked up at him with wide eyes. "I...I thought you knew they..."

"We'll discuss this later." Stanley continued past her and into his office. Seconds later he passed her again charging to the conference room.

. . .

The door opened suddenly and closed violently. Six sets of eyes glared at Stanley, but they remained calm, they had been prepped as if facing a hostile witness in a deposition. Stanley quickly surveyed the room without focusing on any one person in particular. Their corporate suits and briefcases were familiar props, and their Fortune 50 stench smothered the air in the room. Stanley stood near the door unyielding, the first words would not be his.

"You must be the infamous Stanley Forsythe." It was more a proclamation than a question. Stanley did not acknowledge the man who uttered the words, but he had identified their alpha. To engage him would be to recognize his authority, instead he addressed another man seated on the opposite side of the table.

"You must be lost, because I was not expecting visitors today."

Feeling the need to respond, the man's eyes shifted over to the alpha and then back to Stanley.

"First contact is always awkward," the voice was female, and Stanley shifted his eyes in her direction without moving his head. "But we can forgo the 'we come in peace' salutation."

Stanley smiled, but it was not a warm smile, it was an acceptance of the challenge that had been laid. He walked to the opposite end of the table from the pack and made himself comfortable.

"Welcome to my house," Stanley exclaimed as he spread his arms wide.

"There is a 'for sale' sign in the yard so we thought we would have a look." She looked Stanley in his pupils when she spoke.

"If you had scheduled a showing I would have had a fruit and vegetable tray waiting for you."

"I only eat meat."

"Put it away Nicole," the alpha instructed, "You and Mr. Forsythe can decide whose is the biggest later. I'm sure he's eager to get things started so we can wrap things up as quickly as possible."

Finally, the man said something worth hearing. Stanley looked at him for the first time and even nodded slightly.

"My name is Charles McKinnon, VP of Pharmaceutical Operations for New Wind Pharma. You've already met Nicole Fitzsimmons, Director of Pharma Operations, and I will let the others introduce themselves starting with Frank here."

Stanley half listened numbly as names and titles were spewed at him. Of course, there was a lawyer present, and someone who's title meant they were there to take notes. Stanley had already identified that person because he had been writing on a legal pad since Stanley walked in. With the formalities out of the way, they could ring the bell for round one.

Stanley volunteered Hank to take them on a tour of the warehouse, and the New Wind team was excited for the opportunity. They were corporate employees chained to desks and confined to offices. A few of them had visited one or two New Wind distribution centers, but they had never seen one outside of their own network; and certainly not one with the margins the Distributing Company was consistently netting. Hank knew to give them the white house tour, and had Luke join them to help keep anyone from wandering. It was Luke's first week on the job, and while he had already written up eight employees and showed one the door, Hank figured it would be a good learning opportunity for him.

While the New Wind suits were in the warehouse, Stanley called his management team into the conference room for strict instructions. No document was to be turned over without his approval, and all copiers were to be unplugged and "out of order" signs taped to each one. Stanley adjusted the office thermostats restricting the heat so that there was just enough to prevent frostbite, and he closed the vents in the conference room. The New Wind team was only scheduled to be onsite for one full day, and Stanley was determined to make the day half-full.

NICOLE ASKED the majority of the questions during the tour, and each question was a multipart question depending on the answer. Since Hank answered her questions like a politician on the debate stage, they lingered in the air like pollen, causing headaches and irritation; even as Hank tried not to breathe them in.

Two employees talking and laughing on company time distracted Luke long enough for Nicole to wander over to the receiving area to observe an employee breaking down a pallet that had recently been unloaded from the truck. The employee entered the information from the packing list into the computer and picked up a box and scanned the label with a scanner strapped to her wrist. Nicole noticed the name on the packing list but did not recognize the company. It could not have been a manufacturer; she knew them all. Before she could ask a question, Hank seemed to have appeared out of nowhere. Her opportunity had been lost.

STANLEY HAD to be reminded more than once that New Wind had a signed letter of intent giving them the right to view whatever documents they needed during the due diligence period, including purchase orders and sales invoices.

"I've never heard of a lot of these companies," Nicole proclaimed as she reviewed documents in the chilly conference room.

"They don't just purchase drugs from manufacturers," Charles stated, "they also purchase from wholesalers and distributors."

"And apparently pharmacies as well," Nicole exclaimed as

she held up a document to be presented as evidence. "This company is a pharmacy." She looked directly at Stanley as she spoke with a District Attorney's accusatory tone. Stanley was unruffled.

"As you know, most states allow pharmacies to distribute up to five percent of their inventory without a distributor license."

"Well, they must have a lot of inventory because this is a considerable amount."

"I thought you were here with New Wind Pharma," Stanley responded, "not the Michigan Board of Pharmacy." Stanley turned to Charles. "Are we being audited or are you here to look at financials to make sure the numbers you were told are authentic? You've asked a lot of questions about my suppliers. I'm starting to think you're only here to steal my suppliers. I don't believe a supplier audit is within the scope of your agreement."

"Our scope includes mitigating risk to the company." Nicole exclaimed.

"Which company, mine or yours?" Stanley asked as he slowly turned to face her.

"Both. After the acquisition they are one in the same, but I will only have direct responsibility for one."

Stanley quickly turned to Charles for clarification and found a smirk on his face. If he had looked at Nicole, which he definitely was not going to do, he would have found a similar expression but more triumphant.

"I'm sure you have flights to catch," Stanley mused, "traffic heading to Metro this time of day can be pretty bad, I wouldn't want you to miss your flight."

"Looks like we've accomplished everything you will allow us to on this trip," Charles exclaimed, "so I believe we can wrap this up. I'll give Mr. Davidson a recap of the day's events."

"Yes, I'm sure you will."

The New Wind team members gathered their items.

"Now you can turn the heat back on," Nicole exclaimed, "I'm sure your employees would appreciate that."

"Yes, I'm sure everyone will be glad to see you leave."

THE NEW WIND team settled into the van. It would take a minute or two for the heat to overcome the chill.

"What a piece of work," Charles proclaimed.

"What a piece of shit," Nicole added. "Do we need him after the acquisition?

"From what I've heard, yes, he's good at what he does, and we don't know that business. We tried to operate in that space and failed miserably. I'm sure he knows that."

"He knows..."

9

Q was not Charlie's first thought as she contemplated the move to the Distributing Company, but he was an uncomfortably close second. The fact that he even entered her mind while weighing her options caused her more consternation than the prospect of working with Stanley. They had only been on four dates and started having sex on the third. That was a mistake not because Charlie did not want it to happen, but because she did not expect it to be so fulfilling. Q was an unselfish lover, and she erupted at his will; she fought harder than any man ever had to restrain her orgasms. She did not like feeling vulnerable.

"I have something to tell you," Charlie exclaimed as Q's gifted hands massaged her feet. The look on her face let Q know it was serious. They were nestled deep down in Charlie's soft sofa with jazz playing on a turntable. Charlie believed the best way to listen to jazz was on a LP.

"What is it?"

"Remember the guy Stanley I told you about."

"The one you thought about having some of your people cancel?"

"I said that to you? See, I'm way too comfortable with you; but yeah, him."

"What about him?" Q's hands stopped moving and he sat up on the sofa. "Did he do something to you!?"

"No, no, nothing like that. Look at you swelling up to defend yo' woman."

"Oh, don't get it twisted. Don't think just because I'm a teacher, I can't serve up a two piece."

"Teacher?" Charlie said surprised. "I thought you played bass in a jazz band?"

"I do, but I'm also a high-school music teacher. Between the two jobs I almost make enough to eat after I pay my rent."

They both shook their heads and laughed at the realization that they never had a conversation about where they worked.

"Well damn…" Charlie said as she extended her hand to Q, "we've been on how many dates and have talked for hours on the phone and I didn't even know something simple like where you work? Hi, I'm Charlie…"

"Nice to meet you Charlie, I'm Q. I've already seen you naked though."

"Yes, you have." Charlie let her mind wander but had to refocus. "Anyway… let me elevate my mind; so, I'm dating a teacher…"

"Yep, and I'm dating a…"

"I work for a pharmaceutical distribution company, Davidson Enterprises."

"Davidson, I've never heard of it."

"Pharmaceutical distributors aren't well known outside of the Pharma industry. Everyone has heard of the manufacturers, but we stay in the background. We are the ones who get their drugs to pharmacies and hospitals."

"Oh, so you're a drug dealer…"

"I've heard that one many times, but I actually head up purchasing. I'm a buyer not a dealer."

"So, what's going on with Stanley?"

"My boss is selling the company to one of the big boys and he wants me to transfer to Stanley's facility in Michigan. It's either that or find another job basically."

"Okay..." Q felt like he was just sucker-punched in the stomach, and he hesitated long enough for his breath to return. Charlie watched him intently. She knew no other way than to just drop the bomb. She could not read Q's reaction, because he did not react. His face was stoic, at least he hoped.

"Sooo... you don't want the potential hostile work environment."

"I don't wanna go to jail for killing that fool. What should I do?"

"The Charlie I know doesn't back down from anyone. Is this a good opportunity?

"Well, I guess it could be. I don't know, I've heard horror stories about working for huge companies. I could just become an employee number; a grain of sand on their massive beach."

"Or you could show them what you can do and be a rising star in a new company with new opportunities."

Charlie smiled sheepishly; she pulled him down on top of her. "That's why I'm gonna let you keep courting me."

"Oh, is that what I'm doing?

"According to my grandmother, yes."

Q was rigid, the news he had just received made it difficult to express any form of passion towards her. Intimacy was the furthest thing from his mind, and Charlie knew it. She too had struggled ever since walking out of Bob's office. They were having fun dating and exploring each other sexually but had never really discussed a relationship. Charlie tended to shy away from relationships because they never lasted long enough to meet the definition. She sensed that Q could be different if she let him. The possibility of relocating to Michigan forced her to give serious consideration to what the two of them were and could become.

"So, have you made up your mind?" Q succeeded in not letting the trepidation show in his voice.

"No and having you in my life now doesn't make it any easier."

"Well, that's good to hear, I was beginning to wonder."

"My father and grandmother live in Michigan, so I would be closer to them."

"Yeah…"

No one paused first, it was simultaneous, but the silence and tension haunted the room. It was a new experience for Charlie, and it made her uncomfortable. She reacted the only way she knew how.

"What are we Q? I mean, where are we going with this?"

"Wow, you get straight to the point, don't you?"

"I don't do bullshit, don't have time nor the patience."

"I'm not going to tell you that I love you and beg you not to go, I know that would just piss you off anyway. What I will say is that I love falling in love with you. I want you to do what's best for you and I will do what's best for me. Hopefully one day we can do what's best for us. There are high schools in Michigan. I'm always complaining about the cost of living in Connecticut and New York City anyway. I'm not gon' follow you to Michigan, but I'm definitely willing to do the long-distance thing and see what happens."

Charlie did not immediately respond because all of her attention was on the tears she felt in her eyes. What the hell! She could not let one escape, but Q had already noticed the puddles swelling her eyes. Charlie had never cried over a man.

"I hate you." She did not mean to say what she was thinking but it erupted from her throat like acid reflux. Q understood and did not respond verbally. His body relaxed and he kissed her forehead.

"We'll figure it out." He said as he slid down to a comfortable position. It took less than five minutes for her to arch her back and release her nectar. She looked down at him and sighed. Yes, they would figure it out.

"YES, I'LL DO IT." The words lingered in the stale air in Bob's office long enough for him to hear them ring in his ears several times. His smile was genuine, and the relief in his eyes nearly turned to liquid and leaked down his wrinkled cheeks.

"That's great news Charlie. I think you made the right decision, and I will definitely make it worth the trouble. Your relocation package will cover everything. You won't even have to pack."

"When would you like me to start?"

"Next week..."

It was a statement with the tone of a question. The panicked look on Charlie's face made it a question.

"Next month then? That gives you almost three weeks."

"Does Stanley know I'm coming?"

"He knows about the offer I made you."

"I bet he was jumping up and down with excitement."

"He was jumping up and down, yes..." Bob smiled, and Charlie returned the gesture. "Despite what he tells himself, he does not call the shots, I do. I may have given him too much freedom over the years, but it is still my company; at least for another couple months."

"He thinks the Distributing Company is Stanley Forsyth Inc."

"If he's not careful he won't even be an employee once New Wind takes over. They were on site recently and it didn't go so well. They said he tried to freeze them out of the building and wasn't cooperative.

"I'm sure I'll get the same."

"I'm not worried about you Charlie; you can handle Stanley. In fact, I'm more concerned for him."

Charlie smirked and nodded her head. "I do know people in Detroit."

Carl walked into the Henry County Sheriff's office and identified himself to a deputy near the front desk. The name Carl Jones did not immediately have meaning to the deputy, but when Carl explained why he was there, the deputy waved at a detective who had been working the case, and he was quickly escorted to an interview room where he and the detective were immediately joined by another deputy who had overheard and also had interest in the case.

"I'm Detective Barnes and this is Deputy Wiggins, we've been wanting to ask you some questions for some time Mr. Jones; where've you been?"

"I'm right here right now," Carl answered stoically, gazing the detective directly in the eye.

"I see that, but you've been on the run for months now."

"Not from you."

"Who you been runnin' from Carl? Can I call you Carl?"

Carl nodded his head. "I've been running from whoever was on the back of my truck that night."

"Do you know who they were?"

"Nope."

"Had you ever seen them before?"

"Nope, and I didn't see 'em that night either; they had masks on the whole time, but he said he knew who I was."

Detective Barnes had been taking notes, and he flipped the

page on his notepad. Carl looked straight ahead, never breaking eye contact, even when the detective looked down at his pad.

"Why don't you tell me what happened."

"I picked up the trailer from the yard and drove to the pickup location," Carl started without hesitation, "I signed the log and backed into the dock. I stayed in my truck the whole time."

"Is that typical… for you to stay in your truck?"

"Most times; unless I have a take a leak or somethin'."

"So, you backed into the dock, and then what happened?"

"The trailer door was raised and eventually I felt the weight of the forklift loading the trailer."

"You said eventually… did it take longer than usual?"

Carl's eyes shifted ever so slightly, but his face remained expressionless. "I guess it did take longer than usual, but I didn't think nothin' of it. Maybe the pallets weren't ready, or maybe…"

"Maybe they were being held hostage during an armed robbery."

"I don't know nothin' about that."

"Obviously you do, that's why you're here." Both men glared at the deputy who had just spoke for the first time.

"I'm here," Carl exhaled in frustration, "because I'm tired of looking over my shoulder and I wanna clear my name. Whoever did the this is still out there, and I'm sure they're still looking for me. My life is in danger, and I need your help."

Carl sounded sincere, and Detective Barnes took a beat to assess the situation. He searched Carl's eyes for any hint of deceit but could not decipher what he saw in the abyss. He had questioned enough guilty habitual liars to know that one who never accepts or speaks truth can easily evade detection. Just as the detective broke his gaze and was about to speak, Carl offered more.

"I heard about the bust."

"What bust?" Barnes asked after a pause he knew was too long.

"DEA busted one of the guys from the robbery selling Oxy straight from the stolen bottles. Dumb ass didn't even have the sense to remove the pills and throw away the bottles."

"Like you did... I mean would have done?"

"Like anybody would have done."

Barnes tapped on the metal table with all eight of his thick fingers. The beat was in sync, but it was still annoying. Carl had thrown him a curve and he had to decide whether to swing at it or see if it landed in the strike zone.

"Yeah, I heard something," he said in a noncommittal tone, "what do you know about it?"

"I know he said the driver wasn't in on it. Said they were waiting in a trailer when the driver picked it up. It was all over the news, he was a cop, wasn't he?"

"Former officer..."

"Yeah, and he didn't know the others' names but said they were ex-military or something right?"

"So that's why you're here, you think this clears you?"

"It sure doesn't indict me."

Barnes flipped through his notes reviewing what he had written down. He paused at a note he had scribbled and looked up at Carl.

"You said you didn't get out of the truck, correct?"

"Nope, just got out to chock my wheels."

"And you said you rarely get out, only if you have to take a piss or something, right?"

"Yeah, that's right," Carl answered suspiciously.

Detective Barnes nodded his head. "So, what about paperwork?" He paused to gauge Carl's reaction. Carl's twitch let him know there was something there. "Don't you have to sign something? I mean you're picking up and delivering drugs, even controlled substances, I'm sure you have to sign some type of paperwork, right?"

"My old man is a truck driver," the deputy chimed in, "I think it's called a bill of laden."

Carl's eyes cut the deputy before looking down at the table. "Look," he said as he jumped to his feet, "if you're not gonna help me, you're just wasting my time."

"Oh, we're not done here," the deputy exclaimed, "sit down, I have some more questions."

"But I came in here on my own."

"Yes, and thanks for coming in; I'll let you know when you can leave."

"Am I under arrest?"

"No, at least not yet, but I can hold you for questioning. Give us a minute, we'll be right back."

Deputy Wiggins and Detective Barnes rose from the table and left the room. The tide had shifted to their favor, and they could feel the suspect's cockiness quickly turn to tension. Detective Barnes wanted Carl to be tormented by his nerves for a while. He wanted to get more details about the DEA bust so he would know as much if not more than Carl. He finally had control of the conversation and did not want to relinquish it again. Deputy Wiggins went back to his desk with a sense of urgency.

DEPUTY WIGGINS WAS first to return to the interview room. Close to an hour had passed and Carl had the sense the deputy was early. He was acting on his own.

"Can I get you anything?" The deputy asked. "Water, soda..."

"I'll take some water." Carl responded eagerly.

"You know you can ask for a lawyer at any time."

"Do I need one?" Carl asked curiously. "Am I being charged with something?"

"I'm just reminding you of your rights. I'll be back with that water." Deputy Wiggins walked out, and the door closed behind him. He did not return with the water until one hour and twenty-three minutes later, and Detective Barnes was with him.

"Brought you some water so your mouth won't dry out from all the explaining you have to do." Barnes had a confident smirk after he spit the words out.

Carl accepted the bottle of water and took a swig. "I've already told you everything."

"Everything regarding the robbery, maybe… the idiot dispensing Oxy like a pharmacist told DEA pretty much everything you said. They somehow knew which trailer you would pick up and they waited on the back of it. He wasn't the leader of course, too dumb to pull off something like this. Said when you backed into the dock and the door was raised, they jumped out and robbed the place and blah, blah, blah, but what I'm interested in is the drop location. Said it was a field in the middle of nowhere and that other drivers were there waiting on product, and not just drivers from their crew. So, they knew which trailer you would get and where you would make your stop before heading to the depot to make your normal drop. That's a lot of information for them to know without you telling them wouldn't you agree?"

Carl's eyes briefly shifted to Wiggins before mirroring Barnes' gaze. "Like I said, I don't know those guys. Never seen or talked to 'em before in my life."

"So, what about the other guys?"

"What other guys?"

"C'mon Carl," Barnes said with a chuckle, "let's not play games. The guys who were waiting in cargo vans to unload product from your truck like it was a regular occurrence."

"I just pick up freight and drop it off where I'm told," Carl answered without pause. "I'm just a truck driver."

"So, who told you to pick up freight from a pharmaceutical distributor and deliver it to cargo vans waiting in a field in the middle of nowhere?"

"Don't answer that!" Carl's eyes lifted and looked past his interrogator at the door as it swung open. Wiggins and Barnes looked back over their shoulders at the man who looked like money and power. His suit alone would have covered the closing costs on Barnes' house.

"Who are you?" Barnes asked with a frown. He knew he had to be a lawyer with a big powerful firm, but why was he disrupting his interview?

"I am Mr. Jones' attorney, and unless you're arresting him, which I know you're not, we will be leaving immediately."

No one was more surprised than Carl to hear that the superbly tanned man was his attorney. It also terrified him. Barnes noted the fear in his eyes.

"How did you know he was here?"

"That's not important; what is important is that you release him immediately."

"He came in on his own, he had something to tell us," Barnes exclaimed. "Looks like he still does."

"And I'm sure your detention and questioning has exceeded allowable limits without arresting him so like I said, we will be leaving now. Come on Mr. Jones, you've taken up enough of these officers' time."

Carl hesitated but rose to his feet. He looked at Wiggins and swore he saw him nod his head.

"Looks like he's more afraid of you than us," Barnes exclaimed smugly. "Make sure your client doesn't leave town." No other words were spoken by anyone. The two men left the room and exited the sheriff's station without incident.

There was a rather large character dressed in a far less

expensive suit, leaning on the rear passenger-side door of a black Mercedes. His face was expressionless, as if it was a skill he had mastered. Carl followed the smug lawyer toward the car, and the large man opened the front passenger door, presumably for Carl. Carl stopped in his tracks, prompting the man to pull back the corner of his suit jacket and reveal a dull black revolver. Carl wanted to move but could not; his mind was still trying to decide the direction and pace of his next step. He thought about running, matching the pace of his pulse, but knew it would be futile. He strongly considered walking back into the police station, and actually leaned in that direction, but ultimately chose to accept the invitation of the open door. Carl reluctantly settled into the plush leather passenger seat of the massive Mercedes Benz and fastened his seatbelt. Even under the circumstances, he had to admire the craftsmanship.

They rode in silence until they had successfully merged onto 75 North. Traffic was moving slowly, but at least it was moving. Carl was preoccupied with developing an exit strategy and did not hear the lawyer speaking to him. He faced forward looking through the windshield at nothing in particular. The gruff voice from the back seat startled him and got his attention.

"You can talk with teeth or without, your choice."

Carl focused on the lawyer's moving mouth and eventually heard his voice.

"...My client is eager to speak with you Mr. Jones. You've been a hard man to find."

"I thought I was your client."

"I represent the interests of your employer."

"My employer?"

"Yes, let's just call him your freight broker. What did you tell them?"

"Who?"

"I like you Carl," the amused lawyer said with a smirk, "but let's not do the cat and mouse thing."

"I didn't say nothin' about your client. I was just trying to clear my name from that robbery."

"Ah yes, the robbery... that you planned."

"I had nothing to do with it."

"Of course not; they got the information about which trailer you would be picking up and the location of the drop from someone else. Who else knew that information?"

"Your client."

"You don't have to tell me now, but by the end of the day, you'll be telling your mother's secrets."

Carl glanced back at the backseat passenger who met his glance with a snarl. Carl noticed he was not wearing a seatbelt, and the gun was not visible; it was probably securely tucked away in its holster. A single thought morphed into a plan; an idea Carl himself acknowledged was a bad one. He needed to act without thinking, but his body was paralyzed by thoughts of what could go wrong. Even if the plan was executed flawlessly there were still risks, perilous risks. He had to be willing to die to save his life, and he was not sure if he wanted to remain above ground.

All lanes on 75 North about a half mile south of the I-20 interchange were shut down and traffic was backed up for miles. The multi car accident had strewn debris and fluids, both bodily and automobile, across all lanes and the carnage was catastrophic. Potential witnesses who were close enough to see what happened were either deceased or loaded in ambulances and taken to Grady Hospital in critical condition. If they had been able to recount what had transpired, they would have recalled a Mercedes Benz suddenly swerving out of its lane and rolling over several times before striking a tractor trailer trying to avoid the collision. The chain reaction of panic braking and swerving from automobiles traveling at speeds beyond the posted limit at separation distances closer than legally allowed, resulted in what would later be described on the evening news as utter destruction. 'Only mother nature or an act of God could have caused more damage,' the news anchor dramatically stated before pausing to wipe away tears. She nor her viewers had any way of knowing that one of the occupants of the vehicle which caused the accident died instantly when he was ejected from the backseat through the windshield like a projectile. The driver of the vehicle was strapped to a gurney unconscious but clinging to life and rushed away in an ambulance while the third occupant, who had braced as best he could for the impact, crawled and limped away leaving a trail of blood from the far left lane of the interstate, where the Mercedes had come to a rest upside down, to the dense trees on the side of the road where he had made an escape.

The evening news anchor would report later that night that the driver of the Mercedes Benz died at Grady Hospital from his injuries. There was never any mention of a third passenger, and with all the blood splattered along the interstate, no one would notice or be concerned with the trail of drops leading into the woods. Carl was a ghost.

10

It was not the first time Clint begged God for mercy and reneged on his promise to never do whatever he had done again; and like most habitual mercy seekers, it would not be his last. When Clint found the second envelope without postage or a return address in his mailbox, he tore the letter as he frantically ripped open the envelope in anticipation. There was another mysterious pickup location, but the drop location was keenly familiar. It was a pharmaceutical distributor where he routinely made deliveries, and he wondered if whomever had sent the letter had known. It gave him pause, but taking the job was never in doubt.

"CLINT, you son-of-a-bitch, since when do you stay your fat ass in that trucker's trap? Get over here and grab a pallet-jack and help unload the truck."

Clint was a regular; he had been delivering freight at the location for over two years, and even though it was against company policy, he roamed the loading dock freely like he was an employee. It was common for him to help unload his freight, but he felt the need to keep his distance during this unload. The receiving supervisor who had called out to him stood with a confused look.

"Got some kinda bug," Clint exclaimed with a straight face, "don't wanna spread it around. In fact, I'll probably go wait in the cab."

"It's that time of year," the supervisor exclaimed as he stopped in his tracks, "A nasty bug is going around. Still need you to sign the log though."

Clint watched as the seal was removed and the number verified. The seal was not his primary concern, he expected the numbers to match. His heart raced as the trailer door was raised revealing the load. Clint could see shrink-wrapped pallets and knew immediately it was a full load. Whatever had been taken off had been replaced... with something. He didn't know whether to be relieved or even more worried, as if that was possible. His face had turned a darker shade of red than normal, and perspiration puddled on his forehead; but these symptoms could easily be mistaken for fever.

"Use your own pen," the supervisor yelled as Clint approached the log, "don't need you infecting any of my people. Already got enough off sick with that damn bug."

Clint obliged and watched nervously out of the corner of his eye as the forklift went deeper into the interior of the trailer, each time returning with a wrapped pallet.

"Last one." The driver proclaimed as he backed out of the trailer and dropped the pallet next to the others. Another employee carrying a clipboard counted them and scribbled the number on the bill of lading.

"We're good." He exclaimed and handed the form to another employee for signature. Clint was handed his copy through a slot in the trucker's trap. A receiving clerk grabbed a pallet jack and pulled one of the pallets over to her station. She cut off the shrink wrap and unfolded the packing slip which she scanned and began counting the boxes on the pallet. Clint had seen enough. He fled the warehouse and walked to his cab as fast as his sloppy three hundred pounds would allow. He did not breathe until the security guard waved him through the gate.

The box count was accurate on the pallet, and the barcode on the label identified the product as Testrol 30mg when scanned, which is what was listed on the packing list. The pallet was not broken down to be counted, and every label was not scanned. Generally, only the top label and a few on the sides were checked during the process. It could take days, weeks, or even months before the expiration dates on the labels of the inner boxes on several of the pallets were discovered and an investigation conducted. The manufacturer would be blamed for having shipped expired product and credit would be demanded. The manufacturer would track the lot number and March 1998 expiration date to a handful of distributors who had originally received the product and had previously submitted credit requests for the short dated or excess inventory to be returned. With more pressing product complaints to resolve, the manufacturer would simply issue a credit, and the expired product would be sent for destruction a second time.

THE CUSTOMER SERVICE representative was on a fresh performance improvement plan, and the next time his job performance was questioned and found lacking meant his termination. When the credit request came in for the Testrol, he gave it the attention of someone on a final written warning and the additional scrutiny raised questions. Testrol was a popular medication and was rarely sent to a reverse distributor for destruction. In fact, he and others on the team had joked that half the population was taking the blood pressure medication and every black person over the age of forty. There had been a credit request for the same quantity and lot number within the previous thirty days, and even though it was from a different distributor, it was still suspicious to the mind of someone on a PIP and in need of a win. He flagged it in the system along with a very detailed summary of his findings and moved to the next item in his queue.

The supervisor read the details of the investigation and escalated it to his manager. He made a few edits to make it appear as if he had done the investigation and gratefully received the kudos from his manager. It was further escalated up the chain and eventually the authorities were notified. The supervisor did close the PIP on the representative who had forwarded him the notes along with a 'great job.'

THE RECORD KEEPING was some of the worst the investigators had seen at a reverse distributor. Debit memos didn't always match what was sent for destruction and that was only the beginning of what they discovered. Product meant for destruction had no record the destruction ever happened, and most disturbing was a monthly pattern of a truck backing up to the dock with product meant for incineration, and the product placed into a quarantine area until it was loaded onto another truck, usually the same day, and hauled away. Of course there was no record of this, but an employee fearing retaliation, conquered that fear and became a whistleblower. All it took was immunity and whatever the reward was. She was not involved, but she figured out what was going on and wanted protection from prosecution. The truck would make another drop in six days.

. . .

The truck backed up to the dock as usual. While it was being unloaded, a federal agent pulled the truck driver from the cab and placed hand cuffs on her thick wrists. She did not have to be told she had the right to remain silent. Her face was flush, and the redness seemed to emanate heat. While no words were uttered, her gaze and facial expression were laced with profanity.

A forklift driver started unloading the truck and placed each pallet in an area that was not marked as quarantine, but it was understood the product was segregated and not to be touched. The whistleblower had previously identified the driver as the individual who unloaded the truck every month. An agent watched from a distance until the final pallet was unloaded and placed in quarantine before approaching the forklift driver. The agent didn't have time to identify himself before the culprit jumped off the forklift and ran. The agent had neither the desire nor the physique to give chase, so he alerted the other officers at the location. As soon as the runner pushed the door open and leaped outside two police officers were waiting. He was detained without incident.

The truck driver squeezed all she could get out of her right to remain silent. The only word she literally spit out was 'lawyer,' and a glob of spit landed on the agent's face just underneath his left eye. It trickled down his cheek and he ignored it. Only the driver seemed to be annoyed by the sight of her own spittle.

The forklift driver did not ask for a lawyer, but he asked for a deal. He had watched enough 'Law and Order' to know he was low man on the totem pole and that if he offered up a bigger fish he could walk. He had two vital pieces of information; where the product came from every month, and who at his company approached him about quarantining the product and loading it onto another truck. The product came from

Livonia, Michigan, every month and his job was to be at work 'no matter what' to unload the truck and load it onto another later the same day. For his services, he was paid one-thousand dollars every month in cash. He had been doing it for about a year and a half, and the only name he knew was the customer service manager in the front office.

THE CUSTOMER SERVICE manager exercised his fifth amendment rights with the agents and would ultimately plead the fifth in court as well. He knew whatever the federal agents or judge threatened him with was nothing in comparison to what would happen to him if he talked.

The truck driver did not have a bill of lading, at least not one with a ship from location. When asked where the shipment came from, she had nothing to say. When told they knew the shipment originated in Livonia, Michigan she remained silent and stoic. The only reason the agents knew Livonia was the possible origin point was because the forklift driver stated he had overheard the customer service manager talking on the phone about six months ago. They had very little, and they knew it.

The plan was to wait until the second truck arrived, let the forklift driver load the product, and have the truck followed to its final destination. The quarantined product was not part of a recall, so no urgent need to notify FDA, and there were no controlled substances involved so the agents would not have to involve DEA, which was a relief. No agency ever wanted to involve the DEA. Only coordination with state troopers would be necessary to track the truck.

THE DRIVE through Kentucky was uneventful. The Kentucky Trooper handed off to Tennessee without incident. There was the typical traffic in Nashville, and the driver pulled over at a truck stop close to the Alabama line. The driver did not exit the truck, but the State Trooper watched from a considerable distance as a prostitute climbed up into the cab of the truck.

"Damn lot lizards…" he mumbled to himself. It was a quick encounter, and afterwards the driver exited the truck and disappeared inside the building. After relieving himself and ordering greasy food, he returned to the truck. He was followed to Alabama where an Alabama Trooper took over the tail. He followed the truck as it exited 65 South and headed into Huntsville and onto Highway 72. The truck exited onto a desolate road leading to nowhere in particular. After dropping the trailer, he drove away in his truck and was pulled over by another state trooper when he tried to take the onramp onto Highway 72. The original trooper waited at a safe distance out of sight for the next move.

THIS WAS the easiest job yet. The trailer sat on an old runway at what appeared to be an abandoned airstrip about thirty miles from Huntsville, Alabama. It was ten minutes after midnight and the only light was from the nearly full moon. The strip could only be found if one had the exact coordinates, which Clint had in his possession. He turned off his headlights as he approached and looked around for any signs of life. There were none.

Clint had completed four jobs, which he had been generously compensated for, since he had retrieved that first mysterious envelope from his full mailbox. His first drop off exit 79 had him nauseous for several days afterwards. Tax-free cash fed his vices, and evading capture fed his ego and was as addictive as any illicit drug. He was not on the run, as far as he knew he was not on anyone's radar, but it made him and his jobs more dangerous if he convinced himself Navy Seals were in hot pursuit.

Clint reversed his rig up to the trailer and secured the connection. It was more difficult for him to get in and out of the cab with the extra weight he had gained since upgrading his dining options, but he managed to wobble to the back of the trailer and confirmed the seal was in place. He looked around for the Navy Seals and was convinced he was not in the crosshairs of the scope of a sniper's rifle. He returned to the front and after great effort climbed into the cab of the truck. He drove towards highway 72 which would take him to Interstate 24 to Chattanooga, Tennessee. There he would turn onto 75 South to Atlanta, Georgia for his rendezvous.

NOT LONG AFTER a sign on the side of the interstate thanked him for having Georgia on his mind, Clint noticed a patrol car in his side mirror. He was not concerned, but he did keep an eye on it. The headlights disappeared behind his trailer long enough to have the license plate run through the system and then reappeared in Clint's side mirror. He still was not concerned, he was not speeding, but he was relieved when the car pulled alongside the truck as if to pass. Instead of passing, the Georgia State Trooper turned on his lights signaling Clint to pull over. Clint immediately began sweating profusely and felt as if his heart would pound through his chest. Clint had his license and documentation ready for the trooper as he approached. A second car arrived and parked in front of the truck, and a third parked behind the first trooper on the scene.

"Evening officer..."

"Can I see your logbook?"

"Sure..." Clint noticed another trooper standing on the opposite side of the truck with his gun drawn when he reached for his logbook. "Something wrong officer?"

The officer flipped through the book to the most recent entries. "I don't see a stop in Huntsville, Alabama in here anywhere."

Clint searched for his next words, but his entire body was numb. He was unable to speak. His eyes darted back and forth between the two troopers, and he noticed the third trooper in his side mirror standing near the rear of the truck holding a shotgun.

"What cha haulin'?"

"Drugs...I-I mean legal drugs... pharmaceuticals and stuff." He almost choked on his words.

"Let me see your bill of lading."

"Uh... I... don't have one."

The officer pulled his gun and pointed it at Clint. "Get outta the truck! Keep your hands where I can see 'em!"

"I'm unarmed! Don't shoot me!"

"Get outta the truck now!"

Under the watchful eyes of the troopers, Clint opened the door with his left hand while his right hand was raised above his head. He practically fell out of the truck onto the ground and rested on his large stomach.

"Put your hands behind your back!"

Clint struggled to comply, and two of the troopers were more than willing to help. One put a knee in his back unnecessarily while the other locked handcuffs on Clint's thick wrists. It was no small feat getting him on his feet. They escorted him to the back of the trailer.

"Mind if we take a look?"

Clint shook his head defeated and watched as the seal was cut off and the doors opened. He did not know what they would find in the trailer but was relieved to see wrapped pallets of what appeared to be pharmaceutical product. One of the troopers climbed into the trailer with a flashlight and inspected the pallets. He nodded to the other officers.

"You're under arrest..." One of the officers proclaimed.

"For what? It's pharmaceuticals just like I said."

"You have the right to remain silent..." He was read the Miranda Warning as he was escorted to one of the cars and stuffed into the back seat. He watched the flashing lights from the troopers' cars illuminate the north Georgia landscape. He did not know why he had been arrested, or why he had been stopped. Before long, a massive tow truck arrived on the scene, and his first thought was the envelope filled with cash he had frantically tossed in the back of the cab.

After spending the night in a dilapidated cell, somewhere in north Georgia, Clint was transported to a holding facility in Atlanta at the break of dawn. Thankful to be out of the jail cell and the cot which smelled like death, the interrogation room made him even more nervous. He knew at any moment he would be joined by a good cop and a bad cop asking him questions. He had seen it acted out many times in movies. He tried to mentally prepare for the charade.

Seconds passed like minutes, and the anticipation inflated inside his chest and caused Clint to struggle for every breath he could seize. Periodically he heard footsteps, and at times they seemed to stop at the door, but it never opened. Deprived of sleep due to the circumstances, Clint struggled to stay awake as he waited for whomever was coming. He rested his heavy head on the desk and within minutes he fell sound asleep.

Nothing in particular awakened him, but when he opened his eyes, he saw a figure in a dark suit sitting across from him. Startled, he jerked his body upwards and rubbed his eyes. The stone-faced man came into focus, and Clint glanced around the room for an accomplice. The man identified himself as an FBI Agent and flashed a badge as confirmation.

"What was in the truck?"

It took Clint a few seconds to gather his thoughts and remember where he was and why. “Ummm… drugs.

“What kind of drugs?”

“I don’t know, I just pick up a load and haul it.”

“Where did you get them from?”

“I don’t know, the manufacturer I guess.”

“What’s the name of the manufacturer?”

“I don’t know.”

“Where was the manufacturer located?”

“I don’t remember.”

“The drugs are counterfeit, where did you pick up the load?”

Clint paused and shifted his eyes, searching for the most appropriate answer. Claiming ignorance seemed to be working, so he continued. “I don’t remember.”

The agent stood to his feet, causing Clint to jerk backwards. “I’m sorry Clint, can I call you Clint?”

“Sure.”

“I apologize for wasting your time, Clint. You clearly are the victim here and are in desperate need of a shower, so I’m going to leave, and you should be released shortly.” He walked toward the door.

“I can go home?”

“Well… I wouldn’t just yet. The house you just purchased is currently filled with FBI Agents. They have a warrant to search your home and take anything they find as evidence. Your wife and two daughters are being questioned, but I’m sure they’re innocent victims just like you. I know your wife can easily explain the large cash deposits to your Community First joint checking account which was used as a down payment on your brick ranch sitting on over an acre just outside Memphis. Of course, if your wife knew the cash came from an envelope like the one we found in the cab of your truck, she may be an accessory to whatever your fat, sorry ass is caught up in, but hey... you don't know what the hell I'm talking about do you Clint?"

If flies had been in the room, not only would they had been attracted to his smell, but they would have landed inside his mouth which hung open like his jaw was broken. He hung his head in defeat, and when he raised it again his will folded like a handkerchief.

"I really don't know what was in the trailer, but I picked it up at an old airstrip in Alabama."

The agent returned to the table and sat down across from Clint. "If you tell one more lie, or waste one more second of my time, your teenage daughters are going to end up living with their boyfriends while you and your wife wait for them to visit you in prison."

Clint nodded his head. He did not know names nor faces, but he shared the details of every pickup and drop he had made beginning with the first drop off exit 79. He agreed to help their investigation any way he could; an arrangement he regretted as soon as he learned what it entailed.

11

Livonia, Michigan was not hard to find, but the Davidson Distributing Company was situated in an industrial park located behind a larger industrial park several blocks from a main road. If the intent was to be off the beaten path, Stanley succeeded. When Charlie finally found what she believed to be the right building, she was surprised by its size and appearance. The building looked relatively new and was not what she envisioned when she thought of her new workplace. She was pleasantly surprised.

The move to Michigan had been effortless. Charlie did not pack a single box and had not spent ten cents on the move, including food and gas for the drive. Bob even gave her a bonus which he classified as miscellaneous and made it a part of her relocation package. He did not say it was a reward for her agreeing to an expeditious relocation, but it was understood.

Q drove the entire trip from Connecticut to Michigan with Charlie in the passenger seat. She had commented that she had never been in the passenger seat of her own vehicle but did not complain we he insisted on driving her. Charlie thought for sure it would be the end of their relationship having to sit in a car together for a long road trip, but it had the opposite effect. They enjoyed each other's company, the conversation, and the sometimes miles of silence. They laughed and sang along to various songs when they could tune in an R&B station on the radio, which was sparingly. The conversations about their pasts were personal. Both were comfortable sharing their deepest fears and greatest regrets. The moments of silence felt comfortable; they were not due to the lack of anything to say, but more just soaking up the moment. When the Jeep Cherokee was not filled with sound it was filled with... falling in love.

For the rest of the weekend, they went on dates. Lunch dates, dinner dates, a Sunday brunch date and stay at home dates. They enjoyed the stay-at-home dates the most. Q sat in for a set with a local jazz group at a small jazz club in East Detroit. They asked how long he would be in town, but it was only for the weekend. He had made an impression on his fellow musicians, and while it wasn't New York, Detroit did have an appetite for jazz, and a few places one could get their fix. Charlie smiled from cheek to cheek the entire time he was on stage; the instrument may have been borrowed but he handled it like the other woman.

On the Monday morning of Q's departure, he was anxious and unsettled. He knew he had to leave whether he wanted to or not. What really boggled his mind was the doubt. Not just whether to leave or stay, but if he would come back to live or even visit? If relocating was not a viable option, maybe he should just end it before it was too late; or was it already too late? His shuffling caused Charlie to stir from her sleep. She opened her eyes and wiped away the sleep.

"Want something to eat?" It was an attempt to escape the room and his thoughts.

Charlie smiled and licked her lips. "Do you?" She folded the covers away from her naked body. She asked him to pick a number between one and sixty-nine. He did and they did, and he almost missed his flight.

CHARLIE HAD SETTLED into her bland corporate housing and was eager to start house hunting. She had already peaked at selling prices in the Detroit metropolitan area and compared to Stamford, CT it was like a dream. She had looked at houses near Stamford over the years but could not get past the sticker shock for what she would be getting; even though what she paid in rent for her downtown apartment caused nearly as much agony.

Every parking pace appeared to be occupied with the exception of the four visitor spaces. There was an open space near the front door, and she figured it was her lucky day. Just as she pulled into the space, she noticed the reserved sign. There were several reserved spaces, all occupied by expensive cars with the largest most luxurious car parked closest to the door. She knew it was Stanley's. She backed out of the space and found an unoccupied space near the end of the parking lot. Her walk would be what she referred to as a country mile. The wind did not have the bite of a pure winter wind, but it was enough to confirm that winter was still bitter for only having one season. Michigan winters could be brutal, but it was definitely a four-season state.

Charlie held her badge against the badge reader, but the door did not unlock. She was told that her corporate badge would be programmed to work at the Distributing Company, but apparently that did not happen. She pressed the button on the intercom, only slightly perturbed; she was willing to accept it was an oversight.

"How may I help you?" The voice was female and unwelcoming.

"I'm Charlie Thomas, my badge doesn't work."

"What did you say your name was?"

"Charlie Thomas."

"We don't have a Charlie working here. You say you have a badge?"

Charlie held her badge up to the camera. "I'm from the corporate office but I'm relocating here. This is my first day..."

Charlie welcomed the silence. She knew that meant whomever the standoffish speaker voice belonged to was verifying her story and she would not have to continue the conversation via intercom. After what felt like several minutes, Charlie heard the lock release on the door.

Some artificial smiles need not be attempted. The snarl of one's true feelings is better served as an acknowledgment; particularly when the attempted smile failed miserably. Charlie did not even bother to return the receptionist's facial gesture.

"Have a seat, someone will be with you shortly."

Charlie's body language protested but she did not verbalize her discontent. Fortunately, she had not been waiting long before the door opened, and a dark-skinned man greeted her with a genuine smile. He looked to be in his early sixties, which meant he was probably older.

"You must be Charlie..."

Charlie stood to her feet and walked over to the door without looking at the salty receptionist. Charlie extended her hand, but he pulled her in for a fatherly hug.

"My name is Ephram, but everyone calls me Ram. I'm the security guy".

"It's a pleasure meeting you Ram."

"The pleasure is all mine sista', follow me."

Ram led her through the front office but did not make any introductions. It was as if he intentionally tried to avoid people. Charlie made eye contact with everyone she passed. A few returned the gaze, but most turned away. She had not expected a welcoming party, but a few handshakes and greetings would have been nice. The only non-white person she saw was Ram. She did not know why that crossed her mind, but it always did. The lack of diversity, while prevalent in her industry, was still very noticeable; and she was not expecting it in a city with as many black residents as Detroit.

The office furnishings were definitely not what she expected. The furniture was better than what the corporate office had, and everything looked new. The desks were wood, and the chairs were leather, not the faux crap they had at the corporate office. Bob Davidson was frugal with company money, but apparently Stanley had no problem spending it. The front office area looked like that of a fortune 500 corporate headquarters as opposed to a distribution center tucked away in an industrial park in a Detroit suburb.

The badge reader located at a metal door recognized Ram's badge and released the magnetic lock on the heavy door. He led Charlie through the doorway into the warehouse.

"Hey Ram, can I do the warehouse tour later? I just wanna get settled into my office."

"That's where we're headed. Your office is in the warehouse right next to mine."

"Oh..."

"Yeah... there are two empty offices up front, but I was told to set you up back here. We had to move the new supervisor out of the office so you could have it. Now the two supervisors have to share an office and they're not happy about it."

"Great... I'm making friends already."

THERE WAS a corporate spy being sent to infiltrate them, and under no circumstances was anyone to cooperate with her in any way. There was colorful language used, and threats hurled, but the gist of Stanley's message to his team was clear. Hank left the meeting and had a similar meeting with his direct reports.

The two supervisors, Luke and Robert, were still seething from having to share an office because of the intruder, so the message struck a nerve. The seeds of contempt did not find fertile ground in Ram. He welcomed Charlie with open arms and was ecstatic that she was on site.

"OH, so here is where all the black people are," Charlie exclaimed as Ram led her through the warehouse.

"Yep, more than half of the warehouse is black, but besides you and I, there are no other black supervisors or managers; and technically I'm not a manager and I don't supervise anyone."

"I expected that where I moved from, but I thought things would be different in Detroit."

Ram smirked but did not comment.

Three offices lined a back wall of the warehouse, and Ram escorted Charlie to the middle office. It was the equivalent to having the middle seat on an airplane. Everything negative Charlie had envisioned about her new workspace had manifested right in front of her. The metal furniture was raggedy, the cushions on the chairs were torn, the walls were concrete like the floor, and the room looked like a windowless bunker. Charlie looked around the small office in disgust.

"I'll get you another chair," Ram said sympathetically, "but that's the best I can do. I know where an extra one is up front; they won't even miss it."

"Thanks Ram, every little bit helps."

"Let's go next door to my office and I'll make you a badge."

"Can't you just program my badge to work here?"

"Corporate badges don't work here."

"They work at all the other distribution centers."

"Yeah, but we're on a different system."

Charlie shook her head. "Why am I not surprised." She

followed him next door and waited patiently as the machine went through its cycles, each with its own unique sound, as it produced her badge. The smile it captured could best be described as sexy.

"Just let me know if you need anything from up front," Ram said as he handed her the fresh badge, "and I'll be happy to get it for you."

"Thanks Ram, but I can handle it from here. I know it's a long walk through the warehouse to the front office, but walking is good exercise."

"Well, you'll need someone to let you in, the only ones with access are me, the two supervisors and my boss Hank." Ram flinched from the expression on Charlie's face and took a step back.

"What do you mean I have to be let in? My badge won't let me in the office area?"

Ram answered with his eyes and braced for impact. Charlie's rage monster nearly escaped but she was able to reel it back in. She knew Stanley was the instigator of everything she had experienced since arriving on the property, and Ram was just a player in his game; an unwilling player she sensed. She was thankful for the kindness he had shown her. Ram was thankful for her restraint.

12

The idea was Stanley's, but it had Roman's blessing. Hank, naive to how close he had come to being the sacrificial lamb, had no objections; not that his opinion mattered anyway. What saved him was the need for an extra layer of protection for Stanley. He could not be close enough for blood splatter to put him at the scene of the crime. Hank's only job was to deliver the message to Robert and concoct a story for the Feds of how it could have happened on his watch. He called Robert into his office, told him what was going to happen, and watched unapologetically as Robert wept.

ALTHOUGH THEY WERE INVITED, the two FBI Agents produced a warrant as soon as Hank greeted them at the door. They followed him to his office where they found Stanley standing in a corner with his arms folded.

"Have a seat gentlemen." Hank offered with a smile.

"For the record," Stanley blurted out, "I am opposed to this meeting. My ops manager got carried away when he concluded his investigation and dialed you before dialing me." That was only the first statement the two agents found hard to believe. They suspected there were more to come.

"It's good to put a face with the voice Mr. Forsythe."

Stanley did not respond, but he knew which of the two agents was most senior.

"We won't be needing this," Hank exclaimed as he handed the warrant back to the agents, "we're ready to bend over and spread our cheeks."

"Have you found the missing product?"

"No, but we found everything else." Hank smiled as if he was about to reveal who shot President Kennedy. "After you boys left my office, I got to thinking and I started diggin'."

The two agents looked at each other with a 'this should be good' expression. Hank was not deterred, and he continued with fervor. Over the next thirty minutes he gave testimony as to how his supervisor, Robert Cooper, 'had masterminded a criminal operation the likes of he had never seen before.' The agents took detailed notes from Hank's ardent monologue, and did not interrupt, saving their questions until he finished.

"So... Mr. Cooper entered a fake purchase order into the computer so the true source of the product could not be tracked?"

"Yep, and it wasn't his first time," Hank answered enthusiastically. "I was able to find several fake purchase orders in the system, but I didn't find paperwork to match 'em."

"So, have you determined where the product came from?"

"Sure have; when I fired the son-of-a bitch and told him he was going to prison, he told me who he was working with. Some shady operation out of Florida."

That statement seized the attention of the agents. "Is it Rome Enterprises or one of its many companies?" The lead agent inquired.

"I don't think so," Hank said as he handed over a document.

"This is the actual order Robert received; never heard of this company."

The agents examined the document carefully; disappointment caused their shoulders to slump in their dark grey suits. The document had been printed three days prior to the agents' arrival. The company was a small husband and wife operation located in Ft. Lauderdale. They moved enough product to be profitable, but they were far from being a major player. They were not on the agents' radar. Most of their deals came from maneuvering within Roman's circle, so when Roman called and told them the plan and their part in it, they knew refusal was not an option. The only question was which one would be prosecuted, the husband or the wife.

"So how does the money flow? Who gets paid, and how?"

"Good question," Hank exclaimed, "I wondered the same thing." Hank took a breath and regurgitated the scenario Stanley had presented to him. "Apparently Robert had set up a bank account tied to a dummy company associated with the fake purchase order. When the invoice was paid, the money was wired to Robert's account. He would pay the company on that piece of paper there and keep his cut. Since the drugs were counterfeit, that company probably paid very little for 'em, if anything, and sold them to us for WAC minus whatever discount we received."

"What is WAC?"

"Wholesale Acquisition Cost."

The agents considered everything they had been told. It was either an elaborate scheme on Robert's part or an elaborate story on Hank's. One thing was certain; if it was a story, Hank did not fabricate it on his own. They also knew that Hank did not contact them without Stanley's approval.

"Where is Mr. Cooper now?"

"His whereabouts are not our concern," Stanley

proclaimed. "We fired him and had him escorted off the property. I assume that's when Hank called you."

"I see."

"I assure you, I am looking into this matter personally, and..." Stanley turned and gazed at Hank as he made his next point. "Robert Cooper may not be the only casualty."

"Is the product still in your facility?"

"No."

"Where is it?"

"Your colleagues at FDA saw to it that it was incinerated."

"Well, I guess we're done here," The senior agent proclaimed as the two agents stood in unison.

"I guess you are." Stanley agreed.

Robert had forewarned his wife what was going to happen, but that did not prevent her from breaking down when the agents arrived at the house to arrest him. Robert told her he was guilty but had not explained what he was guilty of, nor did he tell her about the phone call he received the day after Hank called him into his office. He did not recognize the voice, but the message was clear.

His wife listened in disbelief as Robert provided the details to the two FBI agents. His motive was clear. Like most people engaged in criminal activity, it was for the money. He had wanted to retire but could not. No one else at the Distributing Company was involved, a point he had to make several times. He was successful because they were extremely busy. Product was coming in and going out nonstop, it was easy to get his shipments in undetected.

Robert heard shrieks and moans from his wife that he had never heard in all of their years of marriage. By the time he answered all of the questions which were hurled at him, his wife's eyes were dry; there were no tears left in the well.

Robert's heart broke, literally, as he clutched his chest and gasped for breath. He would be taken from his home on a gurney, with paramedics unaided in their fight for his life. The ER doctor called his time of death not long after arriving at the hospital.

THERE WAS no chivalrous act of bravery in the husband's decision to take sole responsibility for selling counterfeit and adulterated medications; he lost the argument with his wife and was forced to face justice alone. Roman did not care which one took the fall, as long as one of them confessed their sins to the FBI and did their part as Robert had.

His was the only name on the business license filed with the state of Florida, so her claim of ignorance was not hard to uphold. He had echoed Robert's story and produced supporting documentation. Roman provided bail money and paid for an attorney to represent him. The loosely formed company was dissolved, and all assets were seized by the government; including counterfeit drugs found on the premises. It was not a career changing arrest, but counterfeit drugs were taken off the street, and one tiny link in the supply chain had been cracked. The FBI kept Stanley's scent in their nostrils, confident that they had only scratched the surface of his involvement... in something.

13

The envelope was in the mailbox amongst mail delivered by the United States Postal Service. It was inconspicuous but familiar, addressed to Clint Hardy with no return address nor postage. Clint stuffed the envelope in his back pocket and walked back inside the house. He placed the mail on the kitchen counter and walked to the garage where he retrieved the envelope from his pocket. There was a single sheet of paper folded inside, with instructions typed double-spaced in the usual font.

Clint had hoped he would not receive another envelope in his mailbox after failing to drop his last load in Atlanta on schedule. When he was released from jail after making an agreement with the FBI, he drove to the location in south Atlanta to find the remnants of a building which was still smoldering. He unhooked and left the trailer on the property; it was not his responsibility once the drop was made, regardless of the condition of the drop site.

The load was to be picked up in Olive Branch, MS, a location close to home. It was only a short drive from his house. The drop was a pharmaceutical distribution center in St. Louis,

MO. The name was familiar to him, it was one of the big companies with distribution centers across the country. Should be an easy job, he thought, he would call his contact at the FBI after he made the pickup.

CLINT WAS familiar with Olive Branch but struggled to find the address listed on the sheet of paper; the rain reduced visibility to practically zero. Clint had no way of calling to see if the pickup was still happening, he was never given a name or a phone number, just instructions. He could only assume plans had not been delayed or aborted due to the severe weather.

If not for the quick sequence of flashing headlights, Clint would have unknowingly driven pass his destination. He pulled adjacent to the tractor trailer which had flashed the lights and lowered his driver side window. The driver of the other truck did the same.

"What's the plan?" Clint asked as rain poured in through his window. He had to yell to be heard over the rain.

"Which one do you want?" the other driver asked, "the plan you're gonna follow or the one you're gonna tell the Feds?"

Clint noticed the man sitting in the passenger seat when he leaned forward and pointed a gun in Clint's direction. Clint struggled to catch his breath due to the sudden acceleration of his heart rate. His face became flush, and his eyes were fixated on the handgun. Desperate thoughts of escape flooded his mind, but they all ended in his death. He took a series of deep breaths which steadied his heart.

"I guess I'll take both," he said feebly. The men did not hear his voice, but they understood the surrender in his eyes. Clint was instructed to follow their truck, and he did.

. . .

Clint was not told the plans until he acknowledged a complete understanding of his options, and the consequences of each. He could be the Fed's 'rat', which would be very short-lived and would also shorten the lives of his wife and daughters, or he could continue the work he was doing, feed specified information to the Feds and risk going to prison if caught. An answer was needed at that moment, and Clint responded as they knew he would.

Clint departed with two loads, both bound for Missouri. The first was to be dropped at a location that had just been made known to him, and the second drop was the location listed in the letter he received in his mailbox. That was also the location he would reveal to the FBI.

Local agents met Clint at the location in St. Louis. They watched as six pallets of product were taken off the truck and lined along Bullock's receiving area. Bullock's Inc. was one of the big three pharmaceutical distributors and had a few more distributions centers than New Wind, but considerably more revenue; at least until New Wind's Davidson Enterprises acquisition was finalized. The facility in St. Louis was Bullock's Specialty Facility, or BSF as it was referred by industry, it purchased drugs from other wholesalers to help supplement the insatiable appetite of Bullock's vast distribution network.

Everything looked normal. The vials were exactly what was ordered, and a thorough inspection did not reveal any abnormalities. The operations manager did not understand why the agents ordered the product to be quarantined while a sample was sent to the lab for verification, but after notifying his director, who notified the corporate office in Phoenix, Bullock's Specialty complied grudgingly. They expressed the need for the government to act expeditiously as customers, and patients no doubt, were waiting on the product. Thirteen business days expired before the results were known.

The label stated 40mcg, but the tests revealed the vials only contained 20mcg of the active ingredient stated on the label. While the active ingredient was authentic, the product was still considered adulterated and was reported to the FDA, which ordered an immediate recall of the lot number and launched an investigation. It started with a request for the pedigree Bullock's received for the product. The request was just a formality, since the FDA had already requested and received a pedigree from Coliseum Pharma Supply, the company that invoiced Bullock's for the drugs. They had also already tracked the drugs back to the manufacturer.

The questioning was intense, and Doug, Bullock's purchasing manager did his best, but he was doomed from the start.

"Who did you purchase the adulterated product from?"

The word adulterated shook him, and his discomfort glared in neon lights. The word was well placed by the FDA agent and the tactic worked. "Coliseum Pharma Supply Company," he answered as confidently as he could.

"What is Coliseum Pharma Supply?"

"They're a distribution company." The agent sat gazing silently at Doug as if he was waiting for the question to be answered properly. Doug was uncomfortable with the silence and looked at his director of operations who was in the office with him. His expression conveyed to Doug that he was on his own. "Th- they specialize in hard-to-find drugs." It was only the second question and Doug's nervous stutter surfaced.

"By hard to find, you mean..."

"Drugs that are in ssshort supply."

"And these drugs are usually more expensive and prone to

counterfeit." It was a statement with the tone of a question, and Doug felt obligated to answer it.

"I-I don't know."

"You're the purchasing manager, correct?"

"Yes."

"And you placed the order for the adulterated drugs in question, correct?"

"I didn't know they were not what the label said, I ordered 40 mcg..."

"But you know the price, correct? You know how expensive the drugs are?"

"Yeah, but..."

"And you know certain drugs are more prone to be counterfeit right? It makes sense, right? The more popular or expensive a drug is that's what the criminals want to counterfeit and pollute our supply chain." The agent paused for effect, and Doug's voice could not snag a breath to form words. The agent placed a document on the desk. "Is this the pedigree you provided our office?"

Doug leaned over and scanned the document. "Yes, that l-l-looks like it."

"According to this, Coliseum purchased the illegal drugs from Davidson Distributing Company who is listed as the authorized distributor."

"Yes, that's what it says."

"So did Davidson Distributing purchase the drugs from the manufacturer?"

"I guess, I don't know."

"Would you like to know how many other companies distributed the product before it got to Davidson Distributing?"

"We only need to track back to the AD per the PDMA." Doug actually smirked when he used the agent's own regulation against him. The agent was not amused.

"Would it surprise you to know that three other companies

touched the product before it was received by Davidson Distributing?" Doug's smirk began to erode. "What would you say if I told you that another Bullock's distribution center was one of the three?"

Doug looked at the director of ops. They both were dumbfounded. "Uh… what does that mean?"

"It means that a Bullock's facility in Dallas, Texas purchased the product from the manufacturer and sold it to a hospital system in the Dallas area; for a profit I presume. That hospital system, for reasons yet unknown, sold the product to a repackager in Louisiana called Gulf Coast Pharmapack, who in turn sold the product to Davidson Distributing. As you know, Davidson Distributing sold the product to Coliseum. Now it is sitting in your warehouse where you intended to sell it for another profit to another hospital system in Indiana; according to the sales manager I spoke with."

"How would we have known all that?" The ops director blurted out to everyone's surprise, including his.

"Well, you could have asked… just because your pedigree only goes back to the AD, you don't have to stop there. You can ask for verification that the AD purchased it from the manufacturer, and if not ask for the entire trail back to the manufacturer. Or here's a crazy thought… only purchase directly from the manufacturer and sell to a final dispenser."

"We did that," the ops director proclaimed, "Bullock's originally purchased it from the manufacturer and sold it to a hospital, which is a final dispenser."

"And yet here it is quarantined in your warehouse."

"Sounds like you need to talk to the hospital."

"Of course, I can't comment on an active investigation, but it is safe to say we will be speaking with every entity involved."

. . .

Coliseum initially balked at crediting Bullock's for the adulterated drugs, at least until it was reimbursed from its supplier. Bullock's legion of attorneys descended on Coliseum with such force that Coliseum succumbed and refunded every cent. A credit was not acceptable because Bullock's vowed to never purchase from Coliseum again. A promise that would be broken in two months when they needed a drug that only Coliseum had, and which they would pay a hefty premium for.

14

The first time Charlie sent Stanley a question via email, he called and told her to never send him an email again. He did not answer her question, but he was clear in his demand. Her second email was an inquiry about the amount of product the Distributing Company purchased directly from manufacturers; she felt the percentage was too low. There was no response. Several days later she sent a third email reminding Stanley that at least twenty-five percent of product purchased should be distributed to the other Davidson distribution centers. According to her numbers, roughly eight percent was currently distributed to Davidson facilities. She braced herself for a phone call but was caught off guard when he walked into her office and slammed the door shut. Both Ram and Luke jumped from the sheer force of the collision felt in their neighboring offices.

"I know you think Bob can protect you," Stanley yelled, "but this is my house! You follow my rules or get the hell out!"

"What rules is you referrin' to massa'?"

Stanley inhaled a deep breath through his flaring nostrils and slowly exhaled through his puckered lips. His anger actually secreted through his pores, and Charlie could smell its musty odor.

"I would offer you a seat, but I don't have one. There's barely enough room in this cell for me."

"Usually, dogs don't shit where they sleep..."

"Just call me a bitch Stanley, no need to dance around it."

"I thought I was clear about not sending me emails." Not only did the conversation shift, but so did his tone.

"You don't answer the phone when I call."

"And I don't respond to emails."

"Well, I can't go to your office to talk to you because my access is restricted."

"Yes, it is."

"Sooo... I will continue sending emails."

Stanley's rendition of a smile was void of meaning. He looked around the small concrete office and then locked eyes with his antagonist.

"What is this about my direct from manufacturer inventory?"

"It is my understanding that it should be twenty percent. For the last two quarters it's been around five percent."

"We purchase enough to maintain our AD status with the manufacturers."

"It only takes two transactions over twenty-four months to be an authorized distributor with a manufacturer;" Charlie countered, "that's not much. And by claiming AD status you don't have to pass a pedigree when you sell the product. You don't have to reveal your shady sources."

"I suggest you voice your concern with the FDA. I didn't write the Prescription Drug Marketing Act, I just use it to my advantage; and twenty percent is Bob's number, not mine."

"And I guess the twenty-five percent the Distributing Company is obligated to distribute to our own distribution centers is Bob's number too?"

"It's definitely not mine. I'm in the business of making money. The margin is higher when I sell externally."

"The other Davidson distribution centers would have higher margins if they were able to sell some of the product you're able to source so cheap. Share the wealth."

"That's not my business model; besides, they'll all be closed soon anyway. Have a good day." He exited less ceremoniously than he entered, but he did close the door behind him. He walked next door to Ram's office and stuck his head in just long enough to say...

"Give her access to the front office."

SEVERAL MONTHS PASSED since the acquisition of Davidson Enterprises by New Wind had been finalized and Nicole apologized to Charlie for not visiting her sooner. While she had not had an opportunity to visit the facility physically, she had made her presence felt. The reserved parking spaces were gone, although the warehouse employees were too scared to park in the spaces even if they were empty. Charlie did not hesitate to park in one of the spaces and took pleasure in parking in the space that had been reserved for Stanley. She also championed several changes Charlie proposed regarding pedigree review and inventory levels, much to the chagrin of Stanley. His protests fell on deaf ears.

Charlie politely declined the new office when Nicole offered it to her; she actually preferred working in the warehouse with the "normal" people. The majority of the people she had encountered in the front office were elitist, and she could not function if she had to "experience" them every day. Nicole understood, and the two women agreed that it was a culture spawned from Stanley; one which he cultivated.

"So, how is Stanley treating you?" Nicole asked earnestly.

"He pretty much avoids me, but I'm good with that."

"I'm not real clear on the arrangement you had with Bob Davidson..."

"He wanted me to be his eyes and ears, he wanted a spy. He gave me the title of inventory manager, but Stanley already has an inventory manager. I do what I can, but Stan has blocked my access to several screens in the inventory management system. And I have even less access in the warehouse management system."

"Well, you've managed to do a hell of a job with what little access you have. I know you've been in Stanley's ass about the inventory because he's been complaining to Bob even though he reports to me. Bob will be gone at the end of the month, and then he will have to deal directly with me."

"Lucky you."

"I'm not Bob Davidson. Things will be a lot different, starting with the warehouse and inventory management systems. We are converting this facility to our ERP system, and you will have access to everything. You will need it in your role as director of inventory management."

"That sounds like a promotion."

"We want to beef up New Wind distribution centers with more product sourced by the Distributing Company. I need you to oversee that."

"I need to take over the pedigree review process. Right now, it's done by Stanley's purchasing manager, if it's being done at all, and I'm not comfortable that the product is vetted properly."

"Effective immediately all pedigrees will be sent to you for review. I'll let Stanley know."

"And we need to audit our suppliers. I want to conduct an assessment of every alternate source vendor, including a site visit. I believe we have over three hundred distributors shipping us product from all over the country, including Puerto Rico, and I've never heard of most of 'em."

"Done. I'll order you a corporate American Express card to use for travel. If you need to hire someone to help with the audits, I'll approve it. I have a budget meeting with Stanley and team tomorrow morning. I'll forward you the invitation and we can discuss the budget for your department then."

"My department?"

"Yes, that's what it sounds like to me. Look Charlie; I need, the company needs someone to not only source inventory for the lowest price, but also from the right sources. Product integrity is just as important as profit margins. We need you to manage that process. If it means cutting off vendors, then that's what we'll do. There are too many investigations going on right now involving the Distributing Company."

"Investigations?" Charlie exclaimed in astonishment. "What kind of investigations?"

Nicole paused; she contemplated if she had been too liberal with information but concluded that Charlie needed to be informed to do her job. From the conversations she had with Bob Davidson and what she had observed on her own, Charlie was trustworthy.

"We just learned most of this ourselves," Nicole started, "but apparently the FBI and FDA are investigating counterfeit product that the distribution company had on premises, adulterated product that it may have been involved with, and other claims of distribution of illegitimate product." Nicole saw that Charlie was genuinely surprised and concerned. "So, you see, this promotion comes with a lot of responsibility. We need you to keep us out of trouble."

Many thoughts competed for attention inside Charlie's mind, but they all had similar themes. Why was Nicole offering her so much? Why was Nicole being so nice to her? What was the catch? Nicole could see the skepticism on Charlie's face and sought to ease her suspicion.

"I know we barely know each other, but I see a lot of myself in you. I suspect that like me, it has not been an easy road for you to get where you are, but you're here because you don't back down from anyone and you get things done. That's what this job needs and that's why I'm offering it to you with my full support." She leaned in closer to Charlie and spoke in a lowered tone. "Plus, it would be good to have a strong female on my team. There aren't too many of us at this level in our business."

Charlie extended her hand with a smile. "Let's give 'em hell."

Nicole grasped her hand firmly. "We're going to do great things."

"Exactly how much of a promotion are we talking?"

Nicole smiled and leaned back in her chair. "I'll have HR type up an offer letter and submit it to you. New Wind's compensation package is very competitive, and based on your salary now, I think you will find your offer generous. I believe in paying for top talent." Nicole saw the approving glow on Charlie's face. She looked around Charlie's office as she stood.

"I understand you don't want to move up front, but can you at least get some new furniture?"

"Oh Definitely."

"Good, this stuff is awful. Log onto the company intranet and order something from our office furniture vendor. I'll see you at the budget meeting tomorrow morning."

"I'll be there. I can't wait to see the look on his face."

Nicole turned as she walked out "It will be the same look he had when he found out he would be reporting to me. It's priceless."

. . .

THE OPTICS WOULD NOT HAVE BEEN good if Charlie and Nicole sat next to each other, so they sat center on opposite sides of the giant conference room table. Stanley's team congregated on one end of the table and Stanley walked in two minutes after the scheduled start time and set at the end of the table with his team. He took note of Charlie when he walked in but did not acknowledge her. Neither did he feel the need to explain his tardiness; primarily because he did not want to give Charlie the satisfaction of knowing it was due to the fact that he had a great distance to walk from the open parking space he found.

"Good morning, everyone," Nicole greeted fervently.

A chorus of halfhearted greetings were hurled in her direction.

"The last time I was in this conference room I could see my breath it was so cold." She looked up and saw the only smile in the room emanating across from her.

"I wanted to take this opportunity to meet the team, discuss our plans for the future, and answer any questions you might have. I know by now you've heard about the closing of two of the Davidson facilities, and the plans to close the Los Angeles facility by years' end. Each employee was either offered a job at the nearest New Wind facility or was given a severance package based on years of service. Let me put your mind at ease and assure you that the Distributing Company is not closing. There will be a name change, but New Wind has big plans for the Distributing Company." Nicole spent time looking at each person in the room as she spoke. She initiated eye contact even if it was not reciprocated. "You all have done an excellent job making this division very profitable, and we look forward to continuing those efforts, even while making necessary changes."

Her last remark took hostage the attention of everyone in the room. They could no longer pretend to be uninterested; Stanley remained poker-faced.

"Anyway, I've done enough talking, why don't each of you introduce yourself and tell me what your role is here at the Distributing Company." After a tense silence as each waited on someone else to start, Charlie decided to take the lead."

"Hello, I'm Charlie," she began, looking at the three individuals sitting with Stanley. She had only met John, the inventory manger briefly, just long enough for him to dismiss her. "I've been here for several months now working with inventory, and I look forward to working with each of you going forward."

"I'm Sam," proclaimed a woman in her early to mid-thirties with long, curly red hair, "I'm the sales manager."

"Great meeting you Sam," Nicole said cheerfully, "I love your hair, it's beautiful."

"Thank you, Sam responded, softened by the compliment."

"Hi, I'm Christine, I'm the purchasing manager."

"Hello Christine, so you're the one who negotiates such favorable pricing."

Christine flashed her barbie smile and tugged at her short skirt as she crossed her long Barbie legs in Stanley's direction. Nicole noted that both young women were very attractive but did not give credence to any accompanying thought.

"Do I need to do this?" Hank asked mockingly. "I've met both of you already.

"No Hank, we know who you are. You're the one who makes sure our customers get what they ordered and on time."

"I'm John, I'm the inventory manager." John made sure to lock eyes with Charlie as he recited his title. Whatever Charlie did in inventory, he wanted to be clear that it was his domain.

"Oh, so you and Charlie work together."

"No not really," John exclaimed.

"I've only met him once in passing," Charlie added. "We've maybe exchanged two or three words."

Nicole's brow arched. "Oh, well that will definitely change, which is a great segue to our first item. Last night, Charlie received and accepted an offer to become director of inventory management for the Distributing Company, reporting directly to me. Congratulations Charlie."

Nicole excitedly led an applause which the others reluctantly participated in while looking at Stanley who sat stone-faced. Charlie nodded and smiled, primarily at Nicole, but also showed gratitude to the others.

"John, you will now report to Charlie, and she may add another person to her headcount to assist with vendor audits."

The four people at the end of the table yelled 'vendor audits?' so loudly in their minds it was almost audible. Stanley did not want his team to know that it was his first-time hearing about any of it, so he struggled to maintain a neutral expression. Charlie fought to remain vanilla as well.

"Charlie, why don't you take a minute to highlight a few of the changes you're initiating."

Charlie, caught off-guard, initiated eye contact with her colleagues and seized the moment. "Of course, I'll bring the team together soon to discuss the details, but I envision an inventory department with a renewed focus on product integrity."

Stanley was on the verge of spontaneous combustion, and there was a noticeable temperature increase in the room.

"I will review all pedigrees prior to the product arriving on our dock. No prescription drugs, including controlled substances, will be received into inventory until I have approved the pedigree. Christine, please let all non-manufacturer vendors know to FAX me the pedigree prior to shipping the product."

Christine's mouth hung open, but no words fell out of it. She was in shock and felt numb. Confident she was heard and understood, Charlie continued.

"We will be implementing a vendor assessment program, including site visits. Any new alternate source vendor will need to be visited prior to shipping us product. All existing suppliers will be visited over the next eighteen months."

Charlie paused and surveyed the room. Christine looked to be on the verge of tears, and John's face was flushed. Sam nervously twisted her red locks, and Stanley was mentally preparing for war. Hank was physically in the room, but his mind was in the warehouse. He was totally checked out from whatever conversation they were having. Charlie decided that was enough for one sitting.

"I know that's a lot to digest, and I don't want to hijack Nicole's meeting, so I'll set up time with each of you to discuss in greater detail. Thanks, and I look forward to working with each of you."

"Thanks Charlie," Nicole exclaimed with a smile. "Does anyone have any questions?" She paused long enough for everyone to say what they were thinking, but no one did. "Okay then... let's move to the budget; we have a new department to fund."

THE MEETING RAN over by the number of minutes which delayed the start of the meeting due to Stanley's long walk from his parking space. John, Christine, and Sam marched straight to Stanley's office with their attitudes in tow. Stanley lingered behind as Nicole knew he would.

"I see affirmative action is alive and well," Stanley exclaimed.

Nicole smirked, but Charlie grimaced with anger. She felt her rage monster trying to surface, but she stomped it back down into her gut.

"You should have talked to me first," Stanley barked at Nicole, "you should have asked my..." Stanley's words dropped to the floor.

"Your what Stanley?" Nicole asked, picking up Stanley's fallen word. "I should have asked your permission?"

"We could have talked before this meeting. I should not have heard the news for the first time with my team."

"Your team? Don't forget, you're the coach, but I'm the GM; and New Wind owns the team, the building, and the land it sits on. We only succeed if we work together. But you're right, I should have talked to you before making an announcement, and I apologize. I literally had a conversation with Charlie yesterday, and HR put an offer together last night which Charlie accepted this morning. She is an asset to the team and will only make us better."

"Is everything she said really necessary?"

"It is if you want to stay out of jail," Nicole exclaimed.

"I see she's been filling your head with her theories."

"No... actually the FBI, FDA and state of California have been filling my head with their theories."

"California?"

"Oh, so the FBI and FDA don't surprise you..."

Stanley turned to walk away but gave Charlie a stern warning before he did. "Just stay out of my way and don't fuck with my margins." With that he exited the conference room. He knew he had to do damage control back in his office.

15

The manufacturer turned over batch records to the FDA confirming that the lot number sold to Bullock's contained 40mcg of active ingredient, not the 20mcg the lab tests revealed. Bullock's executives, cornered by FDA in their corner offices, provided documentation showing the product arriving on their Dallas facility's dock on one day and being shipped to the hospital's storage facility the next day. They did not have the time nor the ability to make any type of change to the product or its labeling. As distributors, they explained, their critical role in the supply chain was to distribute lifesaving medications to pharmacies, hospitals, and other healthcare providers. Without them, medications would not get to the patients who needed them. It sounded like a press release, and they would have gone on and on if they had not been reminded that the product had made its way back to another one of their facilities.

The hospital overestimated their demand for the product, and instead of returning the overage to Bullock's for a credit, they sold it to Gulf Coast Pharmapack who claimed to have customers desperately needing the product. They were also the highest bidder, but that piece of information was not shared with the FDA. Not only was it unethical for the hospital to sell the product, the FDA decried, but also illegal. They did not have a license to distribute product into Louisiana or any other state. The hospital was certain to hear from the Louisiana Board of Pharmacy. While confident the hospital did not alter the product, the FDA could not conclude their investigation of the hospital.

GULF COAST PHARMAPACK already had an open investigation regarding Laprin; the product they purchased to be repackaged had a lot number the manufacturer claimed was not valid. Gulf Coast sourced the product from a company in South Florida, but the investigation had stalled there. The FDA was eager to speak with Gulf Coast regarding the vials they purchased from the hospital.

Peter was Gulf Coast's first line of defense. As general manager, the owners of Gulf Coast relied on Peter to manage the entire operation. Gulf Coast had been a family-owned business from its inception, and the business had never been on the wrong side of the law. They intended for it to stay that way, and it was Peter's job to ensure it did. Once the formalities were out of the way, the FDA agent jumped right in.

"I'm here to ask about this product you repackaged under your label and sold to Davidson Distributing Company." The agent handed Peter an invoice. It's Laprin 40 mcg, correct?"

Peter studied the invoice. "Yes, that's what it says here."

"You billed Davidson for 40 mcg, which I am assuming is more expensive than say 20 mcg correct?

Peter kept his eyes on the invoice trying to figure out where the agent was going with his line of questioning. "Yes, that is correct."

The agent nodded his head as he looked at Peter down his nose. "I'm sure you're not surprised to know that the product is currently quarantined."

"Quarantined?" Peter asked, genuinely surprised. "Why? Where?"

"Let's not do this Peter."

"Do what?"

"Play games."

"I agree," Peter said in frustration, "what do you want from me?"

"The truth."

"What are we talking about here?" Peter was on the verge of putting the agent out of his office.

"The product is quarantined at Bullock's Specialty Distribution because the label says 40 mcg but the amount of active ingredient in each vial is 20mcg. Maybe Gulf Coast put the wrong label on the vials when you repackaged them?"

"No, I can assure you that did not happen."

"Of course, I need all records from that run."

"Of course." Peter did not hide his irritation. "Did you say the product was at Bullock's Specialty? We sold it to Davidson Distributing."

"Who sold it to Coliseum Pharma Supply who in turn sold it to Bullock's Specialty."

Peter looked confused, but when he heard that Coliseum had touched it an alarm went off in his head. Coliseum was one of Roman's companies, and he was sure Roman's DNA was all over the mislabeled product, and he was certain it was not accidental.

"I know, confusing isn't it." The agent exclaimed, responding to the look on Peter's face. "And that doesn't include the companies that touched the product prior to your company receiving it. By the way, is it common practice to purchase prescription drugs from hospitals?"

Peter hesitated before he answered. If he said yes, he would have to explain without any acceptable justification, and if he answered no, he would have to explain the circumstance which led to the one-time purchase. Either way, his company would get a written warning at a minimum, so he answered truthfully as he would later have to do under oath.

"It is not a common practice, but this was not the first time." It sounded very political, even to him. "I can assure you it will be the last," he added for good measure.

"I see..."

'You don't see shit,' Peter thought to himself; even thoughts to himself had a thick accent.

"Tell me," the agent continued, "did you purchase any 20mcg product around the time you purchased the 40mcg from the hospital? Or did you have any on hand at the time you repackaged the product in question?"

"I don't know, let me check..." Peter typed on his keyboard and gazed at his monitor. It took several maneuvers to get to what he wanted, but the information jumped off the screen and smacked him in the face. His face turned red from the blow.

"It looks like we did."

"Was it enough to fill the order for the 40 mcg you sold to Davidson Distributing?"

Peter knew the answer, but he typed a few more keystrokes as if he had to locate the answer. It was an obvious stall tactic, and the agent almost smirked. He knew they did not do it, but the optics were not good.

"Yes, we had quite a bit on hand." Peter cursed his choice of words as soon as they left his mouth. He had been prepped for depositions before, and he knew to just answer the question without offering any detail. This was not a deposition, but it felt like one. The agent pounced on Peter's loose tongue.

"Quite a bit you say… enough that you wanted to get rid of some of the extra inventory that had probably been sitting in your warehouse for a while? Maybe stick a 40mcg label on it because the 40mcg is prescribed more and you can move it faster and for a greater profit?"

"You asked if we had inventory on hand and the answer is yes."

"Of course, I will need documentation on that product as well."

"Of course."

"Just checking every box, you know how things are. One 'i' not dotted or 't' crossed and the whole report is kicked back to you."

"Yeah, I hate when that happens… anything else?" It was time for the agent to leave.

"No not at this time, just the documents I requested, and I'll be on my way."

"Great, I'll be right back." Peter was glad to leave the office so he could curse out loud. He knew he would return without documents, but the stalling would give him time to think. He could have the documents within minutes, but he did not want to hand over anything without first talking with Roman. Peter knew his own hands were clean, but suspected Roman's dirt would stain him as well. His dealings with Roman had finally caught up to him he thought to himself.

"How's it going in there?" Peter recognized the voice immediately. It caught him off guard because he did not know the owner was on site.

"Fine," Peter answered trying his best not too sound nervous, "just fine." Peter prayed he did not want to engage in small talk.

"Good to hear. Is he gone yet? Why is he here anyway?"

"Not yet," Peters responded, ignoring the second question. "I just need to retrieve some documents for 'em."

"Oh, I see... well come to my office after he leaves so we can debrief."

"Of course, see you soon."

Peter had to cut his stall tactics short. He knew his boss was waiting impatiently in his office. He wanted to know why the FDA had shown up unannounced when they had inspected the facility not even a year earlier. The longer Peter procrastinated, the more questions he would have hurled at him. He returned to his office and the agent.

"Looks like I'm going to have to get those to you, it's gonna take longer than expected to round everything up."

The agent smirked; he was not expecting Peter to have the documents. "Forty-eight hours then? I believe that's the definition of readily available. I will be back then."

"Certainly, but you don't have to come back out; I can have them sent to your office by courier."

"It's no bother at all. I may think of something else I need for the report, and I can just pick it up while I'm here."

"Sure, just let me know and I'll have it ready."

"Yes, I'm sure you will."

Peter was glad the agent did not extend his hand for the customary handshake. It was doubtful if he would have accepted it.

"So, what's going on?"

Peter had never seen suspicion in his boss's eyes, but it clouded his pupils like cataracts. Peter had never lied to either of the two owners of the company, partially because they had never asked the right or wrong questions, and he decided at that moment that he would not start then.

"The FDA is investigating product that we repackaged that is mislabeled."

"Mislabeled?"

"Yeah... Label says 40mcg, but contents are 20mcg."

"Did we..."

"Wasn't us," Peter interrupted, "we repackaged 20mcg. It had to have happened further down the chain."

"Do you have any ideas?" Concern was still in his voice, but it was fading.

"No," Peter lied, "but I'm looking into it."

"Good, keep me posted. Our family has trusted you to run the operations for too many years to count, no need to stop trusting you now."

"I appreciate that Sir. I will let you know what I find."

With that, satisfaction prevailed, and Peter confidently smiled and exited the office with furniture from the sixties.

"PETER..." Roman answered after the first ring.

"What the hell did you do Roman?"

"Now that's a question you don't want the answer to even if I knew what the hell you were talking about."

"Laprin 40 mcg, or should I say 20 mcg." The silence on the phone spoke volumes "Shit Roman!"

"Who's asking?"

"Who's asking? I'm asking... the FDA is asking. This is an immune globulin; this is some serious shit. We shouldn't even have it anyway"

"Calm down..."

"Calm down? You said this was a one-time thing. I know we packaged the right product. What did you do when it got to Coliseum? And why did it go to Coliseum?"

"Like I said, questions you don't want answers to."

"Like I said," Peter countered, "I'm not the only one asking; and to get them off my ass I'm giving them yours. All of my documentation is in order."

"Is it?" Roman asked facetiously. "Are you sure about that? Did you even look at the pedigree?"

"I just wanted to give you a heads up." Peter hung up the phone before Roman could respond.

It took him a while to find the pedigree for the Laprin he purchased, and he reluctantly removed it from the file and placed it on the desk in front of him. He could feel his body temperature rise and his nerves surface as musty perspiration. He looked at the document without seeing it, at least not wanting to see it, and he finally examined it for the first time. His initial scan showed three companies possessed the product prior to Gulf Coast receiving it, and the hospital was not listed, which came as no surprise. When he finally studied the document, one company stood out from the others. It looked more like a stain on the paper than a typed name and address, and Peter wanted to stain it even more by wiping his ass with it. It was one of Roman's companies, one Peter knew was engaged in repackaging. 'Son-of-a-bitch!' He screamed it loud enough in his head that he was certain someone heard it.

IT WAS Nicole's final day at the facility before returning to the corporate office in Atlanta, and she just happened to be in Stanley's office when he was told FDA was on the premises. Usually, Stanley would have summoned Hank to entertain the guest, but Nicole was already out of her seat walking to the door. Stanley would not only have to deal with the FDA, but Nicole as well.

"I feel like I need an office here," The agent said with a chuckle as he sat in one of the plush leather chairs in the conference room. Stanley was not amused.

"Oh, so you're here that often?" Nicole chimed.

“Can I get you anything to drink?” Stanley asked before the agent could respond. He could certainly use one himself.

“No thank you, I’m fine.”

“So, what can we do for you?” Stanley asked in an effort to move the conversation along.

“Well, I’m here to talk about some product you purchased from Gulf Coast Repackagers and sold to Coliseum Pharma Supply.”

“What product?” Stanley asked. Coliseum was one of Roman’s companies, which caused Stanley to proceed carefully.

“If we’re speaking about inventory then Charlie should be in here as well, “Nicole proclaimed. She dialed Charlie’s number on the speaker phone in the middle of the table and asked her to come to the conference room immediately. She stated that the FDA was on site and needed to discuss inventory.

“That’s really not necessary,” Stanley exclaimed. Nicole did not acknowledge his comment.

The agent placed a thick folder on the table in front of him and searched its contents for the documents he needed. There were numerous documents in the folder, but the two he needed were near the top of the stack. He slid them across the table to Stanley. Nicole leaned over so she could read the documents as well.

“My ops manager, Hank, manages the shipping and receiving operation,” Stanley said as he studied the documents, “but what is the issue?”

There was a knock on the conference room door and Charlie entered as she knocked. She took a seat next to Nicole.

“This is Charlie, our director of inventory management,” Nicole announced.

“Nice to meet you, Charlie.”

“You as well.”

“So,” the agent continued, “the first document is for the sale of 40mcg from Gulf Coast to Davidson Distributing, and the second is for the sale of the 40mcg product from Davidson Distributing to Coliseum Pharma Supply."

Stanley scanned the documents and handed them to Nicole so she could stop leaning over his shoulder. Charlie and Nicole reviewed the documents on their own.

"Okay…" Stanley said hoping the agent would get to the point of the visit.

"Coliseum sold the drugs to Bullock's Specialty, which I believe is also a customer of yours, and the drugs have 20mcg of active ingredient instead of the 40mcg identified on the label.

"How would you know that?" Nicole inquired.

"The product is quarantined, and we had it tested."

"What prompted the quarantine and testing?"

"I can't say Ma'am, it's an active investigation. I will say that we have confirmed that the manufacturer's product contained 40mcg of active ingredient."

"It seems to me that when Gulf Coast repackaged it, they made a labeling error," Stanley said matter-of-factly. "Hopefully it was just an error, and nothing more dubious."

"Yes," the agent responded, "that *is* the logical first thought isn't it."

"But you're here," Charlie interjected, "So you're obviously not convinced that is the case."

"We're just checking every box Ma'am."

"Of course."

"I am curious though," the agent continued, "Bullock's Specialty is a customer of yours, so why wouldn't they purchase the product directly from you instead of waiting until you sold it to Coliseum and then purchase it from them?"

'That's a good question' both Charlie and Nicole thought as they looked at each other. Charlie glanced over at Stanley awaiting his answer. She knew Coliseum was one of Roman's companies.

"Of course, I can't speak for Bullock's," Stanley exclaimed, "but maybe they didn't need the product when we had it in our inventory."

"Ahh," the agent said as he reached back into his folder, "I logically thought the same thing; but this purchase order from Bullock's is for the day after you sold the product to Coliseum." He waived the purchase order in the air but did not share it. "It's almost as if they were waiting until Coliseum purchased it from you."

The room was silent as everyone chewed on what the agent had just served. At a minimum, it was not a good look.

"And here's the thing," the agent continued animatedly, "they paid more for it from Coliseum than they would have paid if they had purchased it from you." The room was still silent and very still. "And on top of all that, they only paid slightly above WAC. After all those transactions, I believe it was a total of six different entities, they still basically paid the price the manufacturer would normally charge; for the 40mcg that is. How does that happen?"

'Very strategically,' Stanley thought to himself.

"Yeah, how *does* that happen?" Nicole asked genuinely curious. She was still learning the trading business; she was accustomed to the standard business model.

"I would love to teach a class," Stanley mused as he grinned at Nicole, "but then if everyone knew our secrets, we wouldn't be so valuable would we." Indeed, that was why Stanley believed Nicole needed him more than he needed her. In fact, he did not need her at all.

"One more small thing," the agent exclaimed, "I will need a copy of the bill of laden and any other document showing the shipment from Davidson Distributing to Coliseum."

Stanley's eyes shifted for the first time, and it did not go unnoticed by Charlie.

. . .

After another thirty minutes of hypothetical scenarios, and questions which opposing counsel would have objected to as being 'leading the witness,' the FDA agent surmised that he had everything he needed for the time being and would contact them if his office needed anything further. Stanley saw it as an opportunity to flee, but Nicole asked him to stay.

"Well, that was interesting." Nicole exclaimed after the agent had left them alone in the conference room.

"Sounded like a fishing expedition to me," Stanley moaned.

"Well, he had a lot of bait on his hook." Charlie countered.

"So, the obvious question is, did we know the product was mislabeled when we purchased it from Gulf Coast and sold it to Coliseum?"

"Of course not," Stanley fired back at Nicole as if he was insulted.

"Do you think Gulf Coast sold us adulterated product?"

"That would be my guess," Stanley answered, "but we had no way of knowing."

"Well, do you think it was nefarious? How well do you know this supplier?"

"We've been doing business with them for years, and we've never had anything like this happen."

"What about Coliseum?" Charlie asked. "Isn't that one of Roman's companies?"

Stanley shot her a look but did not answer the question.

"Who is Roman?" Nicole asked.

"Roman Caesar..." Charlie scoffed, "One of the most crooked players in the game. I don't trust him as far as I can spit him out."

"This is no place for your jaded opinions Ms. director of inventory management or whatever your title is. Roman is a trusted trading partner and unless you have evidence saying otherwise, I suggest you keep your opinions to yourself."

"You're right," Charlie conceded, "in my current position I cannot act on unfounded biases."

"What about the short amount of time between transactions?" Nicole asked. "I mean the optics are not good."

"One could argue," Charlie interjected, "that Coliseum was brought in just to make money on the deal."

"An argument that sounds like a desperate attempt to defame not only Davidson Distributing Company, but another highly respected company as well."

"Tread lightly Charlie," Nicole rebuked, "we're all on the same team here." Stanley almost smirked at the reprimand.

"Of course," Charlie said assuredly, "I was just wandering if we shipped the product to Coliseum or if we shipped it directly to Bullock's?"

"We would have shipped it to Coliseum, right?" Nicole looked at Charlie, but her question was directed at Stanley.

"Stanley?"

Both women looked at Stanley as he shifted in his chair. He gazed at Charlie as if trying to shoot lasers from his eyes.

"I believe in this unique case we shipped directly to Bullock's."

"Why would we have done that?" Nicole asked concerned.

"I believe it had something to do with the timing of Bullock's order from Coliseum. They wanted the shipment expedited so to help a valued customer we shipped the product directly to Bullock's."

Nicole's concern grew to distress. "And the documentation you send to the FDA will reflect the shipment going directly to Bullock's?"

"Yes."

"So, Charlie's hypothetical argument has validity... at least on the surface." Nicole did not offer it as a question because she knew he would not answer it. “Shit.” Nicole’s throbbing head fell into the palms of her hands for support. “I ask again, did we know the product was adulterated?”

“No.”

Roman was not physically present for the meeting with the two FDA agents, but muted, he listened to every word from his office in Miami. The head of operations for Coliseum called Roman from the conference room speaker phone prior to the agents entering the room. One of the agents was very familiar with Roman’s enterprises and was the reason why so many investigations had stalled. He was the beneficiary of numerous monetary gifts that not even the IRS could trace. The other agent was a taut, by the book investigator, who carried a copy of the Code of Federal Regulations with her to every meeting, internal and external. It was her presence which caused Roman to listen in stealth; otherwise, he would have let his team handle it on their own.

The head of operations for Coliseum gave abbreviated answers to the questions asked by the female agent. He paused before answering to give the other agent an opportunity to change the tone of the question or just disregard it altogether. Roman was pleased with his interference. The meeting at Coliseum was only a formality, agents were present when they received the product, so they could not have tampered with it, but they still had to check the box on their list.

While the FDA chased hypotheticals and studied potentially forged documents hoping to uncover hidden facts, the FBI focused on one man, who they believed was the key to everything. When they arrived at his house a teenage girl answered the door and was flashed a badge by a man in a dark suit. He identified himself and asked was her father home. He was not, but she called for her mother.

"Hello Ma'am," the agent said as he flashed his badge and identified himself. "May I come in?"

She pondered the question and what her response should be. "My husband ain't here," she finally said hoping that would cause him to leave. She was a homely looking woman, and it was obvious she did not have a bra on under her large t-shirt which she wore as a dress. It was easy for the agent not to look.

"I understand, but I only have a few questions."

She turned to her daughter. "Call yo' daddy and tell 'em to get home now." The girl disappeared and her mother turned back to the agent. "Don't I need a lawyer or somethin' if you wanna talk to me?"

"That's your choice Ma'am, but I was really just hoping to ask you a few questions. I was hoping to avoid getting a warrant and coming back with a van full of agents to search your house for evidence, but you can have your lawyer present when we return. We may be heading down that path anyway."

Again, she pondered the agent's words and an appropriate response. She could think of nothing appropriate, so she regressed to the distraught wife.

"Can you just wait 'til my husband gets home? He's the one who takes care of everything, I don't even work."

"When do you expect him back?"

"He's just over at our old trailer park at that whore Bridget's house. He thinks I don't know, but I know where he goes in the middle of the day. She ain't nothin' but a slut; been a slut since high school." She turned and hollered back into the house. "Send him a 911!"

"I'm..."

"Don't say sorry, cause I'm not. It keeps his fat ass off of me. I get the money; she can have the rest of him."

"Well can I come in until he gets here?"

She stepped aside so he could enter. “It ain’t my time you’re wastin’.”

The agent declined everything she offered to eat or drink, but he did accept the seat on the living room sofa. The furnishings were modest but new, and surprisingly comfortable. Two teenage girls loitered in the background, more curious than anything.

“These are our two daughters; you probably already know their names bein’ FBI and all.”

“Hello ladies.”

The girls smiled and waved.

“Clint will do anything for his girls; they don’t want for nothin’.”

“So, Clint’s a good provider, but like most marriages you manage the finances?” The agent asked hoping to initiate a conversation around money.

“That’s about right, we just better managin’ money you know?”

“I know, if not for my wife no bills would ever get paid on time. In fact, we just deposit our checks into one account, and she gives me an allowance.”

“You sound like Clint. He gives me the checks to deposit, and I give him what I think he needs to make it ‘til the next check. Mostly it goes to beer, cigarettes and that whore Bridget.”

“What about the cash in the envelopes,” the agent asked while he had her talking freely.

“All of it, I handle everything.” It was not until she said the words that she realized what had been asked. She gazed at him suspiciously, but it was too late.

“So how frequently do the envelopes come?”

“I think we should wait on Clint.”

"On average, how much is in the envelopes?"

"You have to ask him."

"But you manage the money, he brings the envelopes home to you to take care of his daughters, right?"

"You tricked me. You did some of that government mind control on me."

The front door opened, and Clint walked in looking guilty of something until he saw the agent sitting in the living room with his wife; then he became panic-stricken. He thought of running, but he saw his daughters in the kitchen peeking into the living room. He looked into their eyes and felt ashamed. An indignity that could not be ascribed to one particular transgression.

His wife's eyes were conflicted. Filled with the hurt and anger from accepting an unfaithful husband, to the embarrassment and feeling exposed by the agent's questions. 'You were supposed to protect me,' her eyes pleaded when he finally found the courage to look at her, 'you were supposed to protect our girls.'

"It didn't have to come to this," The agent said when Clint sat down in an available chair in the living room. "You haven't been completely honest with us Clint."

"Leave my family out of this," Clint demanded.

"That is totally up to you.

Clint pondered the agent's words as he studied his trained eyes. He understood their meaning and knew the consequences. His dilemma had two faces, the chiseled face of the FBI, and the mysterious face of the individual or organization behind the envelopes. They both kept him up at night and the dangers were equal; there was no lesser evil in his mind. He had to decide which one to stake his family's lives on. The agent knew what Clint was trying to rationalize and offered one last sentiment.

"We can protect you from them, but they can't protect you from us."

And with that, the decision was made. He turned to his wife and told her to take the girls out for a while. He had business to discuss with the agent and he did not want his family involved. She understood and took the girls out to eat at their favorite restaurant; she even let them order dessert.

16

The undisclosed meeting location was an Italian restaurant in Buckhead, several miles from New Wind's sprawling suburban Atlanta campus. Roman had hosted clandestine meetings with various New Wind employees at the restaurant on numerous occasions; all off the record of course. Everything at the restaurant was authentic, from the décor and menu offerings to the accents of the those preparing and serving the tasteful dishes. Roman had commented that it reminded him of the home country, even though he was born and raised in New Jersey and was not Italian.

The meeting was scheduled for 3:00pm to minimize the chance of other New Wind personnel dining at the restaurant during the meeting. The mid-level New Wind litigation attorney was even more nervous than his previous meetings with Roman, partly due to the presence of Stanley. It had always just been the two of them talking informally over his favorite pasta dish. There were no introductions made, and none of their names were uttered.

"We're getting subpoenas and inquiries almost daily regarding the Distributing Company," the lawyer proclaimed.

"The usual suspects? "Roman asked.

"Yes, plus several states. California is the latest and greatest, and their new Governor is really making a lot of noise. It's like she's still campaigning even though she won the election by a California mudslide. One of her campaign promises was to block counterfeit drugs from coming into the state and to make anyone distributing counterfeit drugs subject to hefty fines and prison sentences. She targeted the big wholesalers first because we 'cast the widest net,'" he said using air quotes. "What she did not say was that we also have the deepest pockets and could pay the heftiest fines."

"So, what is the feeling up on the sixth floor?" Roman asked.

"You know New Wind; we're already looking to settle and haven't been charged with anything yet."

Roman shook his head. "Bunch of pussies." He turned to Stanley. "Why couldn't you be acquired by Bullock's? They're quick to give the middle finger to the government alphabets. Even the other one would have been better than New Wind."

"Wasn't my call," Stanley responded.

"Who is Charlie?" The lawyer asked. Roman and Stanley looked at each other reflexively.

"She's my new boss's girlfriend," Stanley mused.

"You report to Nicole?"

"That's one of the names I call her."

"Well Charlie is making more noise than the Governor. She's like a bull in a china shop."

"She's on a mission to clean up the industry," Stanley proclaimed, "and she has Nicole convinced that we're all dirty."

"Well, she's finding your dirt and exposing it," the lawyer proclaimed. "As you know, New Wind has a zero tolerance for drama. They don't like negative attention."

"They?" Stanley asked.

"Like you I'm an employee, but..."

"She needs to be silenced." Roman exclaimed impatiently. "We may not be able to reach the Governor, but we can certainly put a muzzle on Charlie."

No other words were said or needed about the topic. Roman nodded at the waitress and she rushed over to take their orders.

"So, what's new with the states?" Roman asked after his plate was nearly cleaned.

"I guess you heard about Florida, your home state. They're the ones who would give a distributor license to anyone who had a driver's license and could pay the fee, and now they're swinging to the opposite extreme. Have you seen the new application?" He did not give them time to shake their heads. "They ask questions about everyone including your mother. I'm not shittin' you; they ask about your family. They ask for everything short of giving blood, but they do get your fingerprints, and a hefty application fee. Plus, they require a Designated Representative that has to take a test that I heard is hard as hell. Anyone shipping into the state has to have a DR. They're even producing their own authorized distributor list. If you're not on it, then you're not an AD in the state of Florida and you have to pass pedigree; on the form they created I might add."

"Is it in effect yet?" Stanley asked.

"No but they're in rule making. The Florida DOH is having meetings where stakeholders can ask questions and submit opinions. If you can't attend, I encourage you to submit a written comment."

"What about California?" Roman asked. "I heard they're talking some crazy shit too."

"Not as bad as Florida, but close. Other states are considering passing their own pedigree legislation as well. You're gonna have different states requiring different things. It's gonna be a shit show."

"What are the feds doing?"

"Nothing. They've been talking RFID for years, but who's gonna pay for it? And who has the technology to put a chip on every case or bottle from the manufacturer and have it read by the distributors? There is talk coming from our trade organization of having more stringent AD requirements than what PDMA requires. Maybe twelve transactions over twelve months instead of the two transactions over twenty-four months the government requires."

"This is getting ridiculous," Roman exclaimed.

"What's ridiculous is the counterfeit drug problem we have in this country. The counterfeit drugs they're shipping over here from third world countries have lead and God knows what in it. Have you seen pictures of the tablet presses they're using? Talk about unsanitary; I wouldn't let a stray dog piss on it."

"You're so fucking melodramatic," Roman scowled. "We don't buy drugs from overseas anyway."

"How do you know? How can you possibly trace the origins when it exchanges hands so many times? You guys better make all the money you can now, the door is closing."

"You let us worry about that," Roman exclaimed, "you just keep taking my money and telling me what I need to know. In fact, lunch is on you today, you little shit. Now... what's going on with the big distributors that I don't already know about?"

He talked and Roman half listened. He did not offer anything that Roman did not already know, and after ten minutes or so he dismissed him. Roman had more urgent matters to discuss with Stanley alone.

"I'm starting to question the usefulness of that parasite," Roman exclaimed when he and Stanley were alone, "he gives me more of his bullshit than intel."

"He's a rat," Stanley agreed, "but at least he keeps me in the loop as to what's being said down here at New Wind."

Roman waved his hand as if dismissing the entire conversation.

"We need to talk about that Laprin we got from Gulf Coast."

"The FDA has been snooping around sticking their noses in it too. They paid us a visit and Nicole just happened to be on site. Now I have her and her sidekick asking questions."

"Peter is becoming a problem..."

"Becoming a problem?" Stanley snarked, "that guy's too nervous for me."

"We may need to fall on a knife and get cut on this one."

"We?"

"We need to sign an affidavit confessing to knowing the product was adulterated."

"What?"

"Look, Peter reached out to us to ask if we wanted some product he had just repackaged. He said he changed the strength on the labels and offered us a good deal. Yes, we're bastards for taking the product, yes we're complicit, and yes we distributed it knowing it was adulterated; but we didn't alter the labels, Gulf Coast did. It's them they want, not us and all we have to do is cut a deal.

"It's never as simple as you make it sound."

"As usual, I'll do all the work, you just need to cosign."

"So, the shipment you dropped off was picked up somewhere in Olive Branch, MS?"

Clint heard the question, but he was still distracted by the number of suits in the conference room. They shuffled in and out, but at any given time there were no fewer than four FBI agents, including the one who spoke to his wife, all giving Clint their undivided attention. Some took notes, while others had recorders placed on the table in front of them capturing every sound Clint made.

"Mr. Hardy?"

Clint looked at his lawyer, who nodded his head letting Clint know it was okay. Clint retained counsel after his wife told more than a couple of her friends about their visit from the FBI. Each friend told a friend, and each offered advice, but one friend of a friend was having an affair with a lawyer with a firm in downtown Memphis, and she persuaded him to take Clint as a client for minimal fees. The agents had congregated at his firm's offices.

Clint took a deep breath, exhaling it slowly and loudly. His lawyer had already negotiated immunity in exchange for Clint's complete cooperation.

"Yes," Clint finally responded, "I picked up the trailer in Olive Branch, but I don't know exactly where. It was raining cats and dogs that day and I couldn't see ten feet in front of me."

"Did you have an address?"

"I never have an address, only directions. I would've drove right by the place if they hadn't flashed their lights."

"Who is they?"

"Two guys in a truck, one had a gun pointed at me. They told me to follow them, and I did. They dropped their trailer and told me to take it to Missouri. I made two stops in Missouri; the one I told the FBI about and one before I got there. That's what they told me to do.

"Do you know what was in the trailer or where it originated?"

"No Sir, I never know what they have me haulin' or where it came from."

"Can you tell us where the first stop was?"

Again, he glanced at his lawyer and received the nod. "Yep. I remember it being some type of medical campus with a hospital. I don't remember the name, but I remember the location."

"So, it's safe to assume that the adulterated product arrived on your truck, unbeknownst to you of course. They had to have known we would be there, and that we would check the product. What are we missing?"

"In all, how many of these runs have you made after an envelope appeared in your mailbox?" The question came from a different agent, the only skirt suit in the room.

"I don't know... about eight I guess."

"And you have no idea who puts them there?"

"No Ma'am."

"So, you've been crossing state lines with illegal drugs for several months now... do you know what that's called?"

"Whoah," Clint's attorney interjected, "Maybe you didn't get the memo, but my client has blanket immunity. Any attempt to label or criminalize my client's activities will bring this interview to an abrupt end."

"And his immunity with it."

"We're willing to take our chances, are you?"

"Ok, let's take a breath and stay on task." The comment came from the supervising agent seated at the end of the table.

"What was different about this run?"

"It was the first one since I was pulled over in Georgia," Clint answered.

The supervisor looked at the agent assigned to the case. "What happened in Georgia?"

"An overanxious state trooper," the agent sighed. "They were instructed to let the truck arrive at its destination. The state troopers in Alabama and Tennessee followed the truck at a safe distance until it crossed state lines, but some asshole in Georgia was looking to make a big score. He pulled him over, arrested him, and impounded the truck. By the time we got him released it was too late. The building had been burned to the ground by the time Clint got there the next morning. We surveilled the location for several days, but no one ever came back. We were probably being watched as well. We eventually had a truck pick up the trailer Clint dropped."

"And that's how they figured out he was working with us."

"Yes sir."

"And that's when they threatened your family?"

Clint nodded his head slowly.

"We're going to install a camera at your house focused on your mailbox. Hopefully we can capture a suspect dropping the envelope."

"Works for me," Clint exclaimed.

"And we need to know the location of any pickup as soon as you know it."

"You got it."

"We're watching you, Clint."

"You mean you're watching out for his entire family," Clint's attorney interjected. "This is not surveillance, this is protection."

"This is whatever needs to be done to keep counterfeit drugs out of our medicine cabinets counselor. Let's not lose sight of the goal here."

"The way we see it," the lawyer exclaimed, "they're one in the same."

The look he received from the agents was one lawyers received on a regular basis. He was neither surprised nor intimidated. His sole job was to defend his client to the best of his ability. That and keep his adulteress doing what his wife wouldn't.

17

"Why are you returning my product?" The distressed voice on the other end of the phone asked Charlie.

"Because there is a distributor on the pedigree that we don't do business with," Charlie answered matter-of-factly. "They're on our naughty list."

"How am I supposed to know that?"

"I sent a list to all of our current suppliers." There was a pause, and Charlie knew he probably did not read the email.

"Well, I can take them off and send you a new pedigree; who is it?"

"Did you just say you would falsify a pedigree? You've just been added to the list."

Charlie could not hang up the phone fast enough. She sent Christine an email with Stanley copied, letting her know that the Distributing Company would no longer purchase any product from the vendor, nor would she accept the company on a pedigree. She knew Stanley would demand to know why, so she also detailed how he had offered to forge a pedigree. She then logged into the system and flagged the vendor so nothing could be received into inventory, and it would also block anyone from entering a purchase order for the vendor. She appreciated and eagerly utilized the enhanced access she had to the new inventory management system, courtesy of Nicole.

After updating the banned vendor list, Charlie walked to the receiving area to distribute the updated list to the receiving clerks and to tell the clerk who quarantined the product to return it as soon as possible. She found her working tirelessly on five pallets of product lined up at her station. They chatted for a moment, Charlie asked about her baby, and she showed Charlie pictures of the six-month-old.

"I'm sorry," Charlie said after the laughter subsided, "you look extremely busy, but can you please return the product you have in quarantine?"

"Sure, I'll do it right now. I knew that was coming, you don't play. It's like night and day since you've been here."

"I appreciate all the hard work you all do."

"You're the only one who does."

"I see you're working on a big one, did this just come in?"

"Yeah, this is a return from Emperor Drugs. This happens just about every month. The first week of the month we get a large return from Emperor, and usually it's not even the lot numbers we sold them."

"What!? And what do we do with the product?"

"We put it back in salable inventory. We have questions, but everyone is too scared to ask about it. Usually if the lots don't match, we return it or put it in quarantine and send it for destruction. But not Emperor. We were told to process it for credit and put the product back on the shelf. I've even seen product returned in a different language."

"Oh no, no, no, not anymore. Have you started processing this one yet?"

"I was just about to."

"Let me help you."

The two ladies examined the pallets of product comparing the lot numbers received to the lot numbers on the invoice from the original sale. None of them matched.

"We sold Emperor this product a week ago," Charlie exclaimed in disbelief.

"That's how it always is. We ship it to them at the end of the month and they return it the beginning of the month."

"And you say this has been going on for a while?"

"I've been here three years, so it's at least been that long."

"Put this product in quarantine," Charlie instructed, as she turned to walk away, "I'll deal with this."

IT DID NOT TAKE Charlie long to confirm the insidious pattern of transactions. The inventory system only went back twenty-four months, but nineteen of the twenty-four months showed a return at the beginning of the month for most of the product purchased at the end of the month. Panic struck her like the onset of a stroke, her sudden shortness of breath was a result of the acceleration of her heart rate. Anger raged inside of her, pounding her head trying to manifest itself.

She blamed Bob mostly for being so passive. Stanley could not help himself. He was like a wild teenager whose parents were gone for days at a time without calling to check on him. Bob had to know what was going on, did he just look away and count the money? She wanted to ask him, but she heard he had retired and moved out west. Should she have done more? Should she have known? The thoughts in her head were colliding with each other, and she needed to ejaculate them.

Stanley's administrative assistant saw Charlie coming and immediately picked up the phone and alerted Stanley.

"You can't..." The look Charlie fired at her would not allow her to finish her statement. She felt genuine fear. Stanley tried to close his door, but Charlie pushed it open before it could shut.

"We don't have a meeting scheduled," Stanley started.

"How long have we been laundering drugs for Emperor?"

"What the hell are you talking about?"

"Do I need to spell it out for you Stanley?"

Stanley pulled her inside and slammed the door. Charlie jerked her arm away and almost swung at him.

"Get your hands off me!" Charlie warned.

"Calm down, you sound like a crazy woman."

"Yeah, I'm crazy alright... crazy enough to turn yo' ass in."

At that point Stanley would normally tell her to leave, but instead he asked her to sit. Her rant about Emperor captured his attention, and he had to know what she knew.

"What is this foolishness you're talking about drug laundering?" Stanley asked calmly as he walked behind his desk and dropped down in his chair. "And what exactly is drug laundering?"

Stanley's calm demeanor was not contagious; Charlie continued her tirade.

"It's what you've been doing with Emperor Drugs for at least two years but probably much longer. Two years is all I can prove."

"Prove?" Stanley struggled to contain his own emotions; he could not let Charlie know she had rattled him. "There is nothing to prove here. Tell me what you think you know, and I'm sure I can shed light on the misunderstanding."

"Drop the act Stanley and wipe the sweat from your forehead." Charlie leaned forward in her chair and seized his nervous eyes. "The last week of every month we sell Emperor a shit load of drugs and they return them a week later for credit. Not a full credit, but a partial credit, it looks like we keep a percentage as a fee for services. And what they return is not the same as what we sold them. Same drugs, but the lot numbers are always different. I would say we sell them authentic product; they return counterfeit or illegally sourced product; we stock it and sell it without having to pass a pedigree because we are an AD. That is the definition of drug laundering."

A smile slowly stretched across Stanley's face. Charlie could practically hear the names he was calling her in his mind.

"I appreciate you bringing your concern to my attention," Stanley exclaimed, "I will discuss with Hank, I'm sure there is an explanation that does not involve the drug laundering you are accusing us of." He used air quotes to emphasize drug laundering.

"I can't wait to hear what you come up with." To continue the back and forth would just be a waste of her time, and she knew her time would be better spent investigating Emperor Drugs. She left Stanley's office on a mission.

"WHAT'S GOIN' on?" Charlie asked Ram when she returned to her office. "You moving?"

"Somethin' like that." Ram responded as he stuffed all of his personal belongings into a box. "This is my last day."

"What?!"

"Before you go full sista' mode, let me explain." Charlie's hand was firmly planted on her perfectly curved hip, and her lips were already puckered to one side as if whatever words came out of his mouth would be 'bullshit.'

"Ever since Luke got here, he's been making changes like he runs the place, and Hank lets him do whatever he wants. I can't even tell you how many I've escorted out because he fired 'em, not to say they didn't deserve it, but he's definitely made his mark. Hank thinks he's the best thing since sliced bread."

"He can't fire you..."

"No, but he's pretty much taken over the security function, I don't even have keys to the building anymore, and he assigns warehouse access."

"So, Hank fired you?"

"I was offered a 'package.' Ram used air quotes to stress package.

"What kind of package?"

"They'll give me a year's severance if I leave quietly."

"And quietly means you don't report the shady shit they're up to."

"Quietly means my name is Bennet and I ain't in it."

"But..."

"No buts, it's a good deal for me. I've already found another job closer to my house and I can bank that severance money every month. I'm close to retirement and this helps."

Charlie searched his eyes for any sign of deception, and realized he was being truthful regarding his feelings. She softened just enough for sympathy to overtake the anger in her voice.

"I can't help but think this is partly because of me." Before Ram could challenge her, she waved her hand and continued. "All that you've done for me and as much as we talk, I suspect Stanley wants you outta here. That's just my two cent and I'm done. Come here and give me a hug." They meet halfway and embrace as friends. "Thank you.."

"No, thank you," Ram countered, "you've given me hope for my granddaughters that I didn't have before." Ram held the embrace even when he felt Charlie release. She smiled and held on to her friend until he was ready.

IT WAS AN AMBUSH, at least that's how Peter referred to it when what seemed like an army of FDA agents descended on Gulf Coast. They were there when he arrived at the facility, followed shortly thereafter by his boss and owner of the company. They came with empty boxes that he knew would be full when they left.

"What's this all about?" Peter asked the question, but his boss was thinking the same thing. A warrant was handed over which did not answer the question but gave them the right to be on premises and take whatever they wanted.

"Are we under some type of investigation?" The owner of the company asked after scanning the document.

"We're temporarily stopping operations," the lead agent responded, "whatever you have running right now needs to be shut down."

All eyes focused on Peter, whose eyes were closed in what appeared to be prayer.

"Stopping operations!? Peter what is this about?"

"I don't know, but I'm sure the agent can tell us the basis for this intrusion."

The lead agent followed the two men to the conference room, while the other agents gathered documents and seized product. As soon as everyone was seated, the agent laid several documents on the table.

"We have executed affidavits from Mr. Forsythe and Mr. Caesar with Davidson Distributing Company and Coliseum Pharma Supply respectively, stating that you, Peter LeBlanc, knowingly sold adulterated product to Davidson Distributing Company. Specifically, you intentionally placed 40mg labels on 20mg vials of Laprin and contacted Mr. Forsythe to engage in a scheme to defraud and endanger unsuspecting patients."

Peter was unable to respond. He was temporarily paralyzed by shock and disbelief. He could not imagine the depths Roman would sink to save his own ass.

"Peter is this true?"

No response or movement from Peter.

"Peter!"

"Huh, no," Peter exclaimed awakened from his trance, "no this is not true, they're lying... Roman is a liar!"

"They are coconspirators in this scheme," the agent argued, "they are not denying their involvement."

"No, but I'm the mastermind and Gulf Coast is now being raided. Damn Roman, that man is a crook and every business he owns is dirty."

"Yet, I'm sure the records we confiscate will show that Gulf Coast is a regular trading partner with Mr. Caesar and his companies, correct?"

"Peter? Is this true?"

"Well yes, but..."

"We trusted you to do the right thing Peter, we relied on you to run the operations, you know my illness would not let me be as involved as I would have liked to be, or now I guess as I should have been."

"I didn't do this," Peter pleaded, "Roman changed the label before I even received the product. I saw his company on the pedigree, and I know he had to be responsible."

"Was this before or after you received the product into inventory and repackaged it?" the agent asked, "why did you receive the product in if you knew it was adulterated?"

"It was after the fact," Peter sighed after a long pause "I must have missed it on the pedigree at first."

"Regarding the pedigree, I didn't see the hospital you purchased the product from on the pedigree."

"It's Roman," Peter rambled, "he's responsible for all of this, he..."

"That's enough Peter, you sound like a lunatic. Even if what you say is true, you knowingly did business with this man, putting my company at risk."

"But..."

"Pack your personal items from the office, you're fired."

"We may have additional questions for you," the agent exclaimed, "don't go far."

18

Charlie had made the one-hour drive to Flint every other weekend for several months. On the weekends she didn't visit her father, she looked at houses with the real estate agent stipulated by the relocation company. He was an adequate real estate agent, but she had to remind him more than once that she was only in the market for a house, not a man. 'Just find me a house,' she finally told him, 'I can find a restaurant on my own. If you can't do that, I'll tell the relo company to find me another agent.' With a renewed focus, he found the perfect house in Southfield, and Charlie made an offer that was accepted in less than an hour without a counteroffer. It was below asking price, but within the buffer of the sellers' inflated listing. She had a quick closing and had been in the house less than a week and was anxious to tell her father in person.

Charlie had a key to her father's house, but she always rang the doorbell. The brick house on the west side of Flint was filled with mostly fond memories, but her teenage years were tumultuous. She fought with her father about boys, the tightness of her clothes, the lack of material on her clothes, the typical concerned father versus oppressed teenage daughter battles. She smiled when she thought of those times as an adult, but there had been nothing to smile about back then. She lost her mother when she was young, and her father did the best he could to raise his only child while working at the General Motors assembly plant. The work was hard and steady, and Charlie was raised the same way.

He opened the door and kissed her forehead.

"Hi Daddy."

"Hey baby girl; why didn't you use your key?"

"You might be in here entertaining a lady or something."

"Yeah right...get in here funny ass."

They went inside and she made herself comfortable on the leather sofa inside what he called his man-cave. He reached for the purple bag and two glasses as usual.

"This ain't a purple bag day, Charlie exclaimed."

"Oh, I see..." He reached for the Crown Reserve, and she shook her head. "Oh, it's like that?"

"Yep, bring it out."

He reached inside a locked cabinet and retrieved a locked box. He carefully removed the bottle of Crown XR from the box and grabbed two shot glasses.

"I might need that larger glass you had at first."

"Oh no," he replied, "not for this, you're lucky I love you. You're the only other person on this planet that gets some of this." He filled the small shot glasses halfway and gave one to his daughter. "Now, what is so bad you had me break out the XR? The bottle is already half empty."

"Or half full," Charlie exclaimed.

"Whatever, when it's gone it's gone. I can't get this anymore."

Charlie smiled, but her smile soon eroded from the weight

of her thoughts. Her father became burdened as well; he did not like to see his daughter in that state.

"Take your time baby girl; whenever you're ready, I have all night."

"I don't, not if Nana wants her scalp scratched."

Charlie's paternal grandmother lived with her father, and it was part of their routine that whenever Charlie came over, she would scratch her scalp. Charlie did not mind doing it, it was how they spent quality time together.

Charlie emptied her shot glass and her father poured Crown Royal from the purple bag into the original glasses he had. He handed one to his daughter.

"How long have we been doing this?"

"I can't remember a time when we didn't," he responded with a warm smile.

And neither could she. The brown liquor had a calming effect, and the minutes of silence allowed them to savor its smoothness appropriately.

"I just moved into my new house," she exclaimed as if the liquor lubricated her rusted brain and released a memory.

"Oh yeah, where?"

"Southfield."

"Good..." he said nodding in approval, "good, that is a good suburb for us."

"Why does everything have to be about us?" She framed the word us in air quotes.

"This is not a Crown XR conversation baby girl."

"Indeed."

Charlie emptied her glass and looked at her father as if she wanted him to pour her another. He had already put the bottle back in its case and had no intention of bringing it back out that evening.

"So, I got this fool at work doing some crooked shit and it's stressing me out." She sounded like a teenager, and she knew it when she heard the whine in her voice. The question she could not answer was her motive at that moment. Did she want consolation from her father or a refill?

"Why is what *he's* doing stressing *you* out?"

"Because it impacts me. It impacts the company."

"Have you called him out?"

"Come on daddy, you know me... of course I called his ass out; he thinks he's above the law. He's gotten away with it for so long even I'm beginning to think he's untouchable."

"So, what exactly is he doing?"

Charlie sighed as she thought about what to tell her father. It was as if talking about it would make her feel dirty and stain her father as well. She had always been honest with her father and appreciated his counsel. He was full of 'life lessons' as he called them. She felt comfortable talking to him about anything but discussing illegal activity that she was aware of and had not reported made her uneasy.

"I won't go into detail, the less you know the better, just in case..."

He saw the seriousness on her face, and he became serious as well. Charlie began recalling at a high level what her concerns were. She recalled what she suspected and what she could prove, and what the potential consequences were, not only legally but for patient safety as well. Her father listened intently, without interruption, and when she concluded he retrieved the bottle of XR from its case and filled the two shot glasses.

"You're sleeping here tonight, right?"

"Aww hell..." She knew she was in for a long night of him 'droppin' knowledge' as he called it, so she decided to go to her grandmother's room before he started.

. . .

Her grandmother's hair was thinning, but it was still thick enough to offer resistance to a fine-toothed comb. Charlie parted her grandmother's hair and scratched her scalp with the comb agitating the dandruff. She then applied hair grease to the exposed scalp with her index finger and repeated the process until her entire scalp had been scratched and greased. Her grandmother talked the entire time and Charlie's troubles momentarily faded to nothing. Some of the stories her grandmother told were repeats, but there was also a new revelation that Charlie cherished. The only time Charlie focused on what she was doing was when her grandmother told her to scratch harder.

Eventually the conversation took a turn down a deserted yet well-traveled road. Charlie knew it was only a matter of time.

"Have you settled down with one man yet baby?"

"Dang Gramms... you make me sound like a hoe... I mean hussy; and no, I haven't settled down with one man. Well... there is this one guy, but..."

"But what baby? Ain't no good man gon' wait around 'til you figure it out."

"How you know he a good man Gramms?"

"Because you never singled out one man before. He must be good..."

"Yeah, he good at somethin'."

"Charlie don't make me laugh," she said as her body shook with laughter, "you know I'm tender headed."

"I haven't known him long enough to know if he's a good man or not, but it was lookin' good."

"Was?"

"Just as we were getting serious, I moved back to Michigan. He lives in Connecticut, and I don't know about a long-distance relationship."

"Well baby ain't no distance greater than God. If it's His will..."

"I know, if it's meant to be it will be."

"Amen."

"I don't know... I got too much goin' on right now to be worried about a man."

"Like that white man gettin' on your last nerve at work?"

Charlie stopped scratching and greasing and looked at her grandmother curiously. "How do you know about a man stressin' me out at work?"

"Chile you talk just as loud as yo' daddy, and he loud as a train comin' down the tracks. I may be old but I ain't def."

"And how you know he's white?"

"Can't nothin' but a white man cause so much strain at work. From the cotton field..."

"To corporate America..." Charlie finished. "I know that's right Gramms!"

"But don't you give him your peace."

"Ma'am?"

"Yo' peace and joy come from God and no man can take it from you, you have to give it to 'em and don't you ever surrender yo' peace and joy to no man, you hear me?"

"Yes Ma'am. Unfortunately, I have my Momma's temper, and I go off on him too quick."

"Oh, you didn't get that temper of yours from your sweet mother, that's your daddy all day. I know my son and you get your short fuse from him."

"But I remember Momma always going off on him, they were always arguing. It seems like she always started it."

"He earned every name she called him; yo' daddy could make Jesus cuss him out. He couldn't stop chasin' women even when he had a good one at home. Yo momma was a saint for puttin' up with that man. If anybody in Heaven yo momma there gettin' some rest."

"I love you Gramms."

"I love you baby."

Charlie leaned over and hugged the back of her grandmother's neck and shoulders; her face settled in a patch of dandruff she had just scratched to the surface.

OVERNIGHT TURNED into the entire weekend, and the empty bottle of Crown XR was added to the collection. Charlie left Flint early Monday morning and drove straight to the office in Livonia. Fortunately, she had visited Genesee Valley mall over the weekend and had several new outfits at her disposal.

"I REBUKE YOU SATAN!"

Stanley gazed at Charlie awkwardly, taken aback by her response to his line of questioning. He stood in the doorway of her office undeterred. "Our inventory levels are the lowest they've been in years."

"Maybe your buyers need to do a better job of purchasing product."

"Maybe you need to stop turning away product at the door. What is this blacklist you have for distributors?"

"I don't have a *blacklist* whatever that is." She stressed blacklist with air quotes. "I have a list of suppliers that I do not want to see on a pedigree."

"That *you* do not want to see! Who made you the final say on who is on a pedigree or who we purchase product from?"

"*Our* boss did."

Stanley's body jerked from the restraint of holding back his verbal response. His body language spoke volumes.

"And how does one make your infamous list?" Stanley asked calmly.

"By distributing counterfeit or adulterated product, by failing to provide verification of a transaction or AD status, by facing disciplinary action by the state or government, basically for being like the Distributing Company. I'm sure we're on a few lists."

"If you're not careful, your name will appear on a list."

Charlie jumped up from her chair. "Was that a threat?"

Stanley smirked and turned his back on her. "Satan doesn't make threats," he uttered as he walked away.

19

When Charlie pressed the button on the garage door opener clipped to the sun-visor, she had just turned the corner onto her street and her house was four houses from the corner. She did not see the shadowy figure enter her garage when the motorized chain lifted the garage door. The door leading inside the house was always unlocked for her convenience and the intruder found it convenient as well. Charlie pulled her Ford Explorer into the garage and pressed the button again, causing the door to close and secure her inside. She grabbed her phone and dialed her father's number as she walked inside the house; he insisted that she call to let him know that she made it home safely whenever she returned home from a visit. Just as he answered he heard her scream.

The blow to the back of her head stunned her, as intended, and the intruder crushed her phone with heel of his boot. The second blow knocked her to the ground, but she was only down a few seconds. He watched her rise to her feet and take a boxer's stance with her guard up; the stance her father taught her when she was a girl. Charlie could not see his smile under the mask, but she lunged forward and grabbed the mask and pulled enough to briefly see skin. He struck her a third time, but she had already shifted her weight to kick him behind the knee, so she did not catch the full force of his blow. 'Always go low', her father had taught her, 'even the largest man will fall if you take out his legs.'

Flat on his back, the intruder swept Charlie's feet knocking her to the ground as well. He immediately climbed on top of her, and during the scuffle he managed to grab a syringe from his pocket and inject the contents into Charlie's neck. The last thing she heard before blacking out was, "here's some counterfeit drugs for you bitch."

She was bruised, and bleeding from her nose and mouth. He stood over her cursing her for fighting back. It did not go as planned. He was to slip in, stun her and inject her with the needle. It was to appear as a self-induced drug overdose, but between her injuries and the mess made during their struggle, nothing appeared self-induced. He heard the sirens in the distance getting closer. He ran out of the house and disappeared into the darkness, careful to lock the doorknob on the back door behind him.

THE BEEPS from the machine monitoring her heart and oxygen levels were the first sounds Charlie heard in the fog of her mind. They were in the distance but getting closer, and when she finally managed to open her eyes, she saw her father smiling down at her. She tried to move, but the pain was intense and spread from her head to her waist. She grimaced and squeezed her father's hand.

"It's okay," he consoled, "don't try to move, just rest."

"Where am I?" She looked around the room and answered her own question. "What happened?"

"I don't know, I heard your scream on the phone, and I

dialed 911. The police found you on the floor unconscious. We almost lost you."

The doctor walked into the room and immediately started her examination of Charlie.

"Good to see you awake and talking," she said with a warm smile.

"What's wrong with me?"

"Well, besides the drug in your system that would have killed you if the police had not gotten there when they did, you appear to be fine, considering. You have a few bumps and bruises, but you don't appear to have any head trauma or internal bleeding."

"It hurts if I even think about moving."

"I use a great concealer that will cover up the bruise on your face and the knot on your head until they heal. We're about the same complexion so it should work fine for you."

"Thanks Doc. You know a sista' has to look good even when in a hospital bed."

"Do you feel like talking to the police officer waiting outside? He's the one who found you and he has a few questions."

"Sure, might as well get it over with."

The doctor waved the officer in, and he entered with pen and pad in hand. The doctor stayed in the room but took a step back and stood near Charlie's father.

"Thank you," Charlie exclaimed as the officer walked over to her bed and stood next to her, "I understand you saved my life."

"Just doing my job Ma'am, but you're welcome. I just want to ask you some questions if you don't mind."

Charlie nodded her head. "Okay."

"What happened Ma'am? Whatever details you can remember will be helpful."

Charlie stared up at the ceiling and her eyes moved from

side to side as she tried to remember what had transpired. As the images flashed in her mind her body became tense.

"Was I... Did he..."

The police officer was confused but the doctor stepped forward and grabbed her hand.

"No, we don't believe so," she said compassionately, you were fully dressed when the officer found you, and we didn't see any signs of sexual trauma or penetration."

Charlie exhaled a sigh of relief; her father did as well. It took a minute for her to settle herself from the thought, and the officer waited patiently. Pain, whether physical or emotional, when manifested was impossible to measure or comprehend. The images that crammed her thoughts elicited uncontrollable pain in her body.

"I walked into my house, and someone came up from behind. He hit me in the back of my head, and I fell."

"This person was already in the house?"

"Yes."

"We didn't find any signs of forced entry, could it have been someone you know? Does anyone else have a key to your house?"

"No, no one has a key but me."

"Are you sure it was a male?"

"Yes, his voice was definitely male. He had on a mask, so I didn't see his face, but he was a male, a little taller than me, he had on jeans and a black sweatshirt."

The officer wrote everything down. "So, we have a black male, about six feet tall, wearing jeans and..."

"I didn't say he was black."

"Oh... I..."

"Assumed he was black," her father interjected. "Y'all always assume it was a black man."

"Sir, that's not what I meant..."

"It was a white man," Charlie exclaimed, "during our struggle I was able to grab the mask, and I saw part of his skin."

"Okay, what else do you remember?" The officer was eager to continue the questioning.

"We fought, I kicked him in his knee, and he fell but he swept my leg and knocked me down with him. He got on top of me, and we fought some more and then he grabbed a syringe from his pocket and stabbed me in the neck. He said... he said..."

"What did he say?" The officer asked, as if it would help solve the case.

"I don't remember, I must have passed out." Charlie remembered every word he said, but she did not want to tell the officer.

"That's enough for now," the doctor said to the officer, "she needs to rest."

"Sure, sure I understand. Well, if you think of anything else just give me a call." He placed a card on the small table next to her bed. "I hope you feel better soon."

"Thank you. And thanks again for all that you did for me."

The officer exited and the doctor was close behind. "Just one more minute dad," she said when she reached the door, "my patient needs her rest."

"Okay, I'm right behind you." They shared a smile, and he turned to his daughter. "You remember what he said don't you?"

"Every word; and I know who was behind my attack."

Charlie shared the details with her father, and he understood why she did not tell the officer. No need to give the police any evidence that could lead back to her when she closed the circle.

. . .

Charlie missed two days in the office but was back to work with a smile after a couple days of physical rest. Her body was still brittle, and she moved delicately, but she was determined not to let the pain manage her, nor did she fill the prescription for Hydrocodone the doctor prescribed to help manage the pain. She was able to function with just an over-the-counter pain medication. The concealer the doctor recommended worked perfectly, a casual observer would never know her face had been used as a punching bag.

Charlie had considered cancelling her meeting with John, but there were critical matters to discuss. John had not thawed any toward Charlie nor his reporting to her, but he was respectful and did what she asked. Charlie found him useful because she knew he told Stanley everything they discussed, which meant she did not have to engage Stanley. He was also a genius with numbers and spreadsheets and knew exactly how much inventory was on hand at any given time, including the dollar value.

"Come on in John," Charlie exclaimed when John knocked on her open door. "Have a seat."

John did as instructed but looked at her peculiarly. There was something different about her, but he could not determine what it was.

"It's time to start scheduling site visits, and I've prepared a list of vendors I want you to visit." She handed him the list and he looked it over. "We discussed this earlier, but I just want to make sure travel will not be a problem."

"No, I'm single and don't have any kids."

"Sorry you have to do this, but I just haven't had time to go through the hiring process. I'm learning that it almost takes an act of God to get someone hired. New Wind has so many procedures and requirements."

"That sounds familiar," John quipped, "but really, I don't mind. I look forward to getting out of the office."

"Be sure to review the New Wind travel policy, I hear it's strictly enforced."

John nodded and realized what was different about Charlie. She had on makeup; lots of makeup.

"So, the purpose of the visit is to do a PDMA assessment. I have a checklist that I'll email you, and please let me know if you have any questions about it. We have to verify everything. Just saying they have it is not enough; we have to see it. Things like temperature recording records, SOPs, pest control, pedigree review process, everything is on the checklist. Take a tour of the facility and take notes; anything you find deficient or out of the ordinary make note of it. We're not regulators, and we don't have subpoena power, but we have to do all we can to ensure the product we procure is not only authentic, but that it is stored properly as well."

Charlie paused to see if John had any questions, but his eyes had already glazed over.

"And for every manufacturer they claim to be an authorized distributor for," she continued, "we need to see copies of twelve invoices over a twelve-month period. Ask for copies to take for the file if they will give them to you."

"Yes Ma'am."

"In fact, I think we should do the first few together. We have dozens in Florida, we can take a few days in south Florida and hit as many as we can. It'll be a good learning experience for both of us. I will schedule the appointments and book our travel."

"Great," John said indifferently. Charlie knew he was not thrilled about having to travel together for the visits, but it was not done out of spite. She genuinely felt it would be a great learning opportunity. John left her office and headed straight for Stanley's office. Charlie smiled at the thought.

. . .

Stanley seemed distracted, but John kept talking anyway. He complained about having to travel with Charlie and wondered which vendors she would choose. He mentioned Rome Enterprises, hoping to get a reaction from Stanley, but his mind was grappling with other thoughts. From the moment he said he had just met with Charlie, Stanley retreated to a distant place. John finally walked out of the office and doubted if Stanley would know he was gone.

The first five vendors Charlie called in the Miami area declined to let her on site, even after she informed them that the Distributing Company would have to discontinue purchasing if they declined the site visit. Her sixth call reluctantly agreed after the threat of discontinuing purchases, and it was hit and miss after that. In a single afternoon, Charlie informed thirty vendors that the Distributing Company would no longer be doing business with them, and she managed to schedule six site visits. She sent an email to Stanley and Christine, but they had already started receiving calls from the disgruntled vendors. Stanley directed the calls to Christine, and she informed them that there was nothing she could do.

20

What started as a narrowly focused investigation into Medicare and Medicaid fraud, would eventually grow into a far-reaching admonition of alternate source vendors, labeled as the grey or secondary market. Several clinics in and around the Los Angeles area were participating in the 340b program and contracting with several pharmacies to supply the prescription drugs. The investigation found that several pharmacies were billing Medicare and Medicaid the full price of the prescription drugs even though they purchased them at a greatly reduced price under the program. Other pharmacies were filling regular prescriptions with the drugs purchased at the contract price, even though the 340b contract was restricted to low-income patients. They failed to maintain separate inventory as required and co-mingled the 340b inventory with their regular inventory. The 340b program was a federal program so the California AG's office left it to the Feds for enforcement.

What really grabbed the attention of the California AG's office was the discovery of counterfeit drugs found on the shelves at two of the pharmacies investigated. The investigation entered a new phase, one which was in alignment with the new Governor's campaign battle cry, and they pursued it vigorously in collaboration with the California Board of Pharmacy. The first interview was with the pharmacist who allegedly first discovered the counterfeit drugs.

"Please tell us how you discovered the drugs were counterfeit," the investigator asked the pharmacist. The pharmacist was seated behind a tiny desk while the two investigators and the owner of the pharmacy stood over her in the cramped office. She was visibly nervous, and she avoided eye contact with Wilbur, the owner of the small independent pharmacy.

"Well, I opened a five hundred count bottle of Cordol 15mg and counted ninety tablets to fill a ninety-day prescription. I noticed that the tablets were a greenish blue when they are normally a light green color."

"What did you do then?" The investigator was trying his best to take notes in the cramped space.

"I checked the FDA website to see if there was a recall for the drug and that specific lot number but there wasn't anything listed. I contacted the manufacturer to see if they had changed the color and they had not. They asked for the lot number and said it was not one of their lot numbers. They asked me to send them samples for testing."

"And did you?"

She looked briefly at her boss Wilbur and then looked down at the floor. She knew the answer to the yes or no question, but for her it was not that simple.

"I-I told Wilbur about it and... and..."

"And what?"

"Hey, that's enough," Wilbur blurted out, "don't you see she's stressed. She's not thinking clearly."

"You're in enough trouble," the investigator chided, "I would remain silent if I were you; trust me, you'll get your turn to answer questions." He refocused his attention on the pharmacist. "What happened after you told Wilbur here?"

"I don't know... nothing I guess..."

"Aren't you the PIC?"

"Yes, I'm the pharmacist in charge."

"Then it's your license on the line here. You have a responsibility for the efficacy of the drugs you dispense."

"I didn't dispense them to anyone."

"That may help you sleep at night, but..."

"Wait a minute," Wilbur interjected, "How do you know the drugs were counterfeit? Because some customer service clerk at the manufacturer couldn't find the lot number in the system?"

"That's a good question," the agent exclaimed looking directly at the pharmacist, "how did the manufacturer determine they were counterfeit?"

"I sent them samples." The pharmacist lowered her head and closed her eyes. She did not have to open her eyes to know Wilbur was gazing at her, she could feel the heat of his gaze. He wanted to admonish her, but he knew that anything he said would be used against him. The investigator had his pen ready to capture the words as they leapt from his mouth.

"Who did you purchase the drugs from?"

"I'm not involved with purchasing," she said without hesitation, eager to shift the focus away from her.

"Is that you Wilbur?"

"No, I have a purchasing department and a call center, of course it's me." Wilbur was in his late seventies, and his filter was pretty worn with age. He said whatever came to mind with no regard for consequences.

"Who supplied the counterfeit drugs?"

"I have an idea, but I'd have to check my records."

"Well let's go check those records."

. . .

A small distributor in Hawthorne, CA Supplied the drugs to Wilbur's Pharmacy. The investigators were familiar with the distributor, but nothing caused alarm. When they visited the distributor and requested documentation, the investigators learned that the drugs were purchased from the Davidson Distributing Company in Livonia, Michigan. That name was very familiar to them because they had seen it while investigating other cases of counterfeit drugs in California. There was a short list of companies on the AG's radar, and the Distributing Company was near the top.

New Wind Pharma Distributing was not making the profits that Davidson Distributing Company had been accustomed to, and Stanley was furious. When the second quarter earnings were released, New Wind Pharma Distributing was profitable, but margins shrank to levels well below his track record. Stanley blamed Charlie for cutting off suppliers, returning product because she did not like the pedigree, and increasing purchases from manufacturers and inventory allocations to other New Wind distribution centers; both for much smaller margins. And to add insult to injury, Nicole questioned him about the decline.

"What do you mean what happened," Stanley yelled into the phone, "New Wind happened! You happened! Charlie happened!"

"You can't blame all this on the acquisition or Charlie," Nicole countered, "a decline like this in just two quarters looks like sabotage."

"I agree," Stanley exclaimed, "your company has sabotaged my company! You and your sidekick have sabotaged the company not me."

Nicole took a moment to calm herself before continuing the conversation. Getting into an argument with Stanley would accomplish nothing, and she could still feel the dank breath of her boss breathing down her neck.

"Give me an example of what has changed, and how it has impacted the business."

"Really? I'm hanging up the phone now."

The dial tone was announced, so that made it less disrespectful in Stanley's mind. Nicole gained nothing from the conversation she could take to her boss with whom she was scheduled to meet with later that morning. Nicole was aware of the changes but did not understand how they could sink margins, and so quickly. There was still much she did not know about that side of the business, and unfortunately the only person who could teach her was Stanley. One of them would have to succumb, and with each passing moment it looked like it would be her.

Charles McKinnon's office had an unobstructed view of 'the lake', as it was called by New Wind employees; it was actually a small pond with an asphalt walking trail encircling it. Charles stood looking out at the lake through his large office windows, glaring down on the usual suspects circling the lake adorning business casual attire and sneakers. He did not immediately acknowledge the knock on his door, but he eventually invited her in.

"I never see you out there on the walking trail during your lunch break," Charles exclaimed with his back to Nicole. He was still gazing out of the window.

"Lunch break, what's that?"

"Have a seat," he said looking at her reflection in the glass. His office was massive; the décor was minimal but had the obligatory family photographs on his credenza and his Bachelor of Arts diploma from Emory University hanging on the wall. He did not sit in the plush leather chair behind his desk but instead sat next to Nicole.

"I assume you've seen the numbers."

"Yes," Nicole answered solemnly.

"Not what I expected."

"Me neither."

The quietness was not mistaken for peace, Nicole knew Charles well enough to know that he inhabited the eye of the storm. The winds were raging all around him, but he remained in the eye, careful not to maneuver too far in any direction. The prolonged pause made her anxious, and she filled the void with an explanation.

"Things were not as they seemed."

"These things, were they hidden or overlooked?"

"Both."

"Either way, the fault lies with the one doing the searching."

"Agreed." Nicole kept her answers short and direct. She did not want her responses to be misconstrued as a challenge, as that would lead to a deeper discussion of what she had already conceded as fact. Charles seized any opportunity to debate, regardless of the topic, but received very few challengers, and none willingly. His was the most logical mind she had encountered, and the opposite of logic was emotion, which she tried to suppress.

"What caused such a drastic reversal in such a short period of time?" Charles' voice was monotone, and Nicole tried to match it but failed.

"Well, profits are important, yes, but how those profits are attained is equally as important; would you not agree?" She did not expect Charles to answer the question, at least not with a yes or no, so she continued. "We discovered improper activities that..."

"Were these activities illegal?"

"Well, that has yet to be proven, but certainly unethical."

"If one operates within the law or regulation, even though it is a grey, muddy area within the law, does that make it illegal?"

"Technically no, but..."

"But is a word used by one who cannot adequately expound or defend their original thought, so they transition to another."

The rebuttal made it to the tip of her tongue before being captured and swallowed back to the depths from which it came.

"Need I remind you, New Wind acquired Davidson for the Distributing Company. Sure, we gained customers from the closure of the other distribution centers, but make no mistake, the Distributing Company and its very high margins, was the treasure. Stanley seems to have carved a niche in an area you not yet comprehend, and to hinder his ability to operate within that space has proven counterproductive."

"What about the liability to the company?"

"All companies operate with some degree of risk, and we have departments which specialize in risk mitigation, namely legal and compliance; I do not believe those to be your departments. In fact, I am certain of this because you are part of my department, and we are tasked with revenue and profit generation."

"I understand," Nicole muttered.

"Do you... understand?

"Yes."

"Excellent. I look forward to a more favorable Q3." Charles stood and walked behind his desk and sat in his luxurious chair. Nicole had not moved.

"Is there something else you would like to discuss?"

There was plenty Nicole wanted to discuss, but she thought it futile. Retreat was the more logical course of action, but she was feeling emotional. She struggled with her emotions as she sat in the chair across from Charles' judgmental eyes. She convinced herself that showing emotion was a sign of weakness, particularly for a woman, and was detrimental to her career. Climbing the corporate ladder in heels and a skirt was a double-edged sword.

"There's nothing more to discuss," she exclaimed as she stood to her feet.

"You know my door is always open to you."

Nicole nodded her head and walked away.

CHARLIE WAS NOT in her office when the lawyers arrived. She was in Florida conducting site visits with John when he received a panicked call from Christine that their offices were being raided. It was not a raid, but it felt like one to Stanley and his team. Documents were taken from Stanley's office and there was nothing he could do to stop them. Christine's office was also a target, and sales and other relevant records were hauled away as well. It was clear that the focus of the document collection was on purchases from any vendor that was not a manufacturer, and sales to any entity that was not a final dispenser. The vast majority of the Distributing Company's documents fell into those categories.

The California Office of the Attorney General had jurisdiction because The Distributing company was licensed as an out-of-state distributor in the state of California, as it was in all fifty states and Puerto Rico. Stanley faxed a copy of the document handed to him to the New Wind legal department and was told he had to comply. Stanley scanned the document and squinted when he saw the term 'investigation,' which was focused on 'trading in the Secondary Market for Pharmaceuticals.' They claimed to have authority under an Executive Law with a fancy number assigned, and California's Blue-Sky law. Stanley tossed the document into what he called his round file, which was a trashcan next to his desk.

. . .

"Where are all the pedigrees?" The question was hurled at no one in particular, but Stanley's entire team was huddled in his office when the intruder stormed in.

"What pedigrees?" Stanley asked more annoyed that he had stormed into his office without knocking than with the question itself.

"You know, based on what I've already seen I believe you're serious."

"Fuck you." Stanley's filter had been torched, they were just lawyers anyway. Stanley turned to Christine and immediately saw the deer in headlights. "Charlie has the pedigrees, but she's not here."

"Doesn't matter, where's her office?"

"In the warehouse."

"The warehouse, great..." the lawyer responded, "I would love to see the rest of this shit show."

Stanley stood and took several steps toward the man who was much shorter and rounder than him. "That piece of paper doesn't give you the right to speak to us like that."

"I speak how I'm spoken to. If you're an asshole I can be one too; just not as big. Now, who's going to take me back to Charlie's office?"

The stare down was epic, like two gunfighters locked in a duel itching to draw their pistols. Stanley broke the gaze and nodded to Hank. Hank walked to the door and looked back at the lawyer.

"You comin'?"

The lawyer smirked and followed Hank out of the office.

Charlie briefly speculated why she did not receive a call but quickly dismissed the notion. She did not have time to sulk, her attention was needed on the white Porsche she was following in her rental car. The driver of the Porsche, the owner of the company they were auditing, was driving like he was trying to lose her. After trying to convince them to meet him for lunch at a restaurant overlooking the ocean, he finally showed up forty minutes late and Charlie insisted on seeing his facility. She tried to listen to the conversation John was having with Christine, but the white Porsche was weaving through heavy traffic in a city she was unfamiliar with. The Toyota something that she was driving was not built for such maneuvering.

They arrived at a self-storage facility, and Charlie followed the Porsche through the gate after the security code had been entered. John and Charlie looked at each other in bewilderment.

"Hey Christine, I gotta go," John said hastily, "I'll call you back."

"What the hell…" Charlie was in shock.

"Why are we here?" John feared he knew the answer to his question but asked it anyway.

The Porsche parked in front of a storage unit the size of a single car garage. The driver stepped out; his white linen suit and dark shades screamed Miami. He unlocked the padlock and rolled up the door; Charlie and John could see the cases and bottles of drugs from their car.

"You gotta be shittin' me," Charlie exclaimed.

They exited the Toyota and walked over to the storage garage. The temperature was in the mid-eighties, and Charlie figured the temperature was at least ten degrees warmer inside the unit with concrete floors and metal walls.

"These units are not temperature controlled right?"

"No," the proprietor answered Charlie's question.

"I bet it gets pretty hot in there during the summer."

"The drugs are only here for a short time; I turn inventory pretty quickly."

Charlie stared at a puddle of water near the front of the unit. Several cases of drugs were damp. "Did it rain or something?"

"This is Florida, we get a stray shower almost every day."

"I guess rain gets under the rollup door, I see some of the product is wet."

"It's just the boxes, they will dry, there's not any damage to the product. The bottles inside are plastic wrapped in packs of twelve."

"The drugs you ship to us, is this where you store them?"

"Yep, I store and package everything right here."

Charlie noticed a folding table in the back of the unit with several cardboard boxes and other packing supplies. She had a checklist with several items to observe and questions to ask but she had seen enough and was eager to get out of the sun.

"John, do you have any questions?"

The question caught John off guard, but he shook his head. She returned her attention to the man in the linen suit with his eyes hidden behind deeply tinted lenses.

"Do you have any questions for us?"

He was caught by surprise as well but did not hesitate to answer. "No, nothing from me."

"Well thank you for your time," Charlie said to everyone's surprise and delight.

"Is that it?"

"Yes," Charlie answered, "we've seen enough, we have everything we need."

"CALL CHRISTINE back and tell her to shut him off immediately," Charlie exclaimed as soon as they returned to the car. John did not question the directive; he was in agreement.

"That was bad," he said as he dialed Christine's number.

"It has to get better..."

THE SECOND APPOINTMENT LOOKED PROMISING. They pulled up to an office building, which they both agreed was a good sign. It did not appear to have a warehouse, Charlie noticed, but maybe it was in the rear of the building. Once inside, they took the elevator to the third floor and suite 3C. After identifying themselves they were buzzed through the double wooden doors and were told to wait in the reception area. After roughly ten minutes a well-dressed gentleman appeared with a smile.

"Hello, I'm Adam," he greeted as he extended his hand to John.

"I'm John." John was surprised by the firmness of Adam's grip and tried to match it, but Adam had already seized control.

"Come on back," Adam said as he turned so they could follow him. He led them to an average size office that was drowning in clutter. He removed stacks of paper from two chairs around the small conference table so Charlie and John could sit.

"Can I get you anything? Water, soda..."

They both thanked him but declined. After clearing off a third chair he sat at the table with them.

"So, what can I do for you?" He directed the question to John, but Charlie spoke.

"First, thanks for having us, I'm Charlie by the way, the purpose of this visit is just to do a meet and greet and complete our checklist by taking a look at where the drugs are stored and asking a few PDMA related questions."

"Sounds like an audit." Adam half joked.

"Audit has such a negative connotation," Charlie countered, "it's just a way to get to know our suppliers." Adam was not convinced but he manufactured a smile anyway.

"So, what cha got?"

. . .

Charlie started with general background questions about the company, then transitioned to where they sourced product from. They were not authorized distributors for any manufacturer and sourced all of their inventory from other wholesalers and distributors; all domestic. Charlie had three purchase orders for product the Distributing Company had purchased and asked Adam for the corresponding pedigrees and purchasing records from his suppliers. Adam asked his assistant to pull the records and by the time she returned Charlie had completed most of the questionnaire. The remaining questions would be answered as she observed the product storage area. John and Charlie exchanged a brief grin; the visit was going very well.

"There's not much to it," Adam exclaimed as he led them to a closet in the hallway. He opened the closet and, on the floor, next to a few cleaning supplies, a broom, and a vacuum sat a box with the top open to reveal several case packs of drugs. Adam saw the looks on their faces and offered an explanation.

"We very rarely touch the product," he offered, "the product we purchase we already have an order for, and our supplier ships it directly to our customer."

"So, you're like a middleman?" It was the first time John spoke since the greeting.

"We consider ourselves sourcing specialists."

Charlie was amazed that he was able to say it with a straight face, but she had a checklist to complete. The fact that the drugs were stored in a closet, did not necessarily mean that most of the storage requirements were not met, according to the checklist, but it made Charlie uneasy.

. . .

Back in the rental car headed for the third and final appointment of the day, Charlie and John discussed the middlemen, or "sourcing specialists.' They did not know what to conclude, but neither felt satisfied. A broader discussion would be had with the rest of the team.

When they arrived at the location of their third appointment, Charlie had to verify the address. They looked at the large distribution center and then at each other in disbelief. It was what they had expected prior to leaving Michigan, but after the first two site visits their expectations had plummeted. The name of the company they were looking for was on the building, but they still did not believe it was true.

After a warm greeting, and verification of their identities, Charlie and John were asked to sign the visitors log and were issued visitors' badges. They had barely sat down when a middle-aged woman with grey hair came to greet them again and escort them to a large conference room where three other individuals were waiting. A longwinded round of introductions identified an operations manager, purchasing manager, compliance manager, and the grey-haired woman was the vp of something. It was a family-owned business, and her last name was on the building. Charlie and John declined water or soda for a second time and Charlie got down to business.

"Thank you for allowing us to visit," she said with a smile, "we just want to get to know our suppliers and confirm compliance with PDMA requirements."

"Certainly," the vp chimed, "whatever you want to see or anything you need just ask. We don't get too many visits from our trading partners, but we welcome them; we are proud of the work we're doing here."

The compliance manager presented a thick binder to Charlie. "These are all of our SOPs" he said proudly, "you should find anything you need in there."

"Thank you," Charlie said impressed, "I'm sure I will."

"So, what would you like to cover first?"

"Well," Charlie responded to the vp, "if we can start with a tour of the warehouse that will answer a lot of the questions on my checklist. After that we can return here, and I can finish the remaining questions. Does that work?"

"Certainly, right this way."

THE VP LED the group through the office area, stopping in each department to explain its function. When they finally reached the warehouse, Charlie had already learned more about the company than she needed or wanted to know. When the vp placed her badge close to the badge reader and unlocked the mag lock on the door Charlie was immediately struck by the cleanliness of the warehouse. The facility was just over one hundred thousand square feet, and every square foot was spotless. The employees wore blue shirts with the company logo prominently displayed, and the hum of the conveyor belts throughout the facility was an appropriate soundtrack. Charlie was impressed, and the expression on John's face said the same.

They looked like tourists as they walked through the warehouse stopping at each department as the vp proudly provided commentary. It was obviously not the first tour she had conducted but it did not sound rehearsed. The words flowed naturally, as if reciting the family heritage. Charlie took copious notes and answered the appropriate questions on the checklist. John asked several questions, and Charlie was glad to see him engaged. There were two visits scheduled for the next day, and she intended to let John take the lead; unless he was presumed to be the senior person and she was ignored, in which case she would lead the meeting.

Back in the conference room, the vp let the appropriate manager answer Charlie's remaining questions. They were particular from whom they sourced product and conducted an appropriate amount of due diligence on verifying AD status and pedigrees. Charlie was very complimentary in her closing statements and thanked them again for their time and hospitality. It was as close to a perfect visit as she imagined she could experience. John concurred when they were back on Interstate 95 headed to the hotel. They did not discuss 'the raid' any further; Charlie would learn the details when she returned to Michigan.

THE SECOND DAY was almost a repeat of the first. Two suppliers were shut down as soon as Charlie and John made it back to the car, and the third was pending but leaning towards being added to the list of suppliers that the Distributing Company would not do business with nor accept on a pedigree. The experience had been eye opening for John. He had never delved into the purchasing side of the business, that was Christine's job; his job was to manage the inventory regardless of where it came from. After seeing some of the suppliers in Florida, he could not go back to his eyes wide shut mode of operation. His singular focus had been expanded, along with his suspicions about his old boss.

21

The handwriting on the envelope was familiar, and it was addressed to Clint as usual, but 'FBI' was written in the space reserved for the return address which was usually left blank. Clint immediately called his contact at the FBI, and they instructed him not to open the letter until they arrived. Clint was more than happy to obey.

The video recorded a car which was too old and in such poor condition to immediately identify the make and model. The woman who exited the car and placed an envelope inside Clint's mailbox was immediately recognized. Clint did not vocalize the woman's identity, but his reaction to the video confirmed that he knew her.

"Who is she?" The agent asked.

"I-I don't..."

"That's that whore Bridget!" Carol screamed from somewhere behind them. Everyone turned in Carol's direction; they were unaware of her presence in the room. "Your slut girlfriend is involved in this!?"

"What's going on Clint?" The agent asked with an accusatory tone.

"I don't know, I swear."

Carol charged toward Clint with an intent to do harm. "If my girls get hurt because of that bitch, I swear to God I'll kill both of ya!" Carol had to be restrained and was removed from the room. An agent led her outside and stayed with her.

"She's right Clint;" the agent exclaimed, "if the two of you are conspiring somehow, we won't stand in her way next time, and she might get to you before we can haul you off to prison."

"I'm just as surprised as you are to see her on that video."

Carol could still be heard in the background threatening Clint and Bridget to hell and back. It was distracting to Clint, but their daughters were not home, so he did not try to defuse the situation. It would have been a futile endeavor anyway. He wanted to know what was going on just as much as anyone, but Carol was in no position to listen to reason.

The envelope was dusted for prints before the agent carefully opened it and did the same to the letter inside. There were prints on the envelope, but the letter was clean. The prints would be sent to the lab where they identified Bridget Grant, who was already in the system for multiple offenses, primarily meth busts and a few public disturbance charges. The FBI was eager to question their new suspect.

The content of the letter was as expected. The usual instructions along with a pickup location with a two-hour time window and a drop location.

"Make the pickup," the Agent exclaimed.

"What about the 'FBI' they wrote on the envelope? What does that mean."

"Just trying to scare you, it's nothing."

"That's easy for you to say, you're not the one puttin' your life at risk."

"We'll have agents close by."

"Is that supposed to make me feel better? Once they see you, I'm a dead man."

"They won't see us."

"They always see you..."

THE EXPLOSION ROCKED the trailer park like an F5 tornado and caused nearly as much damage. Bridget's trailer was destroyed, as were the trailers on either side of hers, and several others sustained significant damage. There was barely enough left to identify Bridget's body, and it appeared she was home alone at the time of the explosion. After an investigation, the cause would be attributed to a propane tank with a faulty connection, and because evidence of an active meth lab was found at the scene, the investigation ended there. She had died cooking meth with a defective propane tank. Her rap sheet supported the conclusion and the case was closed. The FBI suspected the timing to be more than a coincidence. They did not have an opportunity to get her statement, which would have been that a white man with a beard came to her trailer and gave her one hundred dollars to place the envelope he handed her, inside Clint's mailbox. No, she had never seen the man before, and no she had never placed anything in Clint's mailbox prior to that day.

JUST OUTSIDE OF JACKSON MISSISSIPPI, nearly three miles off Interstate 20, a surveillance team had a small nondescript warehouse in their crosshairs. It was sitting next to a cotton field, which made the only black agent present think about his grandmother and the horrid stories she told about 'pickin' cotton' growing up in Arkansas. It was dawn, nearly ten hours before the two-hour window for the pickup, and no activity had been detected. Nothing would change over the next ten hours.

Clint did not exit off Interstate 20 until seven minutes before the two-hour window was set to expire. He was more nervous than he had been for the first pickup he made after receiving the initial mysterious envelope in his mailbox. He did not know what would be waiting for him three miles down the road, and it gave him no comfort to know that FBI agents were supposedly hiding somewhere waiting to pounce. He wondered if Bridget had been a part of it all along. The FBI had not informed him of her death; he had plans on paying her a visit after he made it back to Memphis.

The exit ramp was a modest incline to the stop sign at the top. Clint did not notice the man standing at the top of the hill until he came to a complete stop. The man appeared to be a hitchhiker. He was holding a sign and may have been asking for food, but Clint ignored him; his mind was roughly nine miles down the road. The man waved his arms wildly and approached the truck. Clint shook his head and tried to wave the man away. The man was close enough for Clint to read the sign and when he did fear gripped his body. Confident Clint had read the sign, the mysterious man slowly walked around the front of the truck to the passenger side and Clint unlocked the door.

“You’re late,” the man said when he was comfortably inside the truck, “I’ve been standing out here for almost three hours.” There were no services at the exit, but several trucks exited and stopped at the stop sign long enough for the man to ascertain the truck and driver. Clint sat motionless; he did not know how to respond. He was not expecting to see a man on the side of the road holding a sign that read ‘Clint there is a new pickup location.’

“There are... uh, people waiting for me...”

“I know, we have eyes on ‘em right now. Get back on the Interstate, we’re going down a few more exits.”

Clint pondered his next move but knew he only had one. He kept straight onto the onramp leading to the unknown.

. . .

USING the perceived cover of darkness, the FBI surveillance team decided to move in. The scheduled pickup window had expired and there still had been no activity, including any sightings of Clint. The last letter placed in his mailbox had shaken him, and they assumed he had succumbed to fear and stayed in Memphis. There would be consequences for his betrayal. The agreement they had with Clint had been breached and he would be prosecuted to the fullest extent of the law. Agents were in route to his house to arrest him.

The barn was approached cautiously, with guns drawn. The barn door was closed but unlocked, and inside they found a trailer as expected. The rush of anticipation energized them. Two agents searched under the trailer and found an envelope, sealed and thick with what they knew to be payment in cash; the acknowledging smiles were infectious. The envelope was indeed stuffed with money, but it was only useful if purchasing property on a Monopoly board. The smiles quickly straightened into clinched lips, as the alleged crime scene felt more like a gag reality show. They instinctively looked up and around the barn for cameras, but none were visible. Still high on adrenaline, they needed a target; something or someone they could thrust their energy and rage onto. The trailer door was not locked, and with guns still drawn and trigger fingers aching in anticipation, the door was raised revealing two wooden pallets. Nothing was on the pallets, and the disappointment hit like a straight right to the temple.

THE OBLIGATORY KNOCK on the door, like the identification announcement, happened after the agents and police officers had already entered the premises by force, splintering the door in the process. The house was surrounded, which is why the large, naked black man trying to escape through the window was quickly apprehended. His erection still full, he yelled out in pain as he was wrestled to the ground full frontal, and his hands were cuffed behind his back.

"Why were you climbing out the window?" The officer asked as he pressed his knee into the center of the man's back.

"Because you guys broke down the door and came in yellin' and screamin'."

"Only guilty people run, you're guilty of something, at a minimum adultery."

"Why you arrestin' me?"

"You tell me..." the officer asked, "you're not under arrest yet, just detaining you until we figure all this out."

"Where's Clint?" One of the FBI agents asked as he stood over the cuffed man.

"Who the fuck is Clint?"

"The husband of the woman you were in there screwing."

Inside the house, Carol was belligerent. Naked, but partially wrapped in a dingy sheet, she confronted the intruders.

"Get out of my house! You can't just barge in here! And you're gonna fix my damn door!"

"Where is he?"

"I'm sure your partners are outside beating his head in right now right now! What did he do? How did you know he was here? You watchin' my house?"

"We're not here for him; we're here for Clint. Where is he?"

"Clint? He's supposed to be with you sorry ass feds. You don't know where my husband is!?"

The agents looked at each other but did not respond to Carol. They continued to search the house but did not find anyone else on the premises.

"Where is Clint? Do *they* have him? You were supposed to protect him!"

The agents walked out of the house leaving the police officers behind.

"So, you just kick in my front door, tell me you don't know

where my husband is and just leave?" No response from the agents. "You're gonna hear from my lawyer! I'm suing the entire government! I'm..."

"Ma'am," one of the police officers interrupted, "we have a perp outside we caught trying to escape through a window. Are you under duress?"

"Am I what?"

"Did he force himself on you? Would you like to report a rape?"

"Do I look like I was raped? Get outta my house!"

Outside, the man had been identified and had no warrants. He was released without an apology but with a stern warning to stay away from married women and the neighborhood; the combination was understood.

THE ABANDONED TRAILER WAS FIRST SEEN from the air. A black helicopter flew overhead and circled before calling it in. The FBI had initiated a search for Clint's truck with instructions to arrest that 'son-of-a-bitch'. It did not take agents long to make the twenty-five-mile trek from the original location to where the trailer had been discovered. There was no sign of the truck, and they assumed Clint had ditched them. The trailer door was opened cautiously, where Clint's lifeless body was discovered. The cause of death appeared obvious due to the bullet sized hole in his head.

SOMEONE WOULD HAVE to notify the next of kin, which meant another visit to Carol. Notifying the next of kin of a death is never easy, but delivering the news to Carol was particularly dreadful. She was sitting on the front porch smoking a cigarette when the government vehicle pulled up in front of her house.

Two suits slowly exited the car, and Carol knew why they were there.

"My daughters are in there!" She yelled, "get the hell outta here!" The men paused and looked at each other.

"I said leave!" Carol screamed louder. "They ain't gonna hear about their daddy from you assholes!"

The two agents gladly got back in their vehicle and drove away. Carol took one last slow drag from her cigarette before smashing it under her right bare foot. The only life insurance policy Clint could get with his health was one for just enough to dispose of him she thought as she stood to her feet. He would be cremated with no memorial service; no sense in wasting money for a service with fewer than ten people and a minister who had never heard of him. She wiped tears from her eyes and retreated inside the house.

22

Charlie received her first invitation to the New Wind corporate office in Atlanta, though it felt more like a summons. She needed to be there in two days, and it was not optional. Nicole sounded like she made the call with a loaded gun pointed to her head and Charlie was unsettled. Something was wrong and she had no idea what it was. The only thing she could think of was the California investigation, which had taken a life of its own. There was not a sheet of paper in her office they had left untouched during the 'raid' while she was in Florida.

FROM THE MOMENT she drove up to the main gate in her rental car, Charlie knew that New Wind was on another level. It was not necessarily the three reddish brick office buildings that made the biggest impression on her, but the campus itself. The three four-story buildings encircled a pond with a stone fountain in the center. The landscaping was plush and colorful, and Charlie immediately felt a sense of pride. The guard asked her name and nodded and smiled when he found it on the list. He handed her a parking pass and instructed her to park in one of the visitor spaces.

"Visitor space?" Charlie asked perplexed, "but I'm an employee."

"Yeah, I know," the guard answered while still managing a smile, "but you're visiting here."

With one statement her pride diminished and was totally demolished when she checked in at the front desk and was handed a visitor badge. The plush waiting area in the main lobby was comfortable, but Charlie would not let herself be impressed. It was only something to look at, but she had no ownership in anything in the building; she was just a visitor.

After roughly fifteen minutes, Nicole exited the elevator wearing a navy-blue pantsuit. Her attire was not the only thing that was all business. Her facial expression and demeanor proclaimed it as well. Charlie stood to her feet and Nicole extended her right hand.

"Thanks for coming," Nicole greeted without passion.

"I didn't think I had a choice."

Nicole turned and headed for the elevator, Charlie followed her, but at a distance. They were the only ones on the elevator and Nicole pressed the button for the third floor. When they passed the second floor, Nicole spoke without looking at Charlie.

"How was your flight?"

"It landed safely, so I guess it was good."

The doors opened and Nicole immediately stepped out of the elevator. Charlie followed her down a long hallway to her office.

"Come in, have a seat."

Charlie saw the smirk before she saw the full face it was etched into. She stopped in her tracks and looked at Nicole as if to say, 'what is he doing here?' It could not have been good, at least not for her, because when she finally looked Stanley in the eye he had the look of victory after war. No treaties, just victory and defeat.

"Please have a seat so we can get started." Nicole's voice had been monotone from the cold greeting in the lobby. She sat across from Stanley at a small conference table with six chairs on the side of her large office opposite her desk. Charlie pulled out a chair as far away from her two adversaries as she could and sat uncomfortably, but with her head held high. She heard both her father and Ms. Geraldine in her head telling her to 'look that white woman in the eye.'

Nicole slid documents across the table to each of them and kept a set for herself.

"These are Distributing Company numbers pre and post acquisition. As you can see, there have been significant drops pretty much across the board. Revenue is down, margins are down, inventory is down..."

"So is risk," Charlie exclaimed, "risk is down significantly but you won't see that in those numbers you're looking at."

"The company's risk tolerance is not our concern," Nicole scolded, "we are a revenue generating department, the company has legal and compliance teams to mitigate risk. In fact, I think you would be a great addition to the compliance team under Jeffrey White."

Stanley could no longer sit quietly. "I think that's a great idea."

"What the hell is this?" Charlie asked angrily. "You had me fly all the way to Georgia to fire me?"

"No, I'm not firing you," Nicole said with the first sign of sympathy in her voice, "but we're moving in a different direction with the Distributing Company. We're going back to the basics."

"You mean you're going back to letting Stanley run a criminal organization. You know he had someone..." Charlie caught herself before she finished her statement.

"Look Charlie, I know this may seem like an ambush, but..."

"May seem like an ambush? Just call it what it is Nicole."

"You fucked with my company, that's what this is." Nicole looked at Stanley with pure hatred. "I want your shit packed and out of my building by the end of the month."

"That's not what we discussed." Nicole addressed Stanley for the first time.

"That's what Charles and I discussed."

And then it all made sense to Charlie. Nicole was the puppet, and her boss was maneuvering the strings. Charlie realized during their conversation that some of his words came out of Nicole's mouth, because they certainly were not her own. She was not just a puppet; she was a dummy and Charles was the ventriloquist. She still looked at Nicole in disgust, but there was a hint of empathy.

"I already spoke with Jeffrey," Nicole exclaimed trying to regain her composure and control of the conversation. "He's eager to speak with you, and I believe he has an open position on his team."

"Am I supposed to be grateful? Oh wow, thank you Ms. Fitzsimmons, I don't know what I'd do without you." Charlie stood to her feet. "Is there anything else?"

"No..." Nicole's voice was burdened with surrender.

Charlie turned to Stanley. "My shit'll be outta your building by the time you get back to Michigan." Charlie dropped her visitor badge on the table and walked out.

AS PROMISED, Stanley returned to the Distributing Company to find his parking space unoccupied and Charlie's office empty. The unadulterated relief and what can best be described as joy caused him to exhale a long, stale breath that had been festering in his core. He immediately called a meeting with his purchasing and inventory managers and his first words were that Charlie was no longer working at Distributing Company. Reactions were mixed.

"Christine, call all of our suppliers and tell them we're back open for business."

"They'll be glad to hear it," Christine exclaimed with an unbridled grin, "I know I am."

"John get our inventory levels back up. I want us to have so much inventory we can't receive it all."

"I remember those days;" John said meekly, "we had product sitting in trailers parked out back. Rumor had it they were even picking product out of the trailers to fill orders. Do we really want that again?"

"Is there a problem John?"

"Uh, no, it's just that I've seen some of our suppliers and..."

"And what?" Stanley walked over to John and looked him in the eye; their noses were almost touching. "You sound like her; what are you her flunky now? What, did she let you touch her fat ass?" John stood motionless and did not respond. "If you can't handle the job let me know right now. I need to know you're loyal John. Are you loyal?" John nodded his head. "I need to hear you say it."

"I'm loyal."

Stanley slapped John's face and held it. "Good to know, now from this point on discontinue all shipments to New Wind facilities until I say otherwise. All product we source we ship to our customers."

"Yes sir."

Stanley double tapped John's cheek with the palm of his right hand before he turned and dismissed him. He asked Christine to stay behind.

. . .

Once again, Charlie found herself leaving Michigan for New York. She needed to breathe and ingest Harlem to strengthen her immune system. She had been under attack on several fronts and felt vulnerable. She sent Nicole an email informing her that she was taking a week off. Nicole asked had she made a decision regarding her future with New Wind, and Charlie did not respond. Her email was not an attempt at conversation, which they had not had since the meeting in Atlanta, it was a time off notification.

Angela was helping a customer squeeze into a form fitting dress that she did not have the right form for when she heard the bell ring on the door. She was too concerned about the potential damage to her merchandise to look up to see who had entered the boutique.

"Sorry sista, but you ain't gettin' all that in this dress, and unless you gon' pay for it we done tryin'." Angela's frustration caused her to inadvertently slip into her street voice, ditching the manufactured customer service persona. Fortunately, the customer laughed in agreement.

"I was wondering how long it was gon' take you."

Angela looked around and saw her friend. They both squealed and ran into each other's embrace.

"Girl! When did you get in town?"

"Last night; you're my first visit."

"I better be! Give me a minute to finish up with this customer."

"No hurry," Charlie whispered, "it's gonna take you an hour to get her out that dress."

"Girl, I miss you."

. . .

After the lone customer in the store was finally convinced that she needed to go up a couple sizes, Angela closed the shop and she and Charlie walked down the street to their favorite pizza restaurant. They caught up over a couple supreme slices.

"So, how long are you here?"

"I don't know." Charlie looked down at the table as she spoke.

"Aww shit... who did what?"

"Just considering my options."

"You're moving back?"

"I didn't say all that."

"But you're thinking about it..."

"I'm thinking about a lot of things.

Angela smiled at the prospect of her friend moving back. Her smiled turned into a smirk. "So, what's up with you and Q?"

Charlie did not smile like a high school girl like she thought she would; she looked down at the table. "Nothing..."

"Nothing? Does he know you're back?"

"Nope, and I'm not back, I'm just visiting. I took some vacation days to come see my girl."

"Bullshit," Angela said disguising it as a cough.

"I thought you was feelin' him. You said the sex was da bomb."

"I am... it is... but, I don't know, the distance thing is not working for me."

"The last time we talked you said he was thinking about moving to Detroit."

Trenches formed on Charlie's forehead, and when she spoke it was in a higher pitch. "I don't know if I want that either. If he moves to Detroit for me, I'll feel pressured. I ain't ready to get married or be committed like that, I'm still working on my career."

"I thought yo' career was tight Miss Corporate America?

That's why you moved in the first place, right..." Angela saw the look on her friend's face and knew she had struck a nerve. "Oh... let me guess, Stanley. Girl, I know people that will take his ass out for a dollar fifty"

"I know your people and I got my own people. I wouldn't even waste their time; I can handle him on my own. I owe his ass anyway for..." Charlie stopped mid-sentence.

"For what?"

"Nothing. Let's get back to the shop, I need a dress for tonight"

Angela wanted to press more about Stanley and whatever he did, but she knew it was best to leave it alone. "What kind of dress? Where you goin'?"

"Harlem. I'm gon' bathe in it and be possessed by it."

"So you need a born-again dress."

"Hell yeah."

AFTER HER HARLEM REVIVAL, Charlie was ready for a word from Ms. Geraldine. Charlie had only told one person she would be in the New York area, and that person was her old friend and mentor. They made plans for dinner and Geraldine insisted on cooking.

Geraldine had a modest brick house in Stamford, CT, that blended in with the other houses on her street. A shiny black Mercedes Benz S class was parked in the driveway and Charlie assumed she had invited other gusts to dinner. Brief disappointment passed through her, but she was still looking forward to seeing her friend.

Geraldine greeted her at the door with a hug that would have thawed the coldest body and heart. It was the hug her grandmother embraced her with and yet was as relaxed as a best friend welcoming her into her home. Charlie thought she had identified every dish Geraldine had prepared from the smells teasing her nose. The exterior of the house may have been common, but the interior was photoshoot worthy. Everything looked and smelled new, and it was obvious that a renovation had been done.

"Your house is beautiful..." Charlie exclaimed in awe as she admired the original wood floors and what she imagined to be new matching wood on the ceilings.

"I recently had a little work done," Geraldine admitted with a coy smile, "come on in, dinner is ready."

"I can smell it." Charlie proceeded to take her shoes off.

"You don't have to take your shoes off," Geraldine exclaimed, "Chile' these floors have seen everything and some." Charlie followed her into the kitchen and was again awed by the craftsmanship.

"This kitchen is amazing. You can't even tell this is an older house; at least not on the inside."

"God is good."

"I see."

Geraldine cut her eyes at Charlie but then softened her expression with a smile. Charlie had been rebuked and forgiven with two quick facial expressions. There were two place settings on the wooden kitchen table which confused Charlie.

"Is it just the two of us?"

"Unless you invited someone."

"Oh, no ma'am, I just..." Charlie thought it best not to mention the Mercedes parked in the driveway, she chalked it up to God being good.

After feasting on smothered chicken, mashed potatoes, collard greens, and cornbread, Geraldine was 'fit to be tied," and Charlie was still trying to think of a time she had tasted better food. She had depleted her compliments on the meal, but after tasting the red velvet cake Geraldine had made from scratch all she could say was "damn..." She meant it as a great compliment, but she still apologized.

"So, what brings you back east?" Charlie took a deep breath and sighed. "That bad huh?"

"Well, I've been keeping you up to date on Stanley and what's going on at the Distributing Company..."

"Have you called the police yet?"

Charlie knew she was not joking. "Nooo, but now..."

"Now what?" Geraldine chided. "Don't get shy now."

Charlie inhaled through her nose and spat the words out. "He put me out."

"What do you mean he put you out?" Geraldine asked perplexed. "He can't put you out."

"Apparently he can." Charlie answered in what sounded close to a whine. She looked deep within Geraldine's eyes and was reminded who she was talking to.

"Miss Geraldine I've been doing my job to the best of my ability, like I always have, and I've been making a lot of progress. Cutting off shady suppliers, refusing suspect product, and making sure the rest of the New Wind facilities get a fair amount of product, just like Nicole and the company wanted; or so I thought..."

"So, what happened since the last time we talked?"

"I don't know... I got summoned to corporate to meet with Nicole and Stanley was there. Nicole is acting funny, and she starts talking this bullshit... I'm sorry, I mean stuff about going in a different direction because the numbers are down. She says there is a position for me at corporate in the compliance department and Stanley beats his chest talking about how he wants me out of his office by the end of the month. I was out by the end of the next day, and I took some vacation time and came here." She paused to take a breath, and Geraldine rested in the silence as well. "At first I blamed Nicole for not having my back, but I realized she was just doing what she had been told to do higher up the chain."

"The thing about corporate America," Geraldine started, "and this is the same now in 2001 as it was in the 50's when I started at Davidson's; there is always a white man higher up. We can only go so high, but..." She stopped her sentence and shook her head. "God is still good." She stood from the kitchen table. "Come with me."

Charlie followed her to the plush living room, and they stopped at a wall of photographs. There were several photographs of a very light skinned male capturing different stages of life. He could almost pass for white, particularly in the older pictures.

"That's my son, Preston." Geraldine picked up a framed photograph off the sofa table. "This is his wife and my granddaughter Emily."

Charlie studied the photograph of Preston and his white wife and gorgeous daughter. The only evidence Charlie could find was a slight kink in her long straight blondish hair.

"You have a beautiful family." Charlie managed to utter the words without them sounding obligatory, which they were not.

"Surprised?"

"A little."

"Well just wait 'til I tell you the story." She walked over and fell down into the oversized leather sofa. Charlie joined her after she studied the family wall. Whatever Geraldine had to say was from a place of great pain, Charlie watched as she sank down into that place.

"I was married..." Geraldine said in a barely audible voice. "He was a good man, but even good men have a breaking point. I didn't tell him I was pregnant, but my body eventually did the talking. I told him a man at work was the father. He knew it was a white man, because I was the only negro in the office; we were negroes back then. My mother's birth certificate said colored, mine says negro..."

"And mine says black. What are we now, Afro American?" Charlie spoke out of turn because she needed to recover from Geraldine's opening statement. She knew it to be only a glimmer of what was to come, and she needed to prepare herself accordingly.

"He thought I had been raped or taken advantage of, but I had not been raped. I was young and dumb. I let myself be taken advantage of and... well...he demanded to know who it was. I told him and he was ready to go right then and kill him, but I begged and pleaded and told him he didn't rape me. He must have heard something in my voice that he couldn't bear because he took all the rage he had for the white man and raised his hand at me. He came down on me with the force of a sledgehammer striking a railroad spike, and later that evening when I got up off the ground, I stabbed him with a kitchen knife." That felt like a good place to pause. Geraldine needed to give her soul a rest and Charlie needed to breathe again; she did not realize she had stopped inhaling and exhaling.

"I was sentenced to ten years but served five months; God only knows why; that was my second break from Davidson Enterprises."

"When was the first?" Charlie asked reluctantly.

"After the first time I slept with Bob." She heard Charlie's gasp before she looked at her face and saw her raised eyebrows. "I came back after about six months, but I should have stayed away."

"Did you come back for the job or for him?"

Geraldine was ashamed but she looked Charlie in the eye when she answered. "Both."

Charlie nodded her head in empathy. "And you worked for him all those years..."

"About fifty in total... he provided for Preston, paid for his college, but never met him. I always suspected that he got me out somehow so his baby wouldn't be born in jail, even though he couldn't claim him. Bob was married, still is to the same woman, she and I get along great, but she has never laid eyes on Preston either; I was too scared she would see her husband in Preston, and... well, no need to break up a home because I was a fool. After Preston, he never approached me in that way again."

"And you never remarried?"

"After what I did to my husband... and I don't mean taking his life with the knife. I took much more than that from him, I took his manhood... his black manhood. I honestly think I killed him more out of mercy than defending myself."

"Wow..."

"That's all you have to say?"

"No judgement Ms. Geraldine."

"You're the first."

The weight that had been placed on Charlie's lap prevented her from getting up to empty her bladder from the sweet tea, emphasis on sweet, that Geraldine had served during dinner. Whatever problems had caused Charlie to escape to New York to avoid were forgotten, at least for the moment, and she sought to comfort her friend.

"Is there anything I can do?"

Geraldine looked at Charlie with a wrinkled brow. "Chile' what can you do for me? I forgave myself a long time ago, and I'll know if God forgave me when I get to the pearly gates. I'm not looking for sympathy, I want you to know that we are strong, always have been, and we are over-comers. Now what are you gonna do about your situation? Is there anything I can do for *you*?"

"I don't wanna back to New Wind."

"Then don't."

"But..."

"A but is something we sit on, and this ain't no time for sitting."

"I've learned a lot, and the Distributing Company has given me good experience. I would love to start my own company, maybe a consulting firm. I'm sure there are other companies knee-deep in this alternate source vendor shit, I mean crap, who could use my experience and expertise."

"I'm sure there are."

"But it takes money to start a business."

"Again, is there anything I can do?"

Charlie looked at her confused.

"When Bob sold the company, he gave a percentage of the proceeds to me. I don't know what was in his mind, guilt or restitution or whatever, but in my mind, I earned every cent. For the last ten years or so I ran that company, Bob was in decline, and he came to me for everything, and I made most decisions; including the decision to sell the company. Even before his mind started deteriorating, he consulted me on business decisions. So, I see it as him giving me my cut."

Again, Charlie was left dumbfounded by Geraldine's latest revelation. She shifted her position on the sofa and felt jittery. She was at a loss for words, but finally spit out what seemed like the natural thing to say.

"Ms. Geraldine I can't ask you for money.""You're not, I'm asking you how much you need?"

"But..."

"There you go sitting on your but again. Look, I received a nice sum of money. I put some in a trust for Emily, I filled Preston's bank account, and I kept the rest for myself. Bought me a new car, updated my house, and the rest Preston can have when I'm dead. Until then, I do with it what I want, and I want to help you."

"I haven't put much thought into it," Charlie exclaimed

feverishly, "I need to develop a business plan and do some analytics. There's marketing, signing clients, I..."

"Tell you what," Geraldine interjected, "you do all that and let me know when you put some numbers together. Just think of me as your angel investor."

"No, you're just my angel."

"I don't know about you," Geraldine exhaled as she stood to her feet, "but I want another slice of that cake."

"Oooh me too."

"Come on back to the kitchen and you can tell me about your man friend you've been avoiding with some cake and coffee."

Charlie smiled, and not just at the thought of the cake. "What did I tell you last?"

BEFORE LEAVING the state of New York, Charlie called a 'break glass in case of emergency' acquaintance and arranged a hookup. She had needs that had not been met since Q's final visit, but she did not want Q's passionate affection; she wanted the raw, carnal opposite of Q with no attachments or expectations. Stix was a drummer she met years earlier at a jazz club in New Haven, CT. He was called Stix not just because of the obvious drummer reference, but he was also tall and skinny. He had a bald head, and his milk chocolate skin was covered in tattoos from the neck down, all the way down.

The rhythm utilized when playing the drum was the same rhythm comprising his sex technique. He could carry a beat for an extended period of time, all night if he needed, but usually his partner tapped out before he lost his erection. Even Charlie's pent-up cravings dried up as Stix was feeling the groove while he was tapping a beat on her backside while she was on her hands and knees groaning in exhausted pleasure.

Just after midnight, nearly paralyzed from the waist down

with painful pleasure, Charlie was glad she had arranged the hookup at her hotel room so she would not have to get up and leave. She felt like she needed to pay him for a service performed, but she felt as if he had equally enjoyed the surprise encounter.

It was not until after a long shower, as she lay in bed basking in afterglow, that she thought about Q. Her thought was more of a question. Should she call him before leaving town? Her answer was quick and concise. He would never know she was in town. Angie on the other hand, answered the phone after only one ring.

"Girl, do you know what time it is"

"Heeeey..."

"You hooked up with Stix, didn't you? Did he tap dat ass?"

"Girl, literally! He played the drums on my ass!" They both laughed hysterically, and the conversation went further downhill after that.

23

"Just find a spot!" Hank yelled at the frustrated truck driver leaning out the driver-side door of his truck. Every dock door had a trailer parked at it and there were trailers dropped along the fence.

"That's what I've been trying to do for the last half hour," the driver yelled back at Hank, "I got other drops to make and I'm gonna be late cause of this bullshit!"

"Just drop the trailer along the fence back there and leave it," Hank yelled back, "Gimmie the paperwork, I'll sign for it."

Hank was outside directing traffic and cursing at anyone spending too much time parked at the dock. Inside, the receiving dock was filled with full pallets stacked as many as three high. Some of the cases of product were being crushed under the weight. Luke was doing his best to manage the chaos, but he was only making his employees angry. The receiving team members were working as fast as they could to get the product received into inventory, and the stockers were behind due to the amount of time it took to find an open pallet location in the racks. The aisles were filled with pallets, making it nearly impossible for the pickers to get to the product to fill orders.

One person, working at a mobile receiving station, had the dubious task of receiving product into inventory which was still on the trailers parked out back. He was handed the packing slips from the two individuals who were tasked with climbing through the pallets in the back of the parked trailers and remove the packing slips which were taped to the shrink-wrapped pallets. The product would be received into inventory, assigned warehouse locations, if available, but remained on the truck. When available locations were depleted, new locations were created such as 39F, which meant the pallet was sitting on the floor at the end of aisle 39.

Mandatory overtime had been implemented for Saturdays, and Sunday overtime was voluntary but encouraged. Employees were paid time-and-a-half for all hours over 40 per week. Many employees complained about the time, but no one complained about the money; except the supervisors who were salaried and ineligible for overtime pay.

HANK SLAPPED Luke on the back when he walked into his office and Hank invited him to 'take a load off'. Luke was happy to rest his large frame and dropped down into the chair in front of Hank's desk.

"Been doin' a helluva job Luke," Hank exclaimed as he sat in his plush chair, "I know things have been kinda crazy lately, but I appreciate it, and the man upfront does too."

"This shit is insane; we might have to start parking trailers on the street." Luke smiled when he said it in jest, but Hank did not. Instead, he had a look on his face that said the opposite.

"Not on the street, but maybe outside the gate."

"But that's not secured..."

"They'll just look like empty trailers to anyone who sees 'em and we'll get 'em behind the gates as soon as we can. We'll lock the trailer doors of course."

"Of course." Luke did not protest further, and he struggled to keep a straight face.

"So, I called you in here 'cause I have something I need you to do. It's the end of the month and I need you to invoice all the open orders."

"But they haven't been picked yet."

"That's okay, we just need to get the money on the books for this month." Hank saw the doubt on Luke's face. "Don't worry, we've done it before, it's just been a while because... well, she's not here anymore."

The first thought that popped into Luke's head was 'well why don't you do it?" But he decided it didn't matter. He knew the real reason was so Hank could keep his hands clean. If something ever happened, it would be Luke leaving the paper trail.

"Will do." Luke said with a heavy head nod.

"Knew I could count on you Luke."

Luke left Hank's office with two plans to put in motion.

Luke reviewed paperwork from the truckers to ensure all refrigerated product and controlled substances got received right away. He did not want to have to issue a recall with the FDA due to refrigerated product left stored outside on a trailer for extended periods, nor did he want the DEA to stop in for an unannounced audit and find controlled substances stored outside the cage and vault. Hank usually managed the process himself, but Luke convinced him to delegate that responsibility to him. Since Luke was responsible for directing where the trailers were parked, he should know what was on the trailers; and Hank agreed. It was almost too easy; Luke had to restrain a smile.

~

THE NUMBERS WERE ONCE AGAIN where they were prior to the acquisition, and everyone was pleased. It did not take long for Stanley to achieve the same elite status with New Wind that he had been bestowed at Davidson Enterprises. When Charlie turned in her notice and left the company, Stanley was free to not only return to business as usual, but he felt even more empowered after receiving the endorsement of Nicole's boss. In his mind, he did not answer to Nicole any longer and was once again King over his domain. When the request from the state of California was placed on his desk, King Stanley immediately filed it in the round trash file. The legal department in Atlanta however, did not.

"TELL 'EM TO GO FUCK THEMSELVES," Stanley replied when Nicole asked him had he received the state of California document. While Nicole no longer had authority over the Distributing Company, she still had to communicate with Stanley in her diminished role. She squeezed the handle on the phone as tight as she could imagining it was Stanley's neck.

"Well, you tried that the first time and what did it get you? I believed you called it a raid." Stanley did not respond, and his silence gave her a small measure of joy.

"So, what do they want," Stanley finally mumbled.

"They want you. They want you to go to Sacramento for a meeting."

"Not gonna happen."

"Well, I don't think you have a choice."

"I always have a choice. Why don't you go? You're ultimately responsible for the New Wind Distributing Company, aren't you?"

It was Stanley who now took joy in Nicole's silence. As enjoyable as it was, he wanted to move the conversation to its conclusion.

"Besides you, who else is going?"

"Well, legal of course, we've retained outside counsel."

"For what!? This is just a meeting, a fishing expedition."

"That's usually how it starts, yes, but legal is concerned it could turn into something more."

"Well, I'm sure I'll hear about whatever comes out of California. Good luck; anything else?"

"Yeah, they requested Charlie."

"Charlie? What the hell do they want with Charlie?"

"Doesn't matter, she's no longer with the company, thanks to you."

"You're welcome." Stanley's final words were followed by the dial-tone.

The phone rang a few seconds after Stanley hung up.

"Did you not get the message when I hung up the phone?"

"What are you talking about?"

"Roman… I thought it was someone else."

"Let me guess… since you fired the pain in the ass you had in-house, it must be the pain in the ass in Atlanta."

"Yeah, and I'm working on getting her fired too."

"Let me know if I can help; anyway… I have a new source overseas and I need to move some product."

"We're full Roman, we're gonna have to start parking trailers at the grocery store down the street."

"I don't need you to sit on it, just receive it into your inventory so we won't have to pass a pedigree. I have customers lined up waiting for it; just unload it off one truck and load it onto another. This drug is hard to get in the states and I can get a shit ton of it."

"Is it legit?"

"When has that mattered? You're starting to sound like one of them. Hell, half the product in your warehouse is questionable."

"I got the state of California crawling up my ass…"

"Relax Stanley," Roman interjected before Stanley could finish, "I'm sure it has the same active ingredient as the brand name."

"So, it's a generic then..."

"You could say that."

Stanley knew it was best not to continue asking questions he did not want the answers to. He simply said 'okay' and hung up the phone.

LUKE'S PLAN was in place, and he had only to set it in motion. There was enough product sitting in trucks both inside and outside the gate to bring in the biggest haul yet, and the easiest. He had truck drivers waiting for the call, but he had to do a test run first. It was a Tuesday afternoon, and Luke stood on the receiving dock at a bay with the door raised, watching Hank do his best at directing truck traffic. A truck entered the property without a trailer, and Hank assumed he was there to move a parked trailer to the empty dock space. Luke watched as the truck backed up to a parked trailer, attached the trailer to his truck and drove away with a trailer filled with drugs. Hank did not pay attention to the truck and Luke smiled; it was too easy.

It was time for Luke to make his exit. He walked into Hank's office at the end of the shift and dropped an envelope on Hank's desk.

"What's this?" Hank looked at the envelope then up at Luke.

"My notice."

"You gotta be shittin' me!"

"I'm sorry, but..."

"Damn right you're sorry!" Hank exploded, "What the hell's goin' on Luke?"

"That's the thing, I don't know what's goin' on, but I ain't goin' to jail."

"Jail? What the hell are you talkin' about?"

Luke inhaled through his nose and spat the words out just as he had rehearsed in his head.

"I've worked for pharmaceutical distributors for over twenty years, and I've never seen anything like this."

"Like what?"

"Where do we get all this product from? I've never heard of most of these companies." Everything Luke had said to that point had been truth.

"Where's all this comin' from Luke?" Hank's voice was less aggressive but still agitated. "You've been doin' a great job here Luke. Is that what you need to hear? You need a that a boy every now and then?" Hank paused, but Luke stood perfectly still and quiet, waiting for it to be over.

"I thought you were happy here," Hank continued. You've taken charge of the employees and turned this place around."

"I'm seeing' a lot of things goin' on," Luke said adlibbing, "and I ain't comfortable with none of it."

"How much?" Hank asked matter-of-factly.

"What?"

"How much more money are we talkin'?"

"This ain't about money Hank."

"Everything's about money."

"Not this."

"What did I tell you the first time we met?"

"Huh?"

"You were standing right about where you're standing now. I told you there was nothin' traditional about this place. I told you to get the product received into inventory, pick it and pack it correctly, and get it loaded on the truck on time. Remember that, Luke?"

"Yeah, whatever..." Luke was growing more annoyed.

"Don't worry about where it came from or where it's going. Remember me sayin' that? We shook hands Luke; I thought you were a man of your word."

"You have my notice." Luke turned and walked toward the door.

"You know what I think of your notice Luke?" Luke stopped when he heard Hank tearing the envelope containing his two week-notice, but he did not turn around. "Leave your badge and key and get the hell off my property! You're fired Luke! You son of a bitch! You're fired!"

"If that's what you need to tell yourself." Luke walked out with a smirk on his face.

LUKE CONTEMPLATED NOT MAKING the call. He had arranged this job himself; it actually was a gift. Nonetheless, Nashville would somehow hear about it, and he knew it would be his ass.

"Everything's set," Luke said unenthusiastically.

"Good, what do you need?" the male voice on the other end of the phone was monotone.

"Nothing, I got this."

"Oh, well... I guess we can end this call since you got this." He made it a point to stress you got this. "I guess I work for you now."

"I didn't mean it like that," Luke exclaimed hoping to end the sarcasm, "I'm just sayin' that I didn't have to do all that we originally planned. The place is a shit show, and the drugs are just there for the taking. It's almost a crime not to."

"The first truck arrived in Miami and the client was pleased."

Whoever was in Miami was always referred to as 'the client' and Luke preferred it that way; the less he knew the better. He didn't even know the name of the man he was talking to. The wire transfers he received were always from a freight forwarding company with a Nashville, TN address, and even that was more information than he wanted to know.

"When do you plan on securing the rest of the loads?"

"I figure one a week for about a month should go unnoticed until it's too late. Like I said, it's a shit show, and no one knows where anything is."

"Seems like we should take as much as we can then; maybe we do two or three a week."

"Too risky..."

"That's not your call."

"But it's my ass on the line if we get caught."

"It's your ass regardless."

And with that final thought it was settled.

24

The New Wind team, which consisted primarily of lawyers, confidently marched into the Attorney General's office nine strong, and were pleased to see only three men and one woman sitting across from them at the massive conference table. Their overwhelming numbers and the fact that the Attorney general himself was not present filled them with confidence. The matter could not be as serious as they thought, and they looked at each other in relief.

Introductions were made, starting with the AG's office. The Deputy AG introduced everyone on his side of the table, and the team from New Wind introduced themselves individually. The only one present that did not attend law school was Nicole.

"So..." the Deputy AG started, "the only person in your rather large group who actually has some responsibility for the Distributing Company and its nefarious dealings is Ms. Fitzsimmons, is that correct?"

"Well..."

"Five people introduced themselves as outside counsel from two different firms. You are a vp in the litigation department at New Wind and the gentleman next to you I believe he said he is a vp and some sort of regulatory counsel with New Wind, and then you brought a paralegal to take notes. Are we here for an initial discussion or a deposition?"

"Quite honestly, we didn't know what to expect," the litigation vp exclaimed, "Your requests thus far have been fairly broad in scope."

"So, it takes nine attorneys to narrow the scope? Your unnecessary show of force while costly, has no impact on today's discussion. For every attorney seated at the table we have ten emails to present to a California Judge and jury."

The confidence the New Wind team had when they first entered the room slowly deflated like a balloon. The litigation vp shifted his eyes before responding.

"Emails from whom might I ask."

The deputy AG looked down at the notepad in front of him. "Stanley Forsythe, and Charlie Thomas primarily, but there were also some shots fired at Ms. Fitzsimmons here from her boss Charles McKinnon. I am certain we requested their presence."

"We are not aware of any such emails."

"Oh, I'm certain you are," the Deputy AG said with a smirk, "I'm sure your outside counsel has combed through all of the records we have requested. If not, we will make them available during discovery."

"Discovery?" He looked around at the other lawyers and they were as perplexed as he was. "Does the California AG plan on taking this to trial?"

"Why yes... it appears as if New Wind is prepping for trial as well; or was the small army of lawyers just for show?"

"I assure you, we take this matter very seriously."

"So where are the individuals who are actually responsible for the activities at the Distributing Company?"

"Well... Mr. Forsythe had a scheduling conflict.

"I see, that happens, even with as much advance notice as we provided. And Ms. Thomas?"

"Ms. Thomas is no longer employed at New Wind."

For the first time the representatives from the AG's office look at each other in surprise. One person jotted notes on a notepad for the first time.

"That's unfortunate, she was the only person who appeared to value product and patient safety over profits."

"Now wait a minute!"

"Before we get into a pissing contest, let's discuss why you are here. Our plan was to ask questions and get answers from the individuals who did not make the trip, but I guess we will have to depose them to get the information we're seeking. We will be sure to issue subpoenas to ensure there are no scheduling conflicts."

The thought of a deposition came as a surprise to the New Wind employees based on the looks on their faces and their sagging shoulders. Their cockiness had withered away, but the highly paid outside counsel remained stone faced; they were not paid to show what they were feeling.

"What exactly is the focus of this investigation?" Nicole's tension erupted as a question. She had been advised not to speak unless asked a direct question, but she could not help herself. It was either let a little out or explode. She felt the disapproving gazes from her team, but did not look directly at any of them; she was laser focused on the opponent in front of her.

"Well, I don't know what your team has shared with you, but our focus is the secondary or 'grey' market as it is commonly called; specifically, the Distributing Company's trading in this market."

"What is the secondary market?" Again, her question was met with disapproval.

"Since your company is a major player in the secondary market, we were hoping you could enlighten us."

Nicole was about to respond when she felt a hand grip her own hand firmly. She swallowed her question and averted her eyes downward to the table in front of her. An uncomfortable silence hovered over the room, and everyone knew the next sound made would be from the California Attorney General's office; it was time for them to show their hand.

"I don't have to tell anyone in this room that we have a counterfeit drug problem in this country;" the Deputy AG declared boldly, "particularly the counterfeit prescription drugs which are distributed to and within the great state of California. Distributors like New Wind, and specifically the Distributing Company, are licensed in California and must abide by the laws of the state of California as well as federal laws concerning the sale and distribution of prescription pharmaceuticals."

His opening statement, while factual, was unnecessary in the minds of everyone else in the room, including the other two members of his office. To their knowledge, there was not a judge or jury listening.

"It is the belief of the California Attorney General's office, that New Wind and its Distributing Company have operated in violation of state and federal laws through reckless secondary market trading resulting in counterfeit, mislabeled, and adulterated pharmaceuticals polluting the distribution network and endangering lives. Quite frankly, I am disgusted by what our office has uncovered, and if it were up to me, your license to distribute drugs to and in the state of California would be permanently revoked before you leave this office today."

"Well in Georgia and the rest of the country, the falsely accused are entitled to their day in court, even though I doubt this will ever see a courtroom. I am sure this is true even in

California. A presentation of evidence of a crime is still the rule of law."

"Yes, evidence... the state will prove that The Distributing Company has operated in and profited from the diversion market, including price diversion through transactions with 340b and other closed-door pharmacies. The state will further prove that the Distributing company knowingly acquired and distributed counterfeit and adulterated pharmaceuticals into the state of California and nationally in what is nothing less than a drug laundering scheme perpetrated with Roman Caesar and his criminal enterprise operating under the Rome Enterprises umbrella. The state plans on filing criminal charges against Mr. Forsythe, and I wouldn't be surprised if the feds throw a RICO charge at Stanley Forsythe and Roman Caesar; we're in contact with the US Attorney's office."

"Those are very serious accusations."

"And this is a very serious matter involving the health and welfare of California residents and American citizens across the country."

"Well, I hope you have more than a few emails."

"The emails are so damaging we may not need to present other evidence, at least not to a jury. We're talking about the prescription drugs that parents and grandparents take on a daily basis not only for quality of life, but for life itself. Drugs we ourselves take for high blood pressure, cholesterol, or after visiting an emergency room."

"Well, it sounds like we're done here," the litigation vp exclaimed as he stood to his feet.

"You came all this way; we can interview Ms. Fitzsimmons..."

"Not today," he said as the others gathered their things and stood, "we have not properly prepared her for questioning."

"We'll issue subpoenas for depositions."

"Yes, I'm sure you will."

The New Wind team left with nothing gained. Their departure was a far cry from their grandiose entrance; they had much to deliberate.

HANK HAD HIS SUSPICIONS, but he could not accept that Luke had been stealing from him. What looked like chaos to others, was actually managed disorganization to Hank. Luke had managed the inbound process during the period when it was like Grand Central Station at the facility, but things had slowed to normal, whatever that was, and there were trailers full of product missing. It would have been easy for Luke to divert a truck knowing the product had already been received into inventory, which also made it impossible for Hank to report it to the police; it would have only raised more questions and there were already enough questions being asked. He had no choice but to tell Stanley; the potential loss was too great to hide.

"HOW MUCH ARE WE TALKING," Stanley asked annoyed.

"I don't know the exact dollar amount," Hank answered looking him in the eye.

"Don't bullshit me Hank…"

"My hand on the lone star flag, I have no idea. The only way to find out is do a full inventory."

"Are there any other options?" We'd have to shut down shipping and receiving for an entire weekend, and I need to move product. I need to get our inventory down, fast."

Hank stood quiet as Stanley pondered the situation.He knew not to even think of words to say because they might fall out of his mouth. He was curious as to why they needed to get the inventory down, it was not the end of the year when they do it for tax purposes. Stanley was gazing at Hank, but Hank knew he was looking through him not at him.

"Hold off on conducting inventory, let me make a call."

Hank nodded and turned and walked out of Stanley's office.

"SO..." Stanley said after getting past the pleasantries, "I recently had some product taken, and I'm hoping you might know where it is."

"I don't steal product."

"No, but stolen product has a tendency to end up in your possession."

"And in your warehouse," Roman stated matter-of-factly, What's the purpose of this call Stan?"

"Do you know where my product is or not?"

There was an extended silence on the phone which answered Stanley's question. He rode out the silence until Roman confirmed.

"I'll give it to you for our standard terms."

"What!?"

"The normal percentage, why should this deal be any different."

"Roman, you know the product was stolen from my facility and now you want me to buy it back? Are you shittin' me?"

"I didn't know where it came from until I received it and saw the packing slips were addressed to the Distributing Company."

"So why didn't you just send it back to me?"

"That's what I'm trying to do now."

"You're trying to sell it back to me."

"Hey, I didn't get this product for free, that's now how it works. I have costs."

"Your costs are minimal Roman; c'mon this is me you're

talking to. I've been doing business with you for as long as you've been in business."

"It's not my fault you couldn't hold on to it!" Roman had grown annoyed with the conversation. "From what I hear it was just sitting there for the taking."

Stanley was livid. "After all we've been through and all the shit we've done, this is how you treat your most trusted trading partner?"

"Don't make this personal Stan, this is business."

"I thought we were better than that… I thought we were…"

"What, friends?" Roman asked cutting him off, "C'mon Stan, you know better than that. There are no friends in this business only people who make money together."

"You're right, keep the product. I'll just report it stolen; maybe I'll even point them south."

"Don't do anything you'll regret Stan…"

Stanley had already disconnected the call. He needed to act quickly and wasted no time gathering the troops. Within ten minutes of hanging up on Roman he had his team in his office.

"UNTIL FURTHER NOTICE all communications amongst this team will be in person. No phone calls, emails, or voice messages. I mean all communications, even personal, am I clear?" All three nodded their heads. "You will make yourselves available regardless of time of day or night, and regardless of what you're doing. Nothing and no one is more important than this team right now."

Hank stood stone faced like a trusted General receiving marching orders. Christine had a deer in headlights look, and her cheeks darkened as Stanley talked. John looked as if he was choking on a question he wanted to ask but could not get it out, most likely due to his body's self-preservation mechanism. Stanley sensed John's uncertainty, but it was not unexpected.

Stanley no longer trusted John, but John was complicit, and that would keep him compliant with Stanley's orders.

"Christine, I want all purchases from Rome Enterprises and all of its subsidiaries to cease until further notice. John, any product we have from Rome I want out of here yesterday; even if we have to have a fire sale."

They both nodded in obedience and agreement. Neither liked doing business with Roman and were glad for even a temporary respite.

"I want our inventory down to just what we need, no spec buying. Send as much product to the other New Wind facilities as they can hold. If we go down, they all go down."

"Go down?" Christine asked reflexively; fear had caused her to react impulsively.

"Just do it," Stanley ordered with a stern voice, "and no one enters this building without my approval, even New Wind people or the alphabet assholes. If they don't have a badge they don't get in, especially anyone from the state of California." Stanley paused as he checked items off the list in his mind. "One more thing," he exclaimed as if just remembering something important, "Any emails to or from Charlie I want printed and on my desk by end of day; do not forward them to me." He stressed his last point with a menacing grimace. "I don't care how old or if they've been deleted, you too Hank."

Hank nodded in the affirmative while Christine and John stood frozen. Stanley gazed at the floor as his mind searched for anything he had forgotten. After what seemed like several minutes to those waiting, Stanley looked up as if he was surprised and annoyed to see Christine and John still standing there.

"Get to it."

They gladly left the office and closed the door behind them. Christine followed John to his office where they huddled behind closed door to try to figure out what just happened. Hank stayed behind; he knew the meeting was far from over.

"Do we still have anything outside?"

"Nope," Hank replied, "the last truck was emptied yesterday."

"We're not doing a full inventory, at least not until the scheduled annual inventory. I don't want any more products cut from customer orders. If we don't have it invoice 'em anyway. If they say they didn't get it dispute it; let them request a credit if they're bold enough."

Hank nodded and smiled. "I'm pickin' up what you're puttin' down boss."

"Do you have an idea what was lost?"

"Pretty much… I had the inventory team do a spot check on all POs received for the last sixty days."

"Do I want to know?"

"No."

"Reach out to our contact at the reverse distributor. We need to return some product on paper for credit. Stay under the radar, we already lost a guy there, just request enough to help offset some of the losses."

"Standard two percent?"

"Offer two, but if they balk, I'll go as high as three. They're still freaked out over what happened."

"Understood." Hank stood looking at Stanley and the floor with shifting eyes.

"Spit it out," Stanley exclaimed sensing his uneasiness.

"Was this Roman?"

"He didn't initiate it, but he ended up with our shit and now he wants to sell it back to us."

"That son-of-a bitch…"

"Don't worry about Roman, just do what we discussed."

Hank tipped his grey cowboy hat and walked out of the office. He knew there was more to the story, and that Stan was knee deep in all of it; he just hoped he was not in over his head. He had never seen Stan so… desperate.

IT HAD BEEN a while since Charlie talked to Q, and when she saw his name on her ringing phone she smiled. It was perfect timing; she had just filled the tub with water and bubbles and was removing her last garment.

"Hey you."

"So, you came to the city and didn't call me?"

Charlie's smile eroded. "I'm good, how the hell are you?" She dropped her brazier on the floor and slowly sunk down into the warm, soothing water.

"Sorry, how are you Charlie?"

"I thought I was about to be chill, maybe even get one off, but you came at me like I stole somethin'."

"You did, you stole my heart, and I don't even think you want it."

Charlie's eyes rolled in her head, and she sank down as deep in the water as she could go without drowning, even though that did not seem like a bad idea at the time.

"There you go," Charlie bemoaned, "you're so dramatic."

"I just don't know why you didn't call me," Q whined, "I thought we…"

"You thought we were what… friends, because that's all we are. I thought we discussed this and had an understanding."

"We talked when I was there, but I guess I misunderstood."

"Look Q, I like you, if I was looking for a husband you would be on the short list, but I'm not. I don't have the time nor desire to be in the type of relationship you want. We're friends, good friends, maybe even friends with benefits as long as you can handle that without attachment, and as long as you don't get married; I'm not that kind of friend to married men."

"I hear you," Q sighed after a long pause, "I just don't know why you didn't call me when you were in New York."

Charlie rolled her eyes again and shook her head in disbelief. "I was in New York to detox, okay? I needed some Harlem healing, and I met up with a few friends while I was there. Some things happened at work, and I just needed to get away."

"Yeah, I did a gig with Stix the other weekend and he told me he saw you. He didn't know that you and I are... friends." There was an emphasis on friends.

"I know how men talk. He told you he hit it and that got you all up in your feelings. I hooked up with Stix because I needed a release without the intimacy or expectations; that's why I didn't call you."

"I hear you," Q conceded, "so what's going on at work that had you so stressed?"

Charlie told him everything. It felt good to unload without judgement. He listened, he consoled and offered encouragement. That was what Q did best, he was attentive, and that was just what Charlie needed. By the time they finished, she was feeling relaxed and craving an orgasm.

"Tell me what you would do if you were here right now," she purred. "I must tell you; I am lying on my back in a tub of bubbles, well not so many bubbles anymore; nothing is covering me now, I'm exposed."

The scene was set, and Q was eager to play along. He took his time and was very detailed. It was like reading an explicit love scene from a romance novel in her free hand while her other hand acted out the scene. They reached the scene's climax together, finishing in unison.

25

The meeting was held in the recently vacated office of Charles McKinnon, the former vp of pharmaceutical operations. Nicole did not publicly cheer her boss's termination, but internally she did cartwheels. It also made her nervous, because she knew his firing was due to the emails outside counsel had discovered, and that she was the recipient of some of those emails. She desperately tried to remember the emails and her response to them. She had found several emails in her deleted folder but knew there were probably more. His termination, while warranted, was more a gesture of good will for the California AG's office. An action that showed that New Wind took the matter very seriously and was already taking action. No one was off limits, not even the head of the operations unit who asked in an email how could New Wind blow up the gold mine while they were still mining gold from it. Mining gold is risky he acknowledged, but some things are worth the risk, and they were sitting on a gold mine.

"And that wasn't even one of the really bad ones," the vp of litigation exclaimed as he looked around at those gathered in the office, "there was much worse generated from the face of the Distributing Company, who is not here I might add."

As if on cue, Stanley walked into the office unapologetically. He did not sit in one of the vacant chairs, he stood along the wall in the back of the office.

"Thanks for joining us Mr. Forsythe," the vp of litigation chided "since you are the reason we are having this meeting in the first place."

"Well let's get this show on the road, I have things to do."

The vp looked at Nicole who just shook her head. There were also two other lawyers in the room from the outside law firm representing New Wind in the California AG matter. The female attorney studied Stanley with a familiar gaze. She knew the type; tall, handsome, athletic, narcissist asshole; he was wearing a very nice suit though.

"It's no secret why we're here today. The two of you have been subpoenaed for a deposition by the California AG's office. Brenda and Mike will be representing us and will be prepping you for the depositions. Treat them as if they worked at New Wind, tell them any and everything. The more they know the better they can represent you and the company."

"I will be retaining my own counsel," Stanley exclaimed, "I don't trust the company nor its counsel to represent my best interests."

Stanley had deflated the air, and life out of the room. No one saw that coming and their recovery from it was slow and arduous. The looks on their faces brought him a twisted level of joy.

"Well, that is certainly your right," The vp stated matter-of-factly," but just know that the company will not be financing any outside counsel other than the firm we have retained."

"I didn't ask you to. I've never asked your company for a damn thing, including your hostile takeover of my Distributing company."

"So why are you even here Stanley?" Frustration filled Nicole's voice.

"The same reason you are," Stanley answered calmly, "to hear what Charlie is planning to say."

"Ms. Thomas has decided to retain her own counsel as well." There was more pain than pleasure in the vp's voice and statement.

"I guess she's smarter than I thought;" Stanley exclaimed, "guess I'll have to defend the Distributing Company against, New Wind and Charlie."

"We're all on the same team."

"Are we? I bet you can't wait to separate me from my company. I bet you've already drawn up the termination papers. What's your plan, to let her run it?""

There was neither acknowledgement nor denial on the vp's poker face, and Nicole looked down at the floor. Mike and Brenda remained stoic; their firm had already started working on a lawsuit against Stanley if needed.

"Well, I have another meeting to get to with my attorney," Stanley said as he stood fully erect from leaning on the wall, "can't be late, I'm being billed by the hour."

"Your attorney is in Atlanta?" The vp seemed surprised.

"Isn't yours? What's the saying... keep your friends close and your enemies closer. We'll be in touch."

Stanley walked out of the office as if he had said something profound that they would not fully comprehend until later.

"This is problematic," the litigation vp uttered after Stanley was gone, "where are we with the lawsuit?"

"Just waiting to see how the California case plays out, but the case against Stanley is strong. With the emails and potential testimony from Charlie..."

"Not happening," Nicole stated shaking her head, "She

wants nothing to do with this. She's only being deposed because she was subpoenaed against her will."

"What exactly did she say when you talked to her?" There was concern in the vp's voice.

"Before or after she told me to kiss her black ass?"

"Do you think she will intentionally hurt us during her deposition?"

"I know she will not intentionally help us. What we... what the company did to her was wrong."

"You mean what Charles did to her. That's why he's no longer with the company."

Nicole rolled her eyes at the vp.

"Are you going to be a problem Nicole?"

"I will answer all questions truthfully," Nicole answered as if reciting a script, "I will only answer the question asked and will not elaborate or offer details or anything else."

"Sounds like you won't need much prep." Debra said it jokingly in an attempt to lighten the mood in the room which was thick with gloom. Everyone knew about the damaging emails and suspect transactions and trading partners, but having both Stanley and Charlie lawyer up only added to the feeling of impending demise. For the first time, the litigation vp was giving serious thought to a settlement.

The DEA was not due for an unannounced visit to the Distributing Company for at least twelve to eighteen months based on when the last cyclical audit was conducted by the Detroit office, but the number of 106's filed in the previous month was concerning and warranted a visit.

Stanley was in Atlanta meeting with his attorney and did not answer the multiple calls to his phone. Stanley's order to not let anyone in the building without his permission rang in the ears of his team when the two DEA diversion investigators tried to gain entry after showing their credentials and notice of inspection. It was Hank's call to make, and he turned them away. He would rather deal with the DEA than Stanley for making the wrong call; and the investigators immediately let him know it was the wrong call. They vowed to return with a warrant.

When the DEA returned armed with a warrant, their team had also grown to six frowning faces, including one field agent carrying a sidearm. An administrative judge was on call in case any immediate enforcement actions had to be taken. Stanley's administrative assistant greeted them with a smile that was both anxious and apologetic and informed them that the warrant was not necessary. She offered her deepest apologies but was basically told to get out of their way. Stanley had returned one of the several calls placed by Hank and left few known curse words unused. He would be on the next available flight back to Detroit.

They were ordered by the group supervisor to cease all controlled substance activities immediately so an inventory could be taken on the items that had been reported as lost on the form 106s; Phentermine and Alprazolam were the drugs in question. Three investigators were sent to the warehouse to enforce the order and guard the controlled substance cage. The usual smiles, even if fake, and pleasantries were forfeited when the initial inspection was refused; it was all business, with an emphasis on enforcement.

"We need to do a full alarm test immediately." The group supervisor's voice was stern and cold.

"Just the cage and vault area?" Hank asked hoping the answer would be yes.

“The entire facility,” the supervisor responded, “all alarm points and sensors.”

“But we’d have to clear out the entire warehouse for that and they’re in the middle of picking orders. Usually when you come in you do the alarm test when it’s more convenient.”

“Usually when we come, we are let in the first time, not when it is more convenient for you. We need it done right now. We also need to conduct an inventory and accountability in the cage and vault.”

“But they’re picking orders right now,” Hank pleaded, “again usually this is done at the beginning or end of shift.”

“Again, if we had been allowed in this morning when my two investigators first presented the notice of inspection we could have accommodated your requests. Unfortunately, we are now pressed for time. One of the investigators in the warehouse will conduct the counts, and you can bring us your biennial inventory for the accountability.”

Hank knew it was futile to argue, and his entire body succumbed to the situation. His shoulders dropped and he slouched over like a man utterly defeated. He knew he was at their mercy as long as they held a DEA registration, which he feared may not be much longer.

“While that is being retrieved, our office has been made aware of at least eight 106s filed so far this month from product originating from this facility. Registrants from as far away as California have claimed not to have received controlled substances you claim to have shipped.”

Stanley’s entire team was present and listened intently to the group supervisor’s weighted words without making eye contact with him.

“I need to see records for all receipts and shipments of these items for the past sixty days.” He slid a printed spreadsheet across the table to Hank. Hank handed it to Christine, who immediately stood to her feet.

"Before you go," the group supervisor exclaimed, "we need to see the invoices and shipping documentation for these eight orders from eight different customers all claiming not to have received the product. These should not take long to retrieve, correct?"

Christine looked at Hank which did not go unnoticed by the DEA team.

"Uhh, no," Christine stammered, "they shouldn't."

"Good, we'll be waiting, and please bring the biennial inventory with you."

"I'll help her," John said eager to leave the room, "call me if you need anything else Hank." John and Christine quickly exited before the supervisor made any more demands.

"Make copies of everything you provide please," Hank exclaimed before they were out the door, "for our own records of course." The last statement was directed at the supervisor.

Seconds felt like minutes to Hank as he sat in the conference room with his unwanted guests. He could see employees gathering outside for the alarm test through the large windows of the conference room. When Christine returned alone, she placed the requested documents on the table in front of the supervisor and copies in front of Hank. Hank quickly scooped up the copies and scanned them quickly. He tried not to show the fear he was feeling. He looked over at the supervisor who studied the documents carefully.

"I don't understand," the supervisor said as he compared the documents for several customers, "on these orders the items were scratched from the picking document, but the customer was invoiced for it."

Hank shot Christine a menacing gaze for not removing the picking sheets from the invoices.

"Why were the items scratched? Did you not have them in

inventory? A picking document would not have been created unless there was inventory in the system, correct?"

"That's correct, but in some cases..."

"Let's walk back to the cage right now," the supervisor interrupted, phrasing his demand as a suggestion, "I want to see your inventory system."

As much as Hank wanted to refuse, he knew he could not. He knew what the supervisor suspected; and that is exactly what he would find. Where was Stanley?

"Soooo, according to this, you received the inventory into your system on the third and on the Fifth you cut it from this order. Let me see the next order."

Hank typed the order number into the Warehouse Management System and the information displayed on the screen.

"Looks like the same thing for this order and I suspect it will be the same for all eight." The supervisor looked at Hank but did not expect an answer to his question.

"What happened to the inventory?"

Hank's body was frozen, and his mouth hung open, but his mind was racing searching for an answer; anything that was not the truth.

"Why didn't you have the inventory that the system said you had?"

"Because we had a theft." The voice was Stanley's, and everyone looked back to see him walking through the cage door. "The product was stolen, and we believe we know who took it."

"We didn't get notification regarding a theft of controlled substances."

"Obviously not," Stanley said in frustration as he gave Hank a scornful look, "apparently an oversight by my ops manager that I will address with him later."

"You said you know who committed the theft?"

"We believe it was a supervisor who recently left. He ran the receiving operation, and while we can't prove it yet, we are still investigating him."

"What's this supervisor's name?"

"Luke, Luke Cartwright."

"Have you filed a police report?"

Stanley looked at Hank for the answer.

"Uhh, no..." Hank responded, knowing his role.

"Please send us a copy when it is filed. How much product has been diverted?" The supervisor asked as he scribbled notes on a legal pad.

"You will have a report of all controlled substances stolen before you leave today," Stanley assured him while looking at Hank, "As for the non-controls, we fear it may be far more substantial."

"Sounds like a pretty severe security breakdown, that's a major problem; anything on camera?"

"We're still reviewing, but he was also head of security, so I fear he may have manipulated several systems. And let me say, I apologize for this morning, my team misunderstood my instructions and unfortunately, I was traveling and couldn't be reached. I caught the first flight I could when I found out what happened so I could apologize in person."

"That rarely happens," the supervisor responded, "and when it does it usually means the registrant is trying to hide something."

Hank absorbed the supervisor's comment and did not launch a counterattack; sometimes the last word is self-evident.

WITH A PROMISE and forewarning they would be back in the morning, the DEA team left the premises. The inventory had been completed, and they planned to do the accountability when they returned. Hank escorted them out and reluctantly walked back to his office; he knew Stanley would be waiting.

"What the fuck Hank?"

"Can I at least sit on my ass before you rip me a new hole?" Hank walked over and plopped down into his chair.

"Why didn't you tell me we had controlled substances missing?" Stanley yelled, not expecting an answer. "Why were they left on the truck? Didn't you know which trucks had the controlled substances so you could unload those ASAP? Who filed the 106s? Please tell me it wasn't us!"

"It wasn't us?"

Stanley continued gazing at him waiting for the other shoe to fall. Hank buckled under the pressure.

"When we denied their claim and told them we shipped the product, they filed a 106 for a loss in transit."

"Dammitt Hank!"

"That's what you told me to do..."

"Not for controlled substances! They had to file a 106 after you told them we shipped it and they didn't get it, and now the DEA is crawling up our ass!"

"I wasn't thinking."

"Obviously not," Stanley chided, "what's wrong Hank, you're better than this."

"What's wrong!?" Hank exploded. "What's wrong!? How the hell am I supposed to keep all the lies, schemes, and misdirections straight!? I don't know up from down half the time, and you leave me here to manage this shit show while you're off rubbing elbows with New Wind assholes! Don't get mad at me when you come back and step in shit!"

"Is that what you think I'm doing?"

"Honestly, I could give a rat's ass what you're doing, but don't ride in on your high horse talkin' to me like I'm, some fool. You're the fool, and you gave strict instructions not to let anyone in, nobody! So fuck you Stanley!"

Hank jumped up from his desk and headed to the door.

"Where are you going?"

"It's either leave right now or hog-tie your ass and drag you around this goddamn warehouse; your call."

Hank stood face to face with Stanley and was unwavering. Stanley had never seen that side of Hank and certainly had not been on the receiving end of his wrath. He wisely stepped aside.

"And it's not just me," Hank said as he walked by Stanley, "you're losing your shit too."

LUKE'S NAME was already in the system when the group supervisor entered it into the database for a query. There was an armed theft at a pharmaceutical distributor in McDonough, Georgia shortly after he quit, and a theft at another distributor where he had been employed as a supervisor in Tulsa, Oklahoma prior to that. He was definitely a person of interest and needed to be questioned as soon as possible.

His last known address was still valid, and Michigan state troopers apprehended him without incident at his apartment in Plymouth. They found packed boxes and luggage in his pickup truck, which led them to believe he was planning to leave town soon. The police report had been filed just in time.

Two DEA diversion investigators were waiting in the interview room when Luke walked in. If he was guilty of something, it did not show on his face, nor his demeanor. He was not under arrest, so he was not handcuffed, but it was understood he was not free to leave. He sat down in the metal chair across from the agents and calmly placed his hands with his fingers interlocked on the metal table in front of him. The Group supervisor introduced himself and the investigator seated next to him. Luke said it was good to meet them.

"Glad we caught up with you before you left," the group

supervisor said with a smile, "It's always better to talk in person don't you think Luke?"

"Sure."

"Where you headed?"

"Out of town"

"Relocating? Tired of the Michigan winters?

"Sure."

"Got a new job lined up yet?"

"Sure."

"Let me guess, a Pharmaceutical distributor." Luke did not respond. "You know Luke, we contacted the local DEA office in the last three places you've worked, and all three registrants, all pharmaceutical distributors like The Distributing Company, had a theft after you turned in your resignation."

"I've never worked at a company like the Distributing Company," Luke quipped, "they're on another level of insanity."

"Yeah, I can't argue with you on that one," the supervisor said with a semi-fake chuckle, "I've only been there once, and it was enough. Still, it's quite a coincidence wouldn't you say Luke?

"Sure."

"This is not a deposition Hank; you can speak freely."

"I don't know what this is to be honest with you."

"I just have a one question..."

"Well ask it, sounds like you're fishing, and I don't like to fish."

"Did you commit the robberies of controlled substances at your previous three employers?"

"No."

"Were you involved in any of these robberies?"

"Now..." Luke said with a smile, "this is where I ask for my lawyer."

26

It was advertised as the best Sunday jazz brunch in Detroit. Charlie had heard of the swank jazz club housed in a renovated historical building in downtown Detroit, but she had never been. It seemed a little too 'uppity' for her, with a famous executive chef offering pricey menu items and elaborate decor. She preferred her dark hole-in-the-wall clubs with thick jazz and everything on the menu was fried, just like her favorite hole-in-the wall restaurants serving fried fish sandwiches on two slices of white bread. The artists that graced the stage at the downtown club were renowned jazz artists, and that particular Sunday she made a reservation to hear a well-known trumpeter and his trio.

Even dressed up in expensive suits and white tablecloths, good jazz was undeniable. The musicians had a swing that surprised Charlie, and the brunch, while expensive, was delicious. She sat alone at a table for two for most of her meal until a slender white man dressed in an expensive suit asked to join her. He was not a musician, and Charlie had never dated a white man, so her initial reaction was to decline. He gave her a lawyer vibe, so her curiosity got the best of her. He smiled and sat down across from her.

"Hello Ms. Thomas," the man said politely, "can I call you Charlie?"

Charlie lowered her mimosa from her mouth and sat it on the table. Her body stiffened and she instinctively looked around the club to see if anyone was watching her. She removed her right foot from her shoe and used it to remove the expensive designer pump from her left foot in case she had to run or fight. Her black dress was form fitting, but she could easily move in it.

"It's just me, and I'm not a stalker." He spoke in a calm and assuring voice. "I won't take up much of your time, I promise."

"Who are you?"

"I represent an interested party in your upcoming deposition with the California Attorney General's office."

"I'm not interested in what your interested party has to say."

"But he's certainly interested in what you have to say." He took a thick envelope out of his jacket pocket and slid it across the table to her. "Think of it as a downpayment, the rest is payable after a favorable deposition."

Charlie slid the envelope back across the table. "Tell Roman Caesar, or whatever name is on his birth certificate, that I can't be bought, especially with his dirty money."

"I really wish you would reconsider. I fear the next encounter won't be as courteous."

"I already had an 'encounter' with one of his clowns, and he got the drop on me, but it won't happen again. Don't let the corporate lifestyle fool you, I'm still a girl from the hood."

"Yes, I'm sure you are." He slid his chair back and stood to his feet.

"I've never been here before; how did you know I would be here?"

A devious smile slowly stretched across his clean-shaven

face. “Would you like to also know the credit card you used to secure your reservation?” Without giving her time to respond, he walked away. He later sent her a mimosa to replace the one he ruined with his presence. She left it on the table untouched.

Luke briefly considered contacting his handler to request a lawyer, but decided it was not in his best interest. He retained his own attorney and did not let anyone but his attorney know about his encounter with the DEA and Michigan state troopers. He asked his new attorney more than once about attorney client privilege. She assured him she was legally bound to not repeat anything he told her. Still not one hundred percent comfortable, he had no choice but to tell her everything.

The DEA and law enforcement were eager to get Luke back in a room, even with counsel present. One of the officers was familiar with the flamboyant litigator and knew she was like a pit-bull. Many often referred to her as a female dog.

“My client did not commit any thefts of controlled substances or any other substance while employed or after leaving the New Wind Distributing Company nor the previous three employers you mentioned when you questioned him earlier without a lawyer present.” The stage had been set, it would be a contentious meeting.

“Yes,” the DEA group supervisor said as he took a deep breath and exhaled, “we established that earlier. I believe the unanswered question is whether your client had any involvement in the planning or execution of said thefts.”

“Why don’t we focus on New Wind right now, since that is the source of your allegation against my client. That criminal enterprise routinely left product, including controlled substances, in trailers unattended on the property, and on occasion outside of the secured areas. There is video proof of this if you check the exterior and receiving dock cameras. Furthermore, said product was received into inventory and placed on customer orders knowing the product was not in the building and the operations leaders engaged in a scheme to deny the customers claims of not receiving the product and bill them anyway."

The group supervisor digested all that was said and suspected it was true based on what he discovered while on site. He looked at Luke who mirrored his stone-faced gaze.

"Even if what you claim is true, how did the perpetrators know how, when, and where to steal the product? Was that part of a 'scheme' as you say by the operations leaders? It seems as if your client is quite knowledgeable about the availability of this product; maybe he organized or at least informed someone who plotted its illegal removal from the property?"

"What my client may or may not be able to recall depends on what the government is offering."

"We are not offering anything."

"Neither is my client. If you had any evidence of any wrongdoing I would be visiting my client behind bars. What you have, at best, is what you referred to my client as coincidence; I believe the courts refer to it as circumstantial evidence. The Distributing Company will be torn to shreds in court and without credible witnesses or evidence, the plaintiff, in this case would be DOA; I know the government likes its acronyms."

She was right of course, but he did not appreciate being reminded of it.

"Give us a minute." The agents stood up unceremoniously and left the room. As much as it felt like victory, Luke's lawyer reminded him it was not.

. . .

A CALL WAS QUICKLY ARRANGED with the DEA diversion investigators from the Atlanta DEA office. Wanda, the diversion group supervisor from the Atlanta office, was particularly interested in what he had to say. Her case involved an armed robbery with an assault with a deadly weapon. The police still had not solved the case, and the truck driver Carl was a ghost, possibly deceased.

Luke had lawyered up and wanted a deal. Everyone on the call agreed that Luke had not been working alone, and that there was someone higher calling the shots, possibly a syndicate or even organized crime. It was also agreed to engage other agencies, including the FBI. What was not so easily agreed to was how to handle Luke. They were certain that any deal would include full immunity, and that was what caused so much dissent. In the end, it was the Detroit supervisor's decision to make, and he wanted to know what Luke was sitting on.

"TIME TO SHOW YOUR HAND," the supervisor exclaimed when they returned to the small windowless room with the standard mirrored glass, "if you want to play this game it's time to put 'em on the table."

"I'm assuming the winner gets full immunity..." The lawyer's question was expected, but it still stung.

"Depends on what he's holding, but yeah, I can convince the AUSA to offer immunity."

"What is AUSA?" Luke asked his attorney.

"Assistant United States Attorney, they handle DOJ, or Department of Justice cases."

"Well Luke, you can't be acting alone, and nothing personal, but I doubt you're the mastermind of all this, so who or what are we looking at?"

"Hypothetically of course."

"Of course, the supervisor answered Luke's lawyer."

She looked at Luke and nodded her approval. He still was not convinced, and was very uncomfortable, but as his father used to tell him, it was time to piss or get off the pot.

"Hypothetically, there may be a person or organization in Nashville, possibly a freight forwarder or at least posing as one, that directs pick-ups and drop-offs of potentially illegally obtained pharmaceuticals; including potentially counterfeit drugs."

"Is this a regional operation or does it extend across the country."

"If it exists, I think it is all over the country."

The supervisor looked at his agent and the officer standing in the back. They were all thinking the same thing. This may be bigger than they originally thought.

"You made some pretty broad statements, we need details; we need to know your involvement."

Luke glanced at his attorney, and she nodded her approval. 'What the hell' he thought. It was time to empty his bladder.

"Certain individuals are employed at pharmaceutical wholesalers, distributors, pharmacy chain distribution centers, and even manufacturer's distribution centers to learn the operation from the inside and determine the best way to get product out basically unnoticed or at least without drawing a lot of attention. They move from place to place in different states."

"And you were one of them?"

"Yes."

"A lot of attention was drawn in McDonough, Georgia; it was an armed robbery, and someone was assaulted. What happened there?"

"That was not us. Our operation involved a truck driver and a supervisor on the inside. What happened there was a rogue group of armed men staged an ambush and robbed the facility. That was the first time controlled substances were involved which got the DEA involved."

"What about here in Livonia, Michigan?"

"Man, that shit was so unorganized we didn't know what was on the trucks. Controlled substances must have been on one of 'em."

"Phentermine was one of the drugs taken and that stuff is basically speed. We're cracking down on rogue weight loss clinics who are selling it like candy."

"Never heard of it."

"Who do you work for?"

"I don't know."

"What do you mean you don't know?"

"I've never met anyone, and they never use names. All I know is there is a freight forwarding company in Nashville that I've seen on some paperwork, but I don't know if it's legit."

"You can provide the name and address?"

"Yep."

"How do you make contact?"

"Phone... why"

"We may need you to arrange a meeting."

"Hell no. If they get any hint that I'm talking to you I'm a dead man."

"We can protect you."

"Bullshit, that's what the other guy thought."

"What other guy?"

Luke dropped his head; he knew he had said too much. He shook his head in frustration. "Look, I told you what I know."

"I think there's more you're not telling us Luke. Your deal is contingent on you telling us everything."

"I need to talk to my lawyer, alone."

"Sure Luke, sure."

ALONE WITH HIS lawyer outside in the parking lot, Luke described what he knew of the full operation, even the part he is not a part of. She did not take notes, but she listened intently to every word. Luke paced as he talked, it was his idea to talk outside to ensure he was not overheard; he knew the information he had would make a much larger case than the couple thefts of controlled substances at a couple warehouses that the DEA supervisor was salivating over. It was much larger, and far more dangerous, which is why he did not want to talk, and his lawyer agreed, at least not just to the DEA.

"MY CLIENT IS a goldfish swimming with sharks," she stated when they were back in the room and seated, "but I am not telling you anything you don't already know."

"It's obvious this is bigger than him."

"Oh, that's an understatement."

"I'm all ears."

"We need more ears at the table, particularly FBI and AUSA who can guarantee not only immunity but also protection if needed. I'm talking totally new identity; I want my client to become a one-hundred-and-seventy-pound black man with stellar credit if necessary."

"A bit much don't you think?" The supervisor smirked. "We're not trying to take down Gotti."

She did not respond vocally, but her facial expression and demeanor suggested they could be.

"I haven't heard anything so far that warrants what you are asking."

"Like I said, bring in more ears if you want to hear what he told me outside."

"It doesn't work like that..."

"Ask the FBI about a truck driver in Memphis who was working with them on a case. Ask them about the envelopes and how he was murdered under their protection. Ask them if they've found any more envelopes."

"Envelopes?" The supervisor asked with a crinkled brow, "what envelopes? What are you talking about?"

"Just ask... I might know where they can find a couple more."

Everyone looked around at each other contemplating the next move.

"Okay we're done here," Luke's lawyer exclaimed as she stood to her feet and tapped Luke on the shoulder for him to stand as well, "anything else will require a larger audience from the government alphabet swamp."

"I don't think your client is just a goldfish."

"Whatever he is, it's not him you want."

"I guess I don't have to tell you not to leave the city," the supervisor warned, "we have eyes on you."

"You're right, you didn't have to tell him."

27

It was a scheduled visit, primarily so the desired attendees would be present. The diversion group supervisor for the DEA Detroit office planned to take an administrative action and wanted Stanley to be present to argue his case; it would at least be entertaining if nothing else. His statement would also likely determine if an Order to Show Cause was issued or an Immediate Suspension Order.

The group supervisor arrived with one of the diversion investigators from his office. They were let in without incident and offered coffee and snacks, which they both refused. The pleasantries were quick and shallow, the purpose of the visit was made clear immediately and without apology. They needed to review camera footage and needed Stanley and Hank present for the review.

As Stanley led the procession to the security room, which was just a room with several monitors displaying the views from all the security cameras on the property, he tried to figure out what Luke had told them. He knew they spoke with him, otherwise they would not have come back so soon demanding to see the cameras. He was sure Luke told them about storing product outside, and how anyone could have stolen it. The warehouse employees knew the product was stored outside and any one of them could have made arrangements to have the trailers stolen; but Luke was the only one who knew about the product stored in the trailers outside the gate. What had Luke told them? He was sure he would soon find out.

"Let's just focus on the exterior cameras," the supervisor said as Hank sat in the chair in front of the monitors, "particularly the area out back where the trucks come in to unload."

"Sure," Hank said as he made a few clicks on the mouse, "what exactly are we looking for?"

"I'll let you know when I see it."

Hank put the camera views on the two monitors from the three exterior cameras showing the rear of the facility. There was a truck parked at one of the dock bays, but there was no other activity.

"Let's go back about forty-five days." There was a confidence in the supervisor's voice that Stanley did not appreciate.

"That's pretty specific," Stanley exclaimed, "again, what are you hoping to find? Maybe we can save you some time."

"Well, I'm looking for the exact time you started storing controlled substances outside on trailers unattended after receiving the product into your inventory."

"Well, we can't help you find something that's not there." Stanley tried to sound as confident as the supervisor; his confidence was superficial, however.

"I don't know if our cameras go back that far..." Hank said timidly.

"Your SOP states you store footage for sixty days before deleting it," the supervisor exclaimed cutting Hank off mid lie, "is your SOP not correct?"

Hank put his head down and vowed to himself not to say another word. A bead of sweat dropped from his forehead onto the keyboard as he maneuvered the mouse, clicking on the date he wanted to display. Stanley noticed the sweat and knew the supervisor had as well. He instinctively rubbed his own forehead and was disappointed by the dampness that met his four fingers. Nothing and no-one had ever caused perspiration to secrete from Stanley's body, and he was a little concerned. Hank may have been right, maybe he was losing it.

"Right there," the supervisor exclaimed as he pointed at the screen, "play it from that point."

Hank reluctantly did as the supervisor asked, and everyone in the room watched as truck after truck waited in line to dump their trailers. Hank was seen on camera haplessly trying to direct traffic and collect paperwork from the drivers. The exact scene played out for hours which bled into days. Hank wanted to find a hole to crawl down into.

"This looks like trucks dropping off product and parking it along the fence out back. Hank, I see you collecting signatures and paperwork, but I have yet to see one single pallet be unloaded; and we've looked at over a week's worth of footage now. I'm sure the FDA would be curious of the temperature on the back of those trucks in the summertime."

"The DEA's only concern is controlled substances," Stanley chimed in, "how do you know, or can prove controlled substances are on those trucks? It's our policy to get those inside the cage and vault right away. We know which trucks have controlled substances when we review the paperwork."

"It doesn't look like he's reviewing anything, just collecting paperwork and moving on to the next."

"And are you making your case on what something looks like?"

"Of course not," the supervisor responded to Stanley with a smirk, "let's keep looking. By the way, your controlled substance pallets are wrapped in black shrink wrap, correct?"

Hank looked at Stanley as they both wondered where the

supervisor was going with the question. Neither man answered the question.

"I'll take that as a yes; at least that's what we were told when we questioned employees on the receiving dock during our initial walkthrough."

Stanley's nerves hardened into anger. His now dry brow had forged irritated crevices, and he grew weary of the game.

"I don't know what Luke told you before he struck a deal," Stanley said angrily, "or what kind of foreplay you're getting out of this, but you're gonna have to get your rocks off somewhere else. What else do you want to see; I have things to do." The bravado was back in his voice, and Hank fought back a smile. They may go down, but they wouldn't be on their knees. Stanley would go down swinging.

The supervisor stood straight up and clenched his fists and released them. The challenge had been accepted.

"Fast forward slowly," the supervisor instructed, "I'll let you know when to stop."

Hank begrudgingly did as he was told, but he made his displeasure known with a loud sigh. Stanley's defiance had emboldened Hank as well.

"There! Right there!" It was not the supervisor's intention to yell, but he was caught up in the moment. "Go back a couple frames and let it play."

Hank knew exactly what it was when he saw it, and it was not good. The video showed a truck pull into the dock area, and the driver jumped down from the cab and opened the trailer door. A pallet wrapped in black shrink wrap can be seen in the trailer. The driver climbed back into the cab and attempted to back into the dock but was stopped by Hank. Luke entered the scene and motioned for the driver to continue but Hank jumped in front of the trailer causing the driver to slam on his brakes. Luke and Hank could be seen arguing until Luke finally threw his hands in the air and walked away. The driver jumped down from the cab again and closed the trailer door. Hank pointed to the fence area and the driver climbed back in his truck and dropped the trailer along the fence with the others. He handed Hank the paperwork and drove away.

"Now..." the supervisor said calmly, "no sound was needed to know what just happened; it was like watching an old black and white silent movie, but in color."

"What do you think happened?" Stanley continued to challenge him.

"A driver tried to deliver a load to the dock and was denied. There was at least one pallet of controlled substances on the truck and Luke knew that and tried to get the product to the dock. An argument ensued, I presume about the controlled substances on the truck, but Hank, being the senior manager of the two prevailed. Now, let's see how long the product stayed outside on the truck."

Hank fast forwarded the footage until a truck is seen retrieving the trailer and backing into one of the dock bays. It was six days after the trailer was initially dropped.

"Six days..." the supervisor said as he shook his head, "Six days of controlled substances left unattended, and six days of that product and whatever else is on the truck sitting outside in July on a hot truck. I assume the product was sent to customers and not quarantined. I will make sure the FDA and Michigan State Board of Pharmacy come ASAP to review this video; and I will need a copy just in case it gets accidentally deleted. Needless to say, we will be issuing an order to show cause for obvious CFR violations, as well as an immediate suspension order due to the severity of the security breakdowns as well as record keeping and storage. It is definitely in the public's best interest that you cease all controlled substance operations immediately."

There was no rebuttal from Stanley, he knew it would be futile, and it was not the time. The final outcome would be decided by an administrative judge, not his stuffy security office.

Three FDA agents arrived early the next morning and reviewed the footage in detail. They were in the security room with Hank for hours combing through footage and recording dates and time stamps. They recorded when the product arrived and the date and time it was moved to the temperature-controlled warehouse. All packing lists and paperwork were matched to the product that sat outside, and manufacturers were contacted to determine what temperature range and what length of time was within allowable parameters. One pallet of refrigerated product was left on a truck for four days and was not quarantined. That product was issued a level one recall, and notices were sent out immediately. For the other ambient product left outside, product disposition would be determined by the manufacturers. Recalls would be issued as necessary. Regardless of the final tally and product efficacy determination, the penalties would be stiff.

Charlie first saw the white Chevrolet Malibu parked on the street three houses down from her house two days earlier but thought nothing of it. The next day it was a silver Ford Taurus, and as she backed out of her driveway, she noticed a black Buick sitting in the same spot. The white male wearing a baseball cap could have been the same guy from the previous two days, but she was not certain. She smiled as she passed, it was not a friendly or timid smile, but a challenging one. She had warned them, so whatever happened next would not be her fault.

28

New Wind suits descended on the Distributing Company like a SWAT team. Senior management from Legal, Corporate Security, Human Resources, and Operations stepped out of the rented full-size van with purpose. A purpose which was stifled when they could not gain entry to the building. When Stanley was alerted of their presence, he gave strict orders not to let them inside. No one present from the Atlanta office had badge access, so they had no way to gain entry.

Calls to Stanley's phone went unanswered, as did calls to the main line. When the police arrived, per Stanley's request, the two uniformed officers were let inside the lobby where Stanley met them and explained the situation from his perspective. The New Wind team could only stand outside and watch. His name was on the lease and all licenses, Stanley explained, and taxes, including state taxes, were paid by the Distributing Company, not New Wind; the Distributing Company was its own entity. No one was being held inside against their will, and employees were free to leave whenever they wanted. The matter with the people outside was a personal matter, and they were trespassing. He also mentioned for good measure how much he and the Distributing Company contributed to the city of Livonia and the police department.

Unfortunately, the officers explained to the furious team from New Wind, there was nothing they could do. No crime had been committed, and after interviewing several employees they confirmed that no was being held hostage, and no one was in danger. They could seek relief through the court, which a director from legal had already initiated through the corporate office after explaining the situation. The team piled back into the van and left, but Stanley knew they would be back as soon as they could get a Judge's ear.

Stanley made preemptive calls to his closest trading partners, including Roman, who had not been in contact with Stanley for an unusually extended period of time. Roman heard something in Stanley's voice he had never heard before in all the years he had worked with him, and he was concerned. Stanley was cracking and sounded on the verge of crumbling like a stale cookie. Their previous call had caused a divide that Roman had intended to address but had not. This latest conversation was a call to action.

Emperor drugs, like most other trading partners contacted, cut all ties with the Distributing Company. Dominic instructed his old friend to never contact him again, but Stanley reminded him it would not be that easy. Whomever was coming for him would be knocking on his door as well. It was the same message for everyone who wanted to wash their hands of Stanley and his company. Betrayal was a bitter pill to swallow, and Stanley spit it back out at them.

THE MAN WEARING the Detroit Lions baseball cap sitting in the tan pickup truck did not notice the three black men sitting in the Cadillac three houses down from where he was waiting for Charlie to make an appearance. He had surveyed Charlie long enough to know her routine and was ready to make a move. When Charlie backed out of her driveway, she glanced at him to make sure he was there and saw her father's Cadillac parked on the street as well. It was not her idea, but her father insisted, with or without her approval. She knew he would overreact if she told him about her meeting at the jazz club and her new stalker, but she knew it would be worse if she had not told him and he found out after the fact.

Convinced Charlie was gone for a while, the man in the Lions cap got out of his car and walked to the back of Charlie's house. The three men in the Cadillac waited and then followed him to the back of the house. The door had been kicked in, and they made their entrance through the door which had been left ajar. Charlie pulled into her driveway, and the man in the cap panicked and tried to escape through the back door but ran into Charlie's father and her two cousins Earl and Craig. Charlie was the only one who called them by their government names, their street name was far more notorious.

"Where you goin' muthafucka'?" Craig did not expect an answer to his question which was more of a threat.

"Yeah," Earl added, "you here now."

"Look, I don't want any trouble." His hands were held in the air.

"You wanted trouble when you broke into my daughter's house!" Charlie's father was about to swing at the man when Charlie walked through her back door.

"Daddy! I got this!" She looked at her cousins and shook her head. "You had to bring these two fools..."

"Hey Cuz," Craig greeted, "you know we got cho' back."

"Hey, just let me go," the man pleaded, "I promise I'll never bother you again."

"Shut the fuck up!" Earl punched him in his gut as he yelled, causing him to fold over and gasp for breath."

Charlie studied the man when she heard his voice. There was a familiarity that made her hairs stand up. He was similar height and build as...

"Roman sent yo' punk ass back to finish me off huh?"

"Who the hell is Roman?" His ignorance was sincere and that threw Charlie for a loop.

"Wait a minute," Charlie's father chimed in, "this the one that jumped you before?"

"Who sent you?" Charlie asked.

Craig retrieved a 9mm from his waist and cocked it before pointing at the man's chest. "Don't make her ask again."

"Stanley...Stanley Forsythe."

"Damn..." That was all she could say.

An unexpected pause did little to dampen the edginess of the situation. The cousins were ready to act, and their target was just hoping it would end soon, one way or another. Charlie was still digesting the name she had been fed but it did nothing for her anger and desire for retribution. She reflected on the surprise meeting at the jazz club when she was offered hush money. She had assumed Roman sent him, but he never confirmed or denied when she said Roman's name. Was Stanley behind that threat as well? Regardless of who was behind it, she channeled her anger on the man in front of her.

"Who the fuck is Stanley?" Craig asked no one in particular, "and where can we find his ass?"

"He works with Charlie," her father exclaimed, "over in Livonia somewhere."

"Oh, I got one for his ass," Earl proclaimed, "as soon as I put one in this muthafucka."

"Leave us alone," Charlie finally said to her father and cousins, "we have some unfinished business."

"Oh hell naw," Earl shouted, "this muthafucka' gon' get got!"

"And he will," Charlie responded, "but it will be by my hand not yours; and definitely not by a bullet; yo' ass can barely stay outta jail now."

Earl and Craig looked at their uncle who nodded his head.

"Wait outside," Charlie instructed, "only one of us is walking' outta here on our own. If it's him, let 'em go."

The three men did as they were instructed. Before leaving, Charlie's father kicked the man on the side of his left knee causing it to buckle and him to drop down onto the other knee before standing up wincing in pain.

"Daddy! I want a fair fight."

"It wasn't a fair fight last time when he surprised you and got the jump on you." He walked out the house before Charlie could respond. Alone in the house, they prepared for battle.

"Get outta here," Charlie commanded as she limped out of the house, "I'm about to call the police and y'all don't need to be around when they get here."

"You alright? Her father asked concerned. In addition to the limp, Charlie had blood trickling from her nose and a few other battle scars."

"I'm okay, go back to Flint."

He nodded and the three men walked to the Cadillac. Charlie dialed 911 and reported the break-in. The intruder was still in her house unconscious, and she needed the police right away.

When the New Wind team returned to the Distributing Company, they were immediately buzzed in by the smiling receptionist. The four police officers and the legal document that was flashed were not needed, as they met no resistance. Stanley greeted them with a smile and handshake when they made it to the office area, as if the incident earlier did not happen. The Atlanta team looked curiously at Stanley and each other and would later ask when they were alone if Stanley was taking medication.

They demanded to have badges which gave them permanent twenty-four-hour access to the building, and badges were made for them with no questions asked. Stanley escorted them to the conference room and made sure they were comfortable.

"Can I get you anything," Stanley asked, "I can have lunch brought in if you like?"

"That won't be necessary," the operations vp quipped, "we had lunch after we left the courthouse after your stunt earlier."

"Did you go to Benny's across the street from the courthouse? They have the best burgers in town."

"No, maybe next time we need to secure a court order we'll keep Benny's in mind."

"I feel like that might be soon," Stanley said with a smirk, "this feels very... legal."

As if on cue, Stanley's lawyer walked through the front door and into the office area. Stanley waved him in. The looks he received as he strutted into the conference room and sat next to Stanley would have made a lesser man uncomfortable, but he was as conceited as Stanley, so he actually enjoyed the moment.

"This is my attorney, Ben; I asked him to join us because well... I believe lawyers should talk to lawyers."

"That's really not necessary," The legal vp exclaimed, "There are no legal actions being taken or discussed today?"

"Maybe not today, but Ben needs to be aware of any potential future actions and discussions as well. I understand you have outside counsel preparing some type of lawsuit where I might be named as defendant?"

As hard as they tried, the Legal and Human Resources executives let a tinge of surprise and awe blush their cheeks. Ben and Stanley smiled in unison.

"We don't feel it's appropriate to discuss company business with your attorney present?"

"Aren't you one of the company's attorneys? If you can be in the room to represent the company's interest, then Ben can be present to represent mine."

"But you are still an employee of the company."

"So fire me now instead of the date you have circled on your calendars down in Atlanta."

"Why does everything have to be a fucking' fight with you!?" The outburst came from the operations vp. "A goddamn test of wills to see who has the biggest dick or who can outsmart the other!" He immediately regretted his eruption of what everyone else was thinking but would not verbalize. He lost control, but did not apologize.

"Is this how you talk to your employees?" Ben asked the question looking to seize the moment. "Maybe we should be the ones seeking relief from a court." Ben wrote every word that spewed from the operations vp's mouth on his legal pad.

"We're not on the record here," The legal vp exclaimed.

"Should we be? Your colleague, who is also my client's superior, just defamed my client's character, and in front of his other superiors at the company. I presume one of you is HR."

"Okay," the human resources vp sighed, "let's just calm down and stay on course..."

"What course is that?" Stanley asked interrupting her. "Why are we, no why are you here?"

"The Distributing Company's DEA registration is suspended," the operations vp said in a slightly milder tone, "and the FDA has about a quarter of the inventory quarantined pending testing and have initiated two recalls with more possible. I'm sure the State Board of Pharmacy will be knocking on the door any second now to conduct an investigation and possibly revoke the distributor registration and shut us down. Why do you think we're here?" He paused to take a breath and to brace for Stanleys smart ass comment, but Stanley sat quiet.

"Who is the antagonist now?" Ben asked in general.

"We're closing the Livonia site." The human resources vp made the proclamation as she tired of the back and forth. "With the impending California AG's complaint, and whatever action that follows coupled with the DEA, FDA, and possible state actions, we're being preemptive with some restructuring."

"Restructuring?" Stanley's question was genuine.

"Yes," the operations vp answered with renewed vigor, "we will be ceasing operations here and moving them to our facility in Memphis, Olive Branch, Mississippi actually; it has the space to accommodate this business model and inventory, and the distribution network in Memphis is outstanding."

"With a new management team, I presume."

"Yes, but we are keeping you on in a different, but important role as we rebuild the business." The operation vp's answer sounded scripted, and Stanley was sure it was.

"Rebuild the business?"

"Yes, but with better guardrails. Look, when not being a criminal mastermind... sorry, strike that, what I mean is you actually have a great business mind for this business model, and we want to capitalize on that. We feel that in a different position, where you can advise instead of dictate, we can still make this business profitable *and* compliant."

"What about my team?"

"They'll be offered severance packages," the human resources vp chimed in, "with stipulations of course, but today is their last day."

"I need to keep Hank to help with the transition."

"We're bringing in an ops manager from another facility to manage the product transfer and other transition duties. Just so we're clear, as of right now, you no longer have any management responsibility or authority for this business." The ops vp looked Stanley directly in the eye as he spoke.

"What about my suppliers and trading partners?"

"Our current partners will be evaluated individually, and a determination will be made on each." The operations vp was sure to stress 'our.' "All inventory not currently quarantined by FDA will be shipped to Olive Branch; trucks will start arriving midweek. Order fulfillment will continue here, minus controlled substances of course, until the end of the month when it will fully transition to Olive Branch."

"That's less than two weeks away; that's pretty aggressive isn't it."

"We've had teams working on this for a while now."

"You'll never make the money I do." Stanley uttered the words as if they were a curse. It was his last act of defiance, at least for the day.

"And we'll never pay the fines you will either," the operations vp exclaimed, "in fact, in the end the Distributing Company will be in the red, and you'll most likely owe us money." He had a fake smile on his face, but he was serious. Stanley did not bother to manufacture a smile, he just stood up and walked out of the conference room.

"OKAY, YOU HAVE OUR ATTENTION."

"And who are you," Luke's attorney asked frankly, "and who are the others in the room and on the phone?"

"I'm special agent in charge Miller, from the FBI Southeast region. On the phone I believe we have AUSA Pam Hall, also from the Southeast region, as well as detectives from the Henry County sheriff's office in Georgia and the DEA diversion group supervisor from the Atlanta, Georgia office. I believe you know the DEA diversion group supervisor from the Detroit office right here and in the back is special agent Banks here from the Detroit FBI office as well."

Luke's attorney jotted down every name and title rattled off. Luke was nervous, and it showed, as much as he tried to be calm.

"I'm Wanda, diversion group supervisor from Atlanta, I'd like to ask a few questions to get things started if that's okay with everyone."

No one objected, and Luke looked to his attorney who nodded his head.

"First, I want to hear from the AUSA on the phone, Ms. Hall, regarding the agreement we have in place. I want to make sure my client doesn't get bit when he throws you meaty bones and you release the dogs."

After receiving necessary assurances, Wanda was cleared to start her line of questioning. She smiled and scooted her chair close to the table so she could lean over as close as she could across the table from Luke. She would have extended a hand if she could reach him. Luke was not fooled by her friendly demeanor, he remained guarded.

"What happened in McDonough, Georgia Luke? Tell me everything, I need to know. Several agencies have been working this case and... well, it's like everyone involved was a ghost."

Luke smiled at what he perceived as a compliment. "There was a truck driver..."

"Carl?"

"Yes Ma'am, Carl."

"Do you know where Carl is?"

"No, dead or playing dead as far as I know."

"I'm sorry, please proceed."

"Sure, Carl was one of our best mail delivery guys, he had no family to speak of, so he worked constantly, never turned down a job."

"Mail delivery?" The question came from AUSA Hall on the phone."

"That's just what we called them. They would get their assignments dropped in their mailbox in an unmarked envelope."

"Assignments?" Again, AUSA Hall.

"Where and when to pick up and where to drop off."

"Pick up and drop off what?"

Luke glanced at his attorney before answering, just in case. "Drugs, and medical supplies; they could be stolen, counterfeit, I believe what you call adulterated, anything."

"Can we get back to Carl please?" Wanda asked in a different tone than she was feeling.

"Carl was supposed to do his normal pickup and drop. Every Thursday he picked up a load, I made sure there was extra product on the dock that was not on the packing slips and Carl would make a stop before he got to the depot and the extra product was unloaded and taken to our customers. The rest of the product was taken to the depot where it was sorted and delivered to the pharmacies, hospitals or whatever."

"You said he was supposed to do his normal pickup," Wanda stated, "what happened the night in question."

"Hell if I know. Some guys with guns were on the back of the trailer and jumped off when the truck pulled into the dock and that's when all hell broke loose. We thought Carl had to be in on it, but he swore he wasn't, and he was really scared for his life. We had him picked up, but there was a bad accident, and Carl was either killed or he walked away; but his body wasn't found with the others in the car."

"And you haven't heard from him since..."

"Nope, dead or playing dead, either way he wasn't talking so..."

"And the guys that robbed the warehouse?"

"Could've been any of you for all I know."

Wanda leaned back in her chair and interlocked her fingers and thumbs, trying to figure out if he was telling the truth. He had no reason to lie, not with the deal he had on the table.

"Anything else?" The question came from FBI agent in charge Miller and was directed at Wanda, who shook her head. "Okay Luke, what do you know about a Clint Hardy out of Memphis?"

"You know as much as I know," Luke said with a smirk, "He was working with you right? He was under your protection... until he wasn't."

"You mean until you killed him."

"I never killed anybody," Luke responded to agent Miller, "you got him killed."

"I don't think you're as innocent as you claim to be," agent Miller blasted, "and I don't think you're low man on the totem-pole either; you seem to be quite knowledgeable about the operation."

"My client never claimed to be the janitor, but he's not a decision maker either. Now if you want to find out who is, I suggest you let my client talk... uninterrupted."

After a tense silence, the AUSA spoke through the phone. "Please continue."

"I'll start with a freight forwarder in Nashville, this is who I technically reported to..."

Luke spent the next hour explaining the structure as he knew it and provided contact information and addresses for anyone and any entity he had information for. He was interrupted frequently with questions, but he was able to tell the story he wanted to tell. The agents took a lot of notes, even though the conversation was recorded. The questioning went relatively smooth, with the only challenges coming from FBI agent Miller. Before sharing his final piece of information, Luke looked at his attorney, who paused before giving the nod.

"One last thing," Luke stated before taking a deep breath

and slowly exhaling, "there were several customers receiving the product we obtained, but there was one big one down in Florida, Miami I think. I don't know his name, but I would say more than half the product went to him. I get the feeling he's a major player in getting product distributed."

"It wouldn't happen to be Roman Caesar, would it?" The question came from agent Miller.

"Like I said, I don't know his name, but... now that I think about it, it seems like Rome was in one of the names of the companies I overheard."

"Any invoices, packing slips or other paperwork that might have a name and address on it?"

"Are you serious?" Luke looked at him in disbelief. "There are no paper trails in this business."

29

Charlie did not know what to expect when she walked into the meeting room at the hotel in downtown Detroit for her deposition. Her lawyer had spent numerous hours with her in prep, reviewing documents, emails, and throwing questions at her to see how she responded. She was surprised to see the video camera; her lawyer had not mentioned she would be recorded. She was also surprised to see lawyers from New Wind in the room, not that it mattered to her; she was there to tell the truth, regardless of who the truth smacked in the face, including her own.

After being sworn in, the three attorneys from the California AG's office jumped right into the deposition. They thanked her for being there, as if she had a choice, had her state her name for the record, then started with general background questions about her education and work history. She was sure they already knew the information, but figured they had to get it for the record. Thankfully, only one attorney asked the questions for the AG's office.

"So, Ms. Thomas, prior to joining the Davidson Distributing Company here in Michigan, you worked at the Davidson corporate office in Stamford, Connecticut correct?"

"Yes."

"And what was your position?"

"I was director of purchasing."

"And can you please tell us what your job function was as director of purchasing?"

"I managed the procurement of all pharmaceutical product for Davidson Enterprises and its distribution centers."

"Including the Distributing Company?"

"No."

"Why not?"

"They purchased their own product."

"I see..." He paused for effect. "Was the Distributing Company a separate company?"

"No, technically it was a Davidson distribution center, but it operated as if it was a separate company."

"So, even though they were under the Davidson corporate structure, they purchased pharmaceuticals separate from Davidson but from the same suppliers?"

"No, I purchased directly from the manufacturers, but they purchased from... alternate sources."

"And by alternate sources you mean..."

"Wholesalers, pharmacies, diverters, anyone they could get product from."

One of the New Wind lawyers jumped to his feet. "Objection!"

"This is not a courtroom sir," another of the California lawyers exclaimed, "this is a deposition."

"I want her comment stricken from the record."

"The Judge will review this transcript and will take any action he deems appropriate. Might I remind you that you are here as a courtesy, a courtesy that can and will be rescinded if there is another outburst."

Charlie's attorney leaned over and reminded her to stick to the facts and to refrain from her opinions or smart-ass remarks. Charlie accepted her guidance and criticism because they were kindred spirits.

"I'm sorry Ms. Thomas, please continue."

"That was it, I have nothing else to add."

"Okay, great." He looked down at his notes. "So, when did you join the Distributing Company?"

"April 2001."

"Was it your choice to join Mr. Forsythe at the Distributing Company?"

"No, New Wind had acquired Davidson, and they shut down everything but the Distributing Company. Mr. Davidson offered me an opportunity at the Distributing Company or a severance package."

"One would think that New Wind acquired Davidson just for the Distributing Company."

The New Wind lawyers wanted to object but thought better of it. Charlie did not take the bait, so he moved to the next question. He picked up a stack of papers and showed them to Charlie.

"There are quite a few emails here from you to various individuals at New Wind. I'm not going to read them all of course, but I would like to discuss the subject matter of a few. It seems that when you first started at the Distributing Company you initiated emails with Stanley frequently, which he never responded to, and then they appeared to stop. Did anything happen?"

"I didn't have access to the front office for a while and he didn't answer my calls, so I had to send emails."

"After reading some of these emails, I'm sure he finally gave you access just to get you to stop."

It was Charlie's attorney who objected and reminded the

counselor to just ask questions seeking relevant facts. He apologized.

"Emperor Drugs... you inquired more than once about why they returned product the first of the month that they had just purchased at the end of the month, and they returned different lot numbers. You even went as far as to call it drug laundering in an email to Nicole..."

"I said potential drug laundering," Charlie exclaimed cutting him off.

"And what exactly is drug laundering?"

"It's just a term I made up."

"I see... I think we all have an idea as to what you meant by it, but I'll move on."

"Please." Charlie's attorney was not amused.

"Who is Roman Caesar?"

Even though Charlie knew Roman's name would come up, the question still caused a visible reaction on her face and body language; one that did not go unnoticed by everyone in the room. Her active mind slowed, and her focus sharpened. Fear never entered her consciousness, nor did any threats whether perceived or real. She thought about her lawyer's guidance; 'keep your smart-ass comments to yourself.'

"Mr. Caesar, through his multiple companies under the Rome umbrella was a trading partner of the Distributing Company."

"And by trading partner, you mean..."

"He bought product from the Distributing Company and the Distributing Company bought product from his companies."

"Was he a good trading partner?"

"What do you mean by good?" Charlie was slightly annoyed by the question. "A lot of product moved between the companies, so I guess he was a good partner."

"Did you ever purchase product from him prior to joining the Distributing Company?"

"No, I only purchased directly from the manufacturers."

"In fact, you instructed Mr. Forsythe to tell Mr. Caesar to never contact you because you would never, and I quote, 'pollute our supply with his dirty product.'"

"I never said that in an email."

"It was a voice message you left on Mr. Forsythe's phone. However, there is an email from you to Nicole Fitzsimmons, your boss, where you call Mr. Caesar and his companies shady and crooked, and state that we should not do business with him."

Her first lesson in discovery was one she would always remember; everything was discoverable. She did not respond because his statements did not contain a question. She later learned why. There was an extended pause, as her attorney warned there would be, to see if she would fill the silence with words.

"What was your role at the Distributing Company Ms. Thomas?"

"I mainly reviewed pedigrees, conducted site visits, managed inventory that went to other New Wind facilities, and..."

"Other New Wind facilities," he interrupted, "so Distributing Company inventory was transferred to the other New Wind facilities as well?"

"Yes."

He looked at his two colleagues and made a note on his legal pad as if they had just uncovered something new and noteworthy.

"You said you reviewed pedigrees. What exactly were you looking for on the pedigrees?"

"Primarily that there were no restricted companies on the

pedigree, and not more than three suppliers including the authorized distributor."

"Why three?"

"Buzz around industry is that is what the PDMA will be recommending, and I've heard it at conferences, so I wanted to be proactive; plus, it just made sense, I've seen pedigrees that were just ridiculous with the number of companies that touched the product."

"What makes a company restricted?"

"Findings from one of my site visits, knowledge of previous counterfeit or adulterated product activity, passing false pedigrees, etc."

"Based on what you just described, is Rome Pharmaceuticals or any of the companies under it on the restricted list?"

"Nope."

"Why not? Based on what you've said in emails and here today, and from what we have discovered about Rome, it just seems like a no brainer."

"Stanley wouldn't let me, I tried."

"Did you report to Stanley?"

"No."

"You both reported to Nicole Fitzsimmons, who has management oversight for the Distributing Company correct?"

"Yes, or so I thought."

He paused and took more notes.

"Did you do any type of verifications of the transactions or just..."

"I started asking for copies of invoices after about three or four months of reviewing pedigrees."

"And prior to you, were pedigrees reviewed for the same criteria?"

"I don't know."

"Were site visits conducted?"

"I have no idea."

"Do you have any knowledge of what type of due diligence was performed on the suppliers, pedigrees or product, prior to you?"

"No."

"Would it surprise you to learn that we could find no evidence of anything being done."

Charlie shrugged her shoulders but did not answer.

"You are no longer an employee at New Wind are you Ms. Thomas?"

"No, I am not."

"Was this your decision?"

"It was mutual."

Charlie drank from the cup of water on the table in front of her. The attorneys from the California AG's office huddled to discuss the next round of questions, which would be conducted by a different lawyer.

The questioning was more intense, primarily against the company and Stanley Forsythe, and numerous emails were reviewed and confirmed for authenticity. The AG's office asked all the right questions, and Charlie did not have to embellish or pepper her responses with sarcasm. She was in her element and seemed to gain favor with the team deposing her. Even the stenographer, the third black woman in the room, smiled with pride a few times as she transcribed Charlie's words. At one point during the questioning one of the New Wind lawyers wrote a single word on his legal pad and underlined it; 'settle!!'

30

FBI agents littered the grounds of the freight forwarding facility in Nashville like leaves on a lawn on a windy autumn day. They unplugged and took equipment, gathered documents, and carried boxes out of the building and loaded them onto vans to be hauled away for thorough scrutiny. Three individuals were brought out in handcuffs, including Luke's direct handler whom he had never met face to face, but had seen in person on several occasions.

The freight forwarding company was legitimate and solvent, but not as profitable as the criminal enterprise. It also laundered money for an organization whose tentacles extended coast to coast, but the Nashville company was home base. No one talked, not even when threatened or offered sweet deals, and the FBI suspected the ladder extended higher than Nashville and the individuals in handcuffs. Unfortunately, nothing on the computers, phones, or in the boxes gave any clue as to who or where they might be. They did find connections to drug counterfeiters and traffickers in South America and Asia but knew that rabbit hole was bottomless. They needed to get someone to talk.

A loaded box-truck bound for South Florida was still sitting at the dock when the FBI swarmed the facility. The truck was released with the grand hope that it would lead them to the infamous customer in Miami. The driver gained a passenger, an armed FBI agent, to chaperone the trip south to make sure it stayed on course. He was also there to make sure the driver did not call ahead with a warning.

The truck arrived in the middle of the night, and both the driver and passenger were sleep deprived. Local agents were in hiding somewhere close to the building which had six dock doors and one man door; the only light was a dim bulb over the man door. The building was not far from the Miami International airport, and there were other industrial buildings in the area but there was no activity. A pickup truck and a Porsche sports car were parked near the man door. The FBI agent made a call and was told his backup was in place and had eyes on the truck. They were ready to move.

The agent instructed the driver to back the box truck to the dock door furthest from the man door with the light and a potential camera, although he did not see one. The driver slid out of the driver seat of the truck and looked around. He knew he was being watched, and it did not take long for the agents and police officers to appear out of the darkness. They surrounded the building and stood out of view as the driver walked up the stairs to the door. He rang the buzzer and looked straight ahead. The camera was in the peep hole in the door. After a couple of minutes, the door opened wide, and the agents stormed the door with guns drawn and entered the building with the driver who was immediately placed in handcuffs.

There were three men inside the building, and the one driving the Porsche was easily identified. The other two were dock workers and claimed not to speak English as they were being handcuffed. A claim which was quickly debunked. The man who was dressed like he was going to a dance club was handcuffed and patted down. There was a revolver tucked in his waist in the middle of his back. An agent retrieved both the weapon and his wallet.

"Mr. Rivera," the agent exclaimed as he looked over the license, "this your place?"

There was no response, and the agent forced him down onto a nearby chair. The two terrified dock workers were taken to another end of the warehouse to be questioned.

"Is that your product on the truck or are you just storing it for someone else?" Still no response other than a smile. "You know your friends over there are probably doing a lot of talking."

"They don't know shit. All they do is load and unload trucks."

"I bet you get quite a few trucks through here."

"Yeah, your mother makes a few deliveries every week."

"Who are you working with?"

"Nobody and anybody. I'm in the business of moving freight. You got a shipment headed to Miami, I can cross dock it for you. Take one of my cards out of my wallet."

"Got any big customers moving pharmaceuticals through here?"

"All my customers are equally important to me, and I don't know what they move, there are no packing lists; I don't ask questions, we just load and unload."

"Who is this load for?"

"I think this one is from the Pentagon, probably some weapons headed to South America or the Middle East. That's why you guys are here right? To make sure they get to their destination."

It quickly became obvious that no information would be obtained from any of the detainees. A search of the premises found no files, records, or paper of any sort other than sticky notes stuck to an extra-large map of the United States secured to a wall. Everything was written in some type of code that no one claimed to be able to decipher. There was one old computer found on a metal desk inside what could be called an office, but there was little hope of finding anything, the organization excelled at not leaving a trail.

No one came that night nor the next night to pick up the product. What they did not know, was that there was an office building across the street from the freight forwarding office in Nashville that rented space with windows facing the freight forwarding location to a company which was an untraceable shell company that paid in cash. The FBI raid had been observed and reported up the chain. Roman had also been warned not to have his men pick up the product. There was a rat, and it needed to be exterminated.

Roman's suspicion focused on Stanley. He had been acting and talking strangely and had even made what Roman perceived as threats. Roman tried to think of someone else to identify as the rat, but he kept going back to Stanley. The team in Nashville had no idea who Stanley was, and they were using their own methods of uncovering the rat. Methods that if someone chose not to talk, left them without the ability to do so, and claims of ignorance were tested to the point that it had to be true. The human body could only endure so much before the self-survival mechanism took over.

THE NEW WIND legal team had hoped to initiate settlement talks and forgo Nicole's deposition, but the California AG's office was eager to question Nicole, especially after what they had learned during Charlie's deposition two days earlier. Immediately after being sworn in and stating her name and title for the record, the vicious attack started, and it was relentless for almost four hours with mercy breaks disguised as bathroom breaks providing the only respite from the attack.

Nicole admitted that initially she made management decisions at the Distributing Company, even empowering Charlie and giving her the ability to make any and all changes she deemed appropriate. Later, while maintaining the title, the authority reverted back to Stanley when the numbers started to slide. It was against her will, but her then boss Charles McKinnon made it clear she did not have a say in the matter. The New Wind attorneys made it a point to stress that the company had fired Mr. McKinnon for his reckless behavior, to which the California attorney applauded them, though it was too little too late, and asked why Stanley had not met a similar fate. There was no response from the New Wind team.

Charlie was removed from the Distributing Company at Stanley's request, with the backing of Charles McKinnon. Yes, Charlie had notified her on several occasions of unethical if not illegal trading practices between the Distributing Company and several of its trading partners, even providing proof, and she took no action. Yes, she was aware of lies told to federal investigators when questioned about adulterated product. Yes, she received an email from Mr. McKinnon instructing her to 'idle the axe that was chopping down the money tree;' and yes, she knew he was referring to Charlie.

The New Wind team stopped objecting when they finally accepted it was futile. The California AG's office had an email, pedigree, invoice, or other type of record which proved each accusation. Charlie had an unnamed file on her computer where she stored meticulous notes, and copies of pertinent documents. It was her CYA file, and the California AG's office struck gold when they discovered it.

The bloodshed was so severe, Nicole requested a leave of absence after her deposition ended when they finally depleted their arsenal and had nothing left to throw at her, not even one last stone from a slingshot. The New Wind team knew there was no way a jury could hear even a sampling of what they had just heard. They had to settle at all costs but contacted their insurance company just in case.

STANLEY ARRIVED at his deposition late, unshaven, in jeans and a Michigan State sweatshirt, and without his lawyer. The team from New Wind did not want to be anywhere near the deposition after barely surviving Nicole's bludgeoning, and they had already retreated back to Atlanta. Stanley refused to be sworn in, and answered the first five questions with 'go fuck yourself', including when asked to state his name for the record. There was not a sixth question. The attorneys from California packed up their belongings and headed for the Detroit airport to see if they could secure an earlier flight back to Sacramento. They already had more than enough to proceed with their complaint.

31

A settlement was not an option without Charlie having regulatory oversight; even after New Wind replaced the management team and were in the latter stages of moving operations to Olive Branch, Mississippi. Even a settlement would cost millions but would be a smaller number than what the AG's office was seeking and would not have an admission of guilt nor the nightmarish court proceedings in front of a jury.

Nicole, who was still on paid leave, made it clear that there was 'no way in hell' she would reach out to Charlie and ask her to come back to New Wind. It was decided that someone from Human Resources would contact her.

The laughter was unexpected, but Charlie was not expecting the call, and it was her immediate reaction. It was better than being cursed out or told to kiss her ass, but it may as well had been, the result was the same. The phone call was brief, and Charlie was thanked for her time.

. . .

News of Stanley's deposition reached the New Wind executive offices in Atlanta and had the impact of a bomb explosion. He was immediately terminated, and the complaint naming him as defendant was filed with the court. It was a move not only to firmly place the bulk of the blame on him, but to also recover a small part of the settlement costs or force him into bankruptcy. Hopefully it would also hold off the New York AG's office who already had the framework for settlements in place with the other two big wholesalers for grey market trading and now had New Wind in its crosshairs. The Distributing Company was by far the worst offender, and New York and Texas were waiting to see what they could learn from the California case.

There was only a skeleton crew left in Livonia, including the operations manager and Stanley. When the operations manager walked into Stanleys office to fire him, he found him slouched in his chair with what appeared to be a self-inflicted gunshot wound to this head. The revolver was found in his lap, and splatter was on the wall behind his body. The police were curious why the serial number had been scraped off the gun but initially ruled it a suicide anyway. After questioning known associates, including Hank, Christine, John and New Wind management and learning all that had recently happened with the deposition, lawsuit, job loss and other work issues, it strengthened their conclusion that he had taken his own life.

Time of death was determined to be the night before the body was found, between four and six in the evening. Others had left for the day and Stanley was in the building alone according to the operations manager. Video footage during that timeframe showed a delivery truck pull up to the front door and the driver exited the truck and rang the buzzer on the front door. He was buzzed into the door a short time later with a package and exited nine minutes later without the package. His face was not visible, and he was wearing sweatpants, a hoodie, and gloves, all skin was covered. The truck was unmarked, and he was not wearing a uniform. The truck was later found in a grocery store parking lot less than three miles away. Their easy suicide case had just become a difficult homicide case, one that was destined to become a cold case.

CHARLIE RELUCTANTLY AGREED TO A MEETING. After learning of Stanley's death, she accepted an invitation to Atlanta to discuss whatever it was they wanted to discuss. She had mentioned the previous call to Geraldine, her angel investor and partner of their fledgling regulatory consulting firm in Detroit, and they had devised a plan to see just how bad New Wind needed Charlie. Geraldine encouraged Charlie to take the meeting.

New Wind flew Charlie to Atlanta on a Delta Airlines flight in the first-class cabin. They reserved a luxury suite, including room service at a lavish hotel near the New Wind Campus in a Northern suburb of Atlanta. She declined the car service, preferring to rent a car instead. When she arrived at the building, an administrative assistant for the operations vp was waiting for her in the lobby and escorted her to an immaculate, well-furnished conference room on the top floor. The usual suspects were waiting inside, including a vp from operations, legal, regulatory, and human resources. They had lunch catered and waiting as well.

The greetings were polite, and the small talk forced but light. They thanked her for accepting their invitation and asked about her accommodations. Charlie assured them all was well and thanked them because it was the right thing to do.

"I heard about Stanley," Charlie said as solemnly as she could, again because it was the right thing to do, "I'm sorry for your loss. I heard they initially thought it was a suicide but found evidence of foul play. Have they arrested anyone yet, or do they have any suspects?" It was the right question to ask but she was also thinking about her cousins Earl and Craig; she had not yet absolved them of being involved.

"No, nothing yet," the human resources vp said in a low voice "It was just a terrible act."

An awkward silence followed which was usually filled with kind words about the deceased. No-one had words they wanted to share out loud so the human resources vp got down to the business at hand.

"We would like to make you an offer."

"What kind of offer?"

"A job offer."

"I told whoever it was that called me that I'm not interested in coming back to New Wind."

"I know," the human resources vp responded as she slowly slid an offer letter across the table to Charlie, "but we're hoping you'll reconsider."

Charlie quickly scanned the letter, but the title and compensation package jumped off the page demanding to be seen. Charlie did not react externally, but her heart rate increased. The legal vp smiled as if he was a vampire and could hear her beating heart. Fearing she had been exposed Charlie stood up from the mahogany conference table.

"I thank you for the ticket and the plush hotel suite, but I'm not interested in ever being an employee of this company again. Maybe you don't know how things went down."

"We are well aware of what happened," the operations vp stated, "and we are truly sorry, we all but forced you out; I would have left too if I were you."

"Yeah, well thanks but... the damage has been done." Charlie walked toward the door as planned. The next move would be on...

"Why did you come here Ms. Thomas?" There it was. The

human resources vp's question caused Charlie to stop and turn around. "You knew you wouldn't accept a job offer, no matter what, and we gave you a hell of an offer. What's your plan? Let's just put everything on the table and stop playing games."

Charlie returned to the table but remained standing. "You first. That offer is too good to be true, but I know it is. What's the story?"

The four executives looked at each other and the vp of legal nodded his head and took the lead. He looked Charlie directly in the eye when he spoke. It was time for everyone to show their cards.

"We're trying to settle this thing with California, but they won't entertain any type of settlement negotiations without you being part of the package. They were very impressed by how you handled or tried to handle the compliance piece."

"And what if you can't settle it?"

"Let's just say it's better to settle. Now, your turn. What is it that you want?"

"I started a consulting firm, and let's just say clients aren't lining up. Gaining New Wind as a client would really help put my firm out in the forefront. I don't want to work for New Wind, but I'd be willing to work with New Wind." It was almost word for word how she and Geraldine had scripted it.

The four executives looked at each other again and knew they had no choice but to agree to terms.

"What are you thinking?" The question was asked by the operations vp.

"The title in your offer letter was director of trade compliance which I would have negotiated to vice president or at least senior director. I assume you need me to have some sort of regulatory oversight of that business and my firm can be contracted to do that. Right now, I am the firm so I would be doing the work. As far as fees, the compensation in the offer letter is acceptable with benefits such as healthcare, vacation, and bonuses factored in. I'm sure the company knows how much it spends on average for healthcare for employees and we can just add that amount to the fees along with whatever annual bonus I would have received. Overall, it won't cost the company any more than if I was an employee."

They understood her rationale, whether they agreed or not, and so far, they had not heard anything outrageous.

"I would counter,' the human resources vp stated, "that the bonus would be paid out as an actual bonus if certain metrics were met by both your company and ours, instead of factoring it into the fees which are guaranteed."

Charlie considered it briefly. "That's fair."

"They will probably want some type of multi-year commitment to abide by whatever stipulations we agree to," the legal vp chimed in, "most likely three to five years. We can structure the term of your contract to match that of the agreed term in the settlement."

"What if you decide to close that business prior to the completion of the term? You've already moved it to Memphis, or Olive Branch, you're already probably thinking along those lines anyway."

"Your contract will still be binding; we will find other consulting opportunities within the company. We really do value what you bring to the table. We would have tried to rehire you even if California wasn't forcing our hand." The operations vp's words were sincere, and Charlie knew it.

"Who would I be working with? After our last meeting, I can't work with Nicole, the trust and respect has been permanently destroyed."

The operations vp raised his hand. "You would be working directly with me."

Charlie nodded her head and stared blankly at the team across from her. Her mind was processing information. Both sides took a moment to process.

"Well, it sounds like we have the framework for a deal." The vp of legal had excitement and relief in his voice. "Of course there are a few other details to iron out, but I would say we have a deal." He stood and extended his hand across the table to Charlie. Charlie paused but eventually stood and shook his hand.

"We have a deal."

"Great, I look forward to working with you. We will take what we discussed here today, and we will send you a contract for you and your lawyer to review."

Charlie let herself smile for the first time, when she was alone walking to her car of course, and the first call she made was to Geraldine.

32

Luke would have to be arrested and have his day in court with the others to get the target off his chest. If found guilty, he was assured a lighter sentence but would need to spend some time in federal prison; at least long enough to warrant an early release. There had to be the appearance that he was caught in the same net as the others, otherwise he would be exposed as the rat. Luke and his lawyer agreed; he had already received threats and feared for his safety. He did not trust the FBI to protect him, federal prison was his only recourse.

Roman proved to be far more difficult to prosecute. Like an onion, there were too many layers to peel, and each layer was as potent as the one before. There were so many individuals willing to take the fall for him and dilute the evidence that had been built against him, that even a desperate RICO case had no chance of sticking. It was nearly impossible to grab and hold a pig in a muddy pen, even if one could catch it. Roman had proven to be quite a slippery pig.

Roman did not step foot inside a courtroom, and the minimal fines he agreed to for his involvement in distributing adulterated and counterfeit drugs were insulting and would have been comical, if it had not been not such a serious matter. The state and federal penalties were not as severe as the crimes, and Roman kept operating with little fear of substantial retribution from the law. Roman still found a way to get his products into the supply chain, even without New Wind, and was not deterred by the pending federal RFID requirements. He figured 'it would be at least twenty years before they got all that figured out.'

TWENTY-ONE MILLION DOLLARS was the California AG's number, and that number could have been higher they claimed. Charlie was not impressed and said as much on the conference call she had scheduled.

"Which one of you was someone's bitch in prison?"

"I beg your pardon?" The litigation vp was taken aback by Charlie's question.

"I said exactly what you thought you heard. I knew New Wind had a reputation of settling in the beginning of the first round, but damn, you guys bend over and spread your cheeks like it's second nature. Twenty-one mil is not a good deal, at least not for you."

"I'm sorry, I didn't know you went to law school."

"I'm sorry, I thought you did based on your title, but I guess I was wrong."

"You understand you're just a consultant..."

"If I was just a consultant, I would just let you get screwed and not say anything, I get paid either way. I am heavily invested in this outcome; my name and reputation are on the line. I know this team is new to working with me, and my in-your-face style forces you to look me in the eye, but I fight for my clients like family, and I get things done. If you just wanted me because the California AG said you had to have me as part of the settlement, then we can tear up the contract right now. If you don't value what I bring to the table, and how I can help make your company more compliant, please let me know now and we can end this call on good terms."

"We value you Charlie," the operations vp chimed in, "and I for one would love to hear what you have to say regarding the settlement. You know far more than we do about what actually happened at the distributing company."

Charlie paused to see if there were any other comments, but the line was quiet.

"Were the bulk of their findings before New Wind acquired Davidson?"

"Yes, you cleaned things up after the acquisition, as much as you were allowed."

"Exactly, and that means something, at least to a jury. We identified a problem and were well down the path of correcting it even before the California AG got involved. New Wind inherited a mess from previous ownership that you were not aware of, at least that's what your lawyer claims. In reality you either knew and were blinded by the money and didn't care, or they hid it from you, and you were too blinded by the money to look. I don't need a confession."

"So, what do you suggest?" The question came from legal.

"We offer up more. We only purchase product from an alternate source vendor if they can prove the product came directly from the manufacturer or from an authorized distributor; no more than one removed from the manufacturer. Any distributor we sell product can only distribute it to a final dispenser, period; and we want a signed agreement. We investigate price diversion; if a company buys our product on a contract like a 340B or a GPO contract with own use restrictions, they can only use the product for that purpose. The states will eat that up because they have a lot of fraud, especially with Medicare."

Charlie couldn't see the heads nodding in the New Wind conference room, but she knew they were at least considering what she had suggested.

"And to really get that number down, we offer up fresh meat."

"What do you mean?" There was concern in the litigation vp's voice.

"I can give them at least one co-conspirator, and maybe a big fish to put on their hook and have them reeling him in for a while to keep 'em busy."

"Who is the co-conspirator?"

"Stanley was engaged in a drug laundering scheme with Emperor drugs, and I have physical proof."

"Drug laundering?" The human resources vp could no longer keep quiet.

"You're familiar with money laundering? It's the same thing but instead of dirty money it's dirty prescription drugs."

"But if we mention this that will just add more to the fine."

"Not if they want the information I have on Emperor."

"I'm sure they already have it."

"Yea, but they don't know how to look and what to look for."

The legal vp was reluctant to keep going but had to ask. "And this big fish?"

"Roman Caesar." Charlie thought she heard laughter on the other end of the phone.

"Yeah, and you might as well give them who really shot Kennedy while you're at it. You'll probably have a better chance with Kennedy. Roman has proven to be untouchable."

"That's what he thinks, but Stanley could have taken him down."

"Stanley is dead."

"Exactly... suicide, right? Who among us really believes Stanley took his own life? Stanley was a narcissist, he was Satan; I can say this now because I said it to his face when he was alive. Stanley did not kill himself; I believe Roman had him killed."

"And you have proof of this?"

"No, but I believe he wants to tell me; or at least he will... by the way, what's my travel budget? I have some site visits to schedule."

"Do you still have your corporate card?" Charlie recognized Nicole's voice.

"No, I cut it up after you fired me."

"I didn't fire you Charlie..." Nicole moaned in a distressed voice. "I'll just send you a new one. Just expense all of your travel like you did before."

"We need to continue negotiations with the California AG," Charlie exclaimed without acknowledging Nicole. "You haven't signed anything yet, have you?"

There was a pause before the litigation vp answered. "Not yet but..."

"Good, don't; bring me to the negotiating table."

Charlie's first visit was to Olive Branch, MS to meet with the team at the distributing company. All of the faces were new to her, but they all knew who she was and what role she played. Nicole attended as well, as the corporate representative to cosign whatever Charlie said and instituted. The two women were cordial, but Charlie declined the lunch invitation.

Any product from any vendor other than a manufacturer could not be received into inventory without Charlie's approval. She had to verify that the supplier had sent proof that their product had either come from the manufacturer or an authorized distributor who had purchased the product from the manufacturer. The only acceptable proof was an invoice; she didn't care if the pricing was blacked out. A block was set up in the inventory management system that only Charlie could release. The same was true for all shipments to other distributors who had not signed the agreement Charlie had recently circulated requiring wholesalers to agree to only distribute the product to final dispensers. Those who refused to sign were no longer customers of the distributing company.

CHARLIE'S second visit was to Emperor Drugs. They initially declined Charlie's request for a visit on the grounds that they had discontinued business with the Distributing Company. Charlie made it known that the visit was not regarding future business, but previous business activities. After further resistance, she made it clear that she could come on her own by invitation, or with the feds unannounced. They conceded to the visit.

Dominic Vanelli did not welcome her with a smile nor a handshake, even though Charlie lit up the room with her retaliatory smile. Michael sat at the small conference table in Dominic's office and identified himself as counsel. Charlie was not offered a seat, but she sat in an empty chair at the table uninvited.

"Like I told you on the phone Ms. Thomas," Dominic stated after exhaling his contempt, "we no longer do business with the Distributing Company, so I don't know why you're here."

"Like I stated on the phone Mr. Vanelli, this visit is regarding all the monthly business you did for the past several years with Stanley through the distributing company."

"Stanley was a friend," Dominic stated solemnly, "his death was tragic."

"I am sorry for your loss. I did not call him a friend, but his death was indeed tragic."

A brief moment of silence was observed for Stanley's memory.

"So, what is this about?" Dominic stared Charlie in the eye and his voice was stern.

Charlie smiled once again. "I like it, straight to the point. You and Stanley were engaged in drug laundering, and I have proof."

"Now wait just a minute..." Michael exclaimed as he jumped to his feet. Dominic raised his hand and Michael dropped back down on the chair pouting like a child.

"Please continue." Dominic's voice was not as stern as before.

"Just about every month for at least two years, but I suspect even longer, Emperor drugs purchased prescription drugs from the Distributing Company at the end of the month and returned drugs at the beginning of the month with different lot numbers. I know this because the Distributing Company tracked by lot number, and the lot numbers we sent you did not match the lots you returned."

Dominic sat with his best poker face, and did not utter any words or sounds.

"Your account was credited for the returned drugs but always for fifteen percent less than what you paid. I assume this fifteen percent was Stanley's fee for taking your dirty drugs and laundering them by receiving them into our inventory and distributing them to other distributors under our authorized distributor status, so we didn't have to provide a pedigree."

Charlie glanced at Michael, who did not have a poker face, and she knew she had hit the bullseye.

"You said you had proof?"

Charlie slid a folder across the table containing two years of invoices and returns along with the corresponding credits and debit memos. Dominic took a few minutes to look over the documents before he closed the folder and slid it back across the table.

"What do you want?" Dominic finally asked. "Is this about money?"

"No... well yes, actually it is."

"How much?"

"That's up to the California Attorney General and whoever else comes after you." Charlie saw the confusion in Dominic's eyes. "Oh, you thought the money was for me? If I accepted your dirty money it would leave a permanent stain on my soul. No, you are going to negotiate a settlement with the California Attorney General which will help offset whatever settlement amount New Wind agrees to. They are very eager to speak with you, and your counsel here should receive a subpoena very soon."

Dominic did not say what he was thinking, but Charlie could read his mind even though she did not speak Italian.

"Also," Charlie continued, "I have documentation proving that some of the drugs Stanley laundered for you were sent to customers in California, as well as New York and Texas; I hear the Attorneys General in those states have heard what California is doing and want to get in on the action as well."

Charlie stood to her feet and smiled at both men. "Have a good day gentlemen; I'll see myself out."

EMPEROR DRUGS WAS NOT the only site visit she had scheduled while in the New York and New Jersey area; there were five other vendors that reluctantly agreed to allow her to visit their facilities. By the time she left, all five were former vendors as none could adhere to the new guidelines. None of the five purchased directly from manufacturers or authorized distributors who had purchased from the manufacturers.

. . .

CHARLIE'S next call was one she dreaded and looked forward to at the same time. She knew the chances were slim that he would agree to a visit, but she dialed the number anyway.

"Rome Pharmaceuticals."

Charlie cringed at the sound of her voice. To Charlie, even on the phone she sounded like someone who got the job because of her looks.

"Hello, is Roman available?"

"Who's calling?"

"Charlie Thomas for New Wind Distributing."

"Oh... please hold."

The salsa music made her head nod to the beat and made her want to dance. She was denied the pleasure of the full song when Roman's voice replaced the music.

"Ms. Thomas, did I hear correctly that you're calling for New Wind? I thought Stanley fired you."

"He would've if he could've, but I didn't report to him; and yes, you heard correctly; I started my own consulting firm and New Wind is a client."

"Interesting... well I guess congratulations are in order. Maybe I can hire you to help me over a few regulatory hurdles. Seems like every agency going after New Wind has their dogs sniffing my crotch now. It's like someone pointed them in my direction."

"You and Stanley were like business partners, I'm sure there were lots of records of transactions in everything gathered from New Wind."

"Yeah... I'm sure you're right." Roman paused to let her know he was calling her bullshit. "So, what made you call me today?"

"Did you get the memorandum I sent to all non-manufacturer vendors? Some significant changes to how the Distributing Company conducts business."

"Yeah, I gave it the attention it deserved. I guess with Stanley gone you can pretty much do whatever you want."

"Are you able to comply with the terms? If so, I need to schedule a site visit; if not we need to discontinue doing business."

The pause spoiled into an extended silence. The call had been cordial to that point, but Charlie anticipated chaos after the quietness.

"I will be traveling over the next two weeks, but I am available after that. Give me your address and I can mail you an invitation."

The unexpected chill surprised her, she would never admit to the brief moment of fear that gripped her before sliding off.

"Why don't I just schedule something with your assistant, I'm sure she needs something to do. I must say I'm surprised. I didn't think you would be able to meet the terms of the new requirements. I didn't think you purchased anything from the manufacturer."

"I don't."

"So you purchase drugs from authorized distributors who purchase them directly from the manufacturer?"

Roman laughed. "Where is the adventure and profit in that?"

"So, what's the purpose of visiting a facility that as of this moment New Wind no longer does business with?"

"So I can take a mugshot. You never know, you might end up missing or something while you're in Florida, and I may need to circulate your picture to help with the search."

"Or I may end up murdered like Stanley."

"Stanley committed suicide, at least that's what I heard."

"Yeah, I heard the same thing, but I also heard the police may have reason to believe he was murdered."

"A reason to believe or evidence?"

"Why don't you give 'em a call and ask; I'm sure they'd be glad to question you."

"You know... I think this is the longest conversation we've ever had. I can see why Stanley hated you so much.

"Good, and I can see why you were able to get Stanley to do your bidding. I'll see you soon."

Charlie hung up the phone with purpose. They had managed to rattle each other on the call, but Charlie was even more confident she could get Roman to confess, at least to her.

NEGOTIATIONS with the California Attorney General's office were moving in a more favorable direction, and the New Wind executive team was pleased. Charlie and the new policies she had implemented had been instrumental in convincing the AG's office that a settlement would be better than a jury trial. They did have a request that the New Wind team found strange. The AG's office wanted to visit the site in Olive Branch to see the current operation. Of course, the New Wind team obliged and a visit was scheduled.

CHARLIE ARRIVED two days early to walk the facility and observe the operation in action. She conducted a mock audit, and while reviewing security camera footage she noticed one of the monitors displayed the view of the front door of the Livonia facility. The security manager noticed her gazing at the screen.

"New Wind still owns the building," he explained, "there's no product but we still have furniture and equipment there, so we monitor the exterior cameras. There hasn't been any activity since..." His voice trailed off and returned to the thought in his head.

"Since what?" Charlie asked.

"Since the day that guy shot himself in the building."

"What was the last thing captured on camera?"

"A delivery truck."

"Do you still have it?" Charlie asked intrigued.

"Yep, give me a sec."

Charlie could barely contain her excitement as the security manager searched for the footage. Maybe there was something that could point to Roman; an assassin's face that could be identified by the police and linked back to him somehow.

"Got it."

Charlie focused on the screen until a delivery truck stopped in front of the building. It was not the familiar brown truck, but a generic truck with no logo. A figure exited the truck and walked to the door and rang the bell.

"Do you have a view of his face?"

"Not on this camera, he hides his face pretty well, but..." He switched to an interior camera view, "we can see his face here."

Charlie's heart imploded when she saw her cousin Earl's face on the screen. Even with the cap pulled down low on his head, she knew it was him. "Dumb ass."

"Do you know him?"

Charlie then realized she had said it out loud. "No... has anyone else seen this?"

"I don't know, why, you think he killed him?"

"Naw, the police ruled it a suicide. Thanks for letting me see the footage, now back to the work at hand. Let me see the alarm tests for this facility."

"Sure."

THE NEW WIND executive team was surprised by Charlie's sudden change of heart when they arrived at the Olive Branch facility. She had been sure of his guilt and seemed confident he wanted to admit it but suddenly she was ready to move on. She also seemed distracted, but her interactions with the guests from California was stellar. They were satisfied with what they saw, and in the end, the settlement amount was a third of the twenty-one million with no admission of guilt.

BETWEEN THE VARIOUS Attorneys General settlements with the big three wholesalers, coupled with much harsher licensing and pedigree requirements in most states, the secondary trading amongst wholesalers all but ground to a halt. The big three either shut down or greatly diminished their operations in that market, and numerous smaller players were forced to shut their doors.

Charlie welcomed the eventual closing of the distributing company. She conceded that just like any business, it was the players that make it bad. Someone would always find ways to break or bend the law for financial gain, even at the detriment of others. Within five months of starting work with New Wind, Distributing Company operations were shut down. As promised, her contract was honored, and she focused on controlled substance compliance. Phentermine was being given out like candy at some weight loss clinics across the country, and Oxycodone and Hydrocodone activity was stirring rumblings within the DEA. Word was starting to spread about new enforcement measures and Charlie was prepping her agency to be at the forefront. She had grown to six clients, including two of the big three wholesalers, and had a staff of three, not including her angel investor and partner.

CHARLIE DROVE to Flint to look her father in the eye when she asked did he know. He looked away and she walked away with no intention to ever return to his presence. When she wanted to see her grandmother he left the house, and she had no words for him, not even in passing. Not only was the relationship damaged, but she was damaged as well. She had to leave Michigan to heal, and the for-sale sign in her yard meant she was never coming back as a resident.

HARLEM, 125th street, Charlie disembarked the train and stepped onto the sacred brick. She smiled at the men feigning for her attention, knowing they did not have a chance with a woman like her but that never stopped them from trying. Charlie strutted as if portraying a Maya Angelou poem and was oblivious to the gentrification.

She walked into the restaurant and was immediately seated. The jazz band on stage was artistic, but a tall cherrywood colored man on stage had all of her attention. Q smiled when he saw her and played his bass even more fervently. Handling it rough but respectful, he hugged its curves and made the strings whine with his caress. Charlie knew it was foreplay and was eager to get to the main course.

THE END

www.ingramcontent.com/pod-product-compliance
Lightning Source LLC
LaVergne TN
LVHW010538160826
845677LV00013B/2918

* 9 7 9 8 9 9 4 1 3 4 1 0 8 *